MW01681262

The Space Between You and Me

ASHLEY B. DAVIS

THE SPACE BETWEEN YOU AND ME

Contact: authorashleybdavis@gmail.com

Cover art by Andrew Davis
Jacket design by Lindsay Heider Diamond
Editing by Auriane Desombre
Author photo by Michelle Patch

ISBN: 979-8-9867087-1-3

Library of Congress Control Number: 2022914183

First Edition: November 2022
10 9 8 7 6 5 4 3 2 1

The Space Between You and Me

1

Apollo

When Junior smiled through the crowd at Purple Haze, it felt like it was just for me. But he treated everyone like they were the only person who mattered in that moment. That's why we all loved him.

As I made my way across the dance floor, I pointlessly swiped a hand through my thick hair. I never slicked it down with gel and always regretted it.

"*Carnal!*" Junior said, shaking my shoulder. Yep. He was already wasted.

"Surprised to see you out after last night," he said with a misplaced grin.

I hadn't touched a drop the night before. I'd just played whatever song he requested on my guitar while he partied solo. I'd hung out until the wee hours when the other transients he lived with started filtering in.

"Couple Red Bulls and lat pulldowns and I'm good as new." I patted my lats for emphasis. I'd never done a pulldown in my life. This fact was very obvious.

He clapped a hand on the side of my neck, laughing. "Okay, *pues*. You remember Jade?" he asked me.

I nodded. How could I forget her when Junior was practically wearing her?

He reluctantly tore his eyes away from his . . . lady friend. "What's new with the Gate Keepers?"

That's what he called our *magikalia* clan—or, *my* clan, I guess, with Junior being an outsider and all. It felt like a reminder that I didn't belong here with him or the other orphaned *magikalia*. Maybe he joked about it to remind me not to take the clan for granted, which would be a very big brotherly thing for him to do, and I wouldn't appreciate it one bit.

"Nothing of note," I said. He didn't hear me because another one of his adoring fans distracted him. Selfishly, I wanted to go back to last night, when it was just us hanging out in his warehouse.

I looked around the club, feeling disconnected. Usually, being with Junior made me feel invincible. I would forget I was an in-betweener—between genders, between magic and sapien, between cared for and cast away.

Sometimes, at the club with Junior, there would be no division between *magikalia* and the sapiens—our nickname for the humans who lived in ignorance of our kind. There would be no difference between me and his group, the wolves, which were orphans among our kind.

I was there because Junior liked me. But for the wolves and some of the sapiens here, he was their leader, brother, friend, and lover. And we were all basking in him, the same current moving through all of us as we burned through another night at Purple Haze.

I swear, clubbing must have been thought of by one of our kind. Clubs were the perfect place for gathering magic by osmosis.

Most of the wolves and sapiens here seemed to follow Junior dogma: he maintained that drugs opened up our absorption lines, allowing us to pull in more magic, to possibly even grab it from the stars.

I wasn't quite so ambitious.

I stepped out the back exit for a cigarette, and I was abruptly alone. The lights of San Alvarez pulsed from the end of the green-lit alley.

I wondered what Jonah was doing. Then I wanted to punch myself.

Being in love with my best friend was a pipe dream. Seriously, I didn't recommend it. I jabbed my cigarette out on the wall (I also do not recommend smoking, for the record) and went back inside. I found Quinn at the bar and pinched her. We leaned our heads together to be heard over the music. Her nose twitched.

"You need to quit," she said. "You're as bad as the wolves. Buncha lost boys."

"I hardly ever do drugs," I said, stealing a drink of her Coke.

She barked a laugh. "If I said that to my parents, they'd slap the color out of my eyes."

I almost spit Coke on her. This was exactly why I'd asked her to meet up. She and Junior were the only people who made me feel more like myself and less like the mess I'd been all summer.

"I've got an addictive personality," I said, chewing an ice cube. "If I didn't have a vice, I would go insane."

"Well, what about competitive rowing or raising lobsters?"

"Are *you* high?" I asked, laughing. Where did she get this stuff? She was a lot like my ex-best friend, Jonah. That's probably why we got along so well. I guess she kind of was my best friend right now, since Jonah and I hadn't talked for months (never mind that I knew exactly how many months, and days . . . and hours).

"Besides," I said, "Those are hobbies. A vice is something you're *supposed* to feel guilty about."

"Well, then smoking's not yours," she said.

"Bingo."

She shook her head, fighting a smile.

I felt itchy and restless as the bass filled our silence. Since losing Jonah, I'd felt like an unmanned kite, waiting for something to grab my string and ground me; not that he'd ever been mine to lose.

"What is it about him?" asked Quinn, watching Junior and the wolves jumping on the floor, sapiens prowling the outer circle.

All summer, Junior had been my anchor. Taking me to his favorite *panaderia* on the strip and going to the pier, the lights of the Ferris Wheel dancing in his brown eyes, the exact same way they danced in the Pacific Ocean at night. So many nights drunk on cheap beer when he'd let me steal one, drunk with movement and light and cruising the strip, but mostly, drunk off magic. I wasn't a wolf like

Junior was, but when I was with him, I felt like I belonged somewhere.

The wolves might not officially be part of the clan—they belonged to no one—but Junior was vital to their clan. Even now, they all revolved around him.

San Alvarez was huge, so there were a lot of *magikalia.* Unfortunately, that meant also a lot of orphaned *magikalia.* At some point, the clan began calling them wolves. Or maybe they started calling themselves that to create their own clan.

Though our kind do not throw magic until twenty-one, sapiens could still sense it, even in a baby. Like any old genetic mutation, magic could skip generations. Whenever it happened, mommy and daddy didn't always take it well.

The clan didn't look down on the wolves. They were just . . . apart, but wolves would always feel that lack of two people who are supposed to want and love them unconditionally. Though if there was anything I'd learned from my privileged position, parents weren't always parents. Sometimes they were just people who turned into mothers and fathers.

I pulled out of my pity party long enough to notice Quinn trying to get the bartender's attention. Apparently, he wasn't very interested in refilling a high-schooler's soft drink.

The magic in the vibration of the music, the connections being made and severed all around me, the lights and pumping blood and sweat and anticipation all begged to be harvested. With the shift in the air from sticky summer to pumpkin-spiced fall, I should have been gorging myself on magic until I popped. Instead, I slipped the guitar pick out of the leather band on my wrist and pushed it back in, wondering how I could feel alone in a city of millions.

"Hello." The deep, clear voice cut through the music. Close.

I looked to find Talbot Erikson, a guy from our clan, standing next to me. He could throw magic, which meant he was over twenty-one. Typically, anyone under twenty-one, like me, was not supposed to be able to access their magic. I kind of didn't fit into our clan's equations though.

"Hi?" I said, confused.

Quinn looked away with the corner of her mouth quirked up.

Talbot was an average-sized drink of water and almost as skinny as me. To top it off, dude had sideburns.

We'd never talked outside of clan meetings, but the buzz in my fingers as he stepped toward me said I didn't mind the sudden attention.

"What are you drinking?" he asked. His glasses amplified the ruthlessly green eyes behind them.

"Nothing." Junior would have laughed at me for that answer. I wondered if I should remind Talbot I was underage.

"Right." He ran a hand through his hair. The movement looked jerky. "You come here a lot?"

Was this actually happening? There was something fragile in the way Talbot's gaze kept sliding off of me.

I tried to break the tension with a joke.

"It's my favorite place to be, aside from Sunday School." Our clan held their weekly meetings on Sundays; see what we did there?

He narrowed his eyes, not pulling them away this time. "Seriously?"

"Not at all."

His mouth twitched up a little. A fraction of a smile. I was going to take it as a win. He always looked so serious.

"What are *you* drinking?" I asked.

He looked at the glass of clear liquid he held. Straight vodka?

"Water," he said, seeming disappointed. I was just happy he wasn't drinking vodka through a straw. Not that I knew anything about *that*.

He cocked his head at me. "Apollo, right?" Something about the movement or the question made me bold. The innocent but direct curiosity of it.

I leaned forward and took a sip from his straw. The water was cool as it coated my insides. Inexplicably, I thought of chugging water with Jonah after playing basketball at the park.

"The one and only," I said, smooth bastard that I was.

He kept staring at his straw. "Anything keeping you here right now?"

Adrenaline or serotonin or something that felt *good* spilled into my body like a faucet had been turned on. It was one thing thinking that something was happening and another for it to actually be happening.

"No," I said.

He set his water on the bar and took off his glasses, cleaning them. Talbot did not fit the glasses stereotype. Jonah in glasses would make more sense, what with his constant reading, sometimes only to the faint glow of his night light. Glasses didn't make sense for Talbot, because his eyes didn't look vulnerable when he took them off. And right now, they had me pinned to the bar.

"Let's go out to Orville Orchards."

I wasn't sure I had heard him right. "The borderlands?" Why would he want to go all the way out there? Why was he asking *me*?

He restored his glasses and raised his eyebrows. He leaned his long body back against the bar, arms crossed over his chest. I watched the lean muscles drawing themselves in.

The people who had been standing nearby were gone. I knew it for sure then. I had to admit, I was thirsty at the idea of Talbot Erikson hitting on me.

"Isn't that where your generation goes to break the rules and be cool?"

He said it in a condescending tone that should have pissed me off. A flame lit inside me instead.

"First of all," I said, "you're barely out of my generation. Certainly not far enough to use that on me. Second of all, you think my generation"—insert air quotes here—"is stupid enough to play around at the boundaries and risk being oofed by a vampiris. Just to prove we're *cool*?" Deploying air quotes again. "That would be a no, Talbot." God, I sounded like Jonah's older sister, Maddie.

His cool expression flickered. Here he was, in the difficult position of hitting on another guy, and I was coming off as an asshole. That was so not my style.

"Why do you keep saying my name?"

I was pretty sure I'd only said it once. I shrugged, smiling, trying to salvage this almost-moment. My fingertips buzzed on a live wire of potential.

"I like it." I didn't, really. It was actually very stuffy. "What will we do out there?"

He shrugged. "Talk." I could smell his body wash. Manufactured man scent. It shouldn't have made my knees weak, but here we are.

He looked embarrassed, tucking his hands back into his pockets. "Want to meet me out there?"

Something was totally Twilight Zone about this—an elder pressuring *me* to break rules. Well, *I* wasn't about to say no.

"Why don't we drive together?" I suggested.

If there was anything that would guarantee me action, it was my car, but only because my guitar was at home. Something about the original (trashed) vinyl seats or maybe the ever-present *parfum de gasoline.*

He was already walking away though.

I looked around for Quinn to say my goodbyes, but she was nowhere to be found. I made my way to Junior. The pill he'd told me he'd be sampling tonight warped his features as his hand kept roaming farther south on Jade's gluteus maximus. He threw his head back, laughing loudly at something. That's how he did everything. All in.

"Apollo!" he said, hooking a massive arm around my neck (not the arm that had been in close proximity to Jade's butt).

"I'm out of here, man. Make good choices," I said, patting him on the shoulder and narrowly escaping one of his unbreakable headlocks.

"Apollo Tormey talking about good choices!"

I was mildly offended. I made good choices. At least one good choice a week, I was sure.

When I glanced back on my way to the door, Junior looked past me, a dark expression on his face that reminded me of the power running through his veins. I followed his gaze to the door closing. I caught his eye again. He lifted his chin at me, but he still had that strange look on his face.

Talbot was already in his car—a freaking Corolla—waiting for me. He watched me through his windshield. Heat flushed through me as I got in the bug and started it.

With the lights of San Alvarez far behind me as I got closer to the orchards, the night pressed hard against my windows. It was a half hour opportunity for Talbot to turn back, but he didn't.

I wondered how often he invited people out here. Guys. How often did he invite guys out here? And what did it mean, coming all the way out here? He obviously wanted to be away from others. Alone. With me?

Something about Junior's look before I left was still bugging me.

Junior had never disapproved of anyone I had taken an interest in. Not that there had never been anyone serious but Jonah, and, well, see above: pipe dream.

Dirt crunching under my wheels, I followed Talbot's brake lights onto the shoulder and stubbed out my cigarette. What if he hated the smell of cigarettes? He had smelled so . . . clean.

I turned off the car and texted Junior, *You had a face. ?*

Junior: *He's not the type you bring home to ma.*

Junior: *Where u going?*

I used voice-to-text to reply, afraid to take my eyes off Talbot's car and have my impending make out sesh disappear.

Me: *Maybe that's the exact type I'm looking for.*

I saw another text from Junior, *Por dios where?* Nerves twisting my guts, I texted back, *Orville's,* and got out of the bug.

I leaned on the Corolla's hood beside Talbot. The engine ticked and the trees seemed to whisper in the gentle wind. He stared out at the rows, as if he could see a damn thing.

"Hey," I said.

The ancient street lights were few and far between out here, so it was hard to see what he was thinking. One could only hope it was inappropriate thoughts.

"It's nice out here, isn't it?" he asked.

I guess if you liked loitering in the sticks in the pitch black.

What I said was, "Sure."

The moon reflected off his glasses. He was so different from Jonah. I had no business thinking about my ex-best friend, comparing him to potential love interests, because he never returned my feelings, but here I was. Doing that. Maybe some sort of self-preservation instinct was kicking in.

He looked at me, and I resisted looking back.

Through the trees, I could see a sliver of light, an outline of a distant window, like it was blocked out. The wind was starting to feel a little chilly.

"When I was a kid," said Talbot, "my mom used to drive me out here. We'd walk through those trees there. She wanted me to understand that my world was enclosed and that if I did not do something about it, it would always be that way for our kind. Imprisoned by our own fear."

"Probably a pretty healthy fear to have there," I said.

Because *vampiria* were fatally attracted to our blood, there was a centuries-old treaty that protected both species by dividing territories. This was so they wouldn't go crazy in the presence of our blood, and we wouldn't get eaten by them. Sounded legit to me.

"It's nice though, isn't it?" he asked. "Being a wolf? You're freed from the limits that control the rest of our clan. Keeping inside the lines, like we're a flock of sheep."

"What's that supposed to mean?" I smiled, trying to hide my disappointment. I had no idea what he was going on about. I just wanted to play some tonsil hockey, like one inning. That's all I was asking for. I get why he might mistake me for a wolf though. I was always hanging around them since Jonah and I stopped talking.

"There's so much more out there the elders don't want us to know about. The things we all might be able to achieve if they loosened the leash." He sounded excited.

"Maybe. But I wouldn't really know," I said. "That's Junior and his clique. I'm just an interloper."

When he turned his full attention back to me, I felt like I was under a microscope. "You're not a wolf?"

"Nope," I said.

He took off his glasses to clean them. I didn't want to make him uncomfortable. Maybe I was smiling too much. Leaning too close.

"What is this?" I asked, holding up the bottle he'd had on the hood beside him.

"I brought it," he said.

Duh. But why? What did this mean?

He looked at his phone. "I gotta go."

"Aren't you going to have some?"

He seemed agitated. "No. Keep it."

"Why are you leaving?" I asked. "We just got here." And gas money didn't grow on trees, particularly not for the ticking, hissing hunk of metal behind me.

He started to walk away, and I panicked. Everything I'd been looking for tonight was right here.

I reached out for his arm. "Hey."

He stared down at my hand.

"Stay," I said, my voice low. It felt like something I couldn't say too loud.

He pushed his glasses up with his other hand. "Let go of me," he said.

I let go immediately. A sickening wave of déjà vu made me stumble back against my own car. Not this again.

"You should go, too," he said.

I didn't move. I watched him get into his car. His dash lights flashed when he turned over the engine. He was staring at me.

Don't overanalyze it. My mom took everything as a sign when she read my Tarot or when I told her about something strange happening, like a seagull shitting on my shoulder on the pier. I really didn't want to think this was a sign that I was fated to be unwanted and alone for the rest of my life.

Don't overanalyze this, I repeated to myself.

Long after he was gone, I still held the bottle, my consolation prize. It sloshed inside, the glass cool and heavy in my hands. I lit a cigarette, catching a glimpse of the label. Patron. Expensive stuff, and he just left it.

I put my cigarette out in the center of the label. Shoving the butt in my pocket, I thought about taking a drink. I wasn't that guy that got wasted and tore around the city, drunk driving. But I did want to be a different guy than the one I was right now.

I pulled out my phone. Junior's response had come twenty minutes ago,

Junior: *On my way*

Me: *Don't worry, DAD, nothing happened*

A noise came from somewhere in the trees, reminding me that I was completely alone out here.

I pushed off the bug and made for the tree line. I kept alongside it. I didn't know exactly where the boundary line was, and I didn't want to stumble past it if the stories about blood-crazed *vampiria* were true.

It seemed like a stupid risk, but I couldn't make myself stop. I wasn't ready to go back to my car and that sad lonely bottle.

There it was again—a strange muffled sound, like tearing paper. Every small noise was amplified out here. We had parked right where the trees began, so the orchard rows weren't that long. I walked a little farther, trying to see through the trees.

The sound was almost sensual. My cheeks got hot. I stood there for fifty-two beats of my heart. Somehow, I caught the light from a street lamp that felt miles away, and I could see someone hunched over, body rhythmically moving. I tried to make sense of it.

Then my brain put it together. This thing was sucking. *Feeding.*

What in the actual fuck?

Instinctually, I reached for my magic. I couldn't use it without being near Jonah, but I needed to feel something right now.

I felt nothing but darkness. Like this thing was suffocating me. And stupidly, selfishly, I wanted my Kindred by my side.

I couldn't hide from the truth that had been dogging me for months anymore.

I needed Jonah.

2

Jonah

"Jonah, get up."

I had been having a really good dream. Then, I was falling, so not so good.

I woke up on the floor, my elbow stabbing me in the hip.

"What the . . ." I tried to say, but it sounded something more like, "Wheat thin . . ."

"Get dressed."

A rush of hot awareness filled my body at the sound of Apollo's voice.

Apollo was in my room.

Something hit me in the face. I peered at it in the dark. A hoodie. Okay.

"What the hell?" I managed to say through a mouth full of fleece.

After pulling the sweater around my head, I realized I'd fallen out of my blankets and was only in my underwear. I ran pretty hot when I slept. "I don't have any—"

Denim flew at my face.

"Would you stop?" I stepped into my pants as angrily as one can perform such a task. Once dressed, I couldn't do anything but acknowledge him. The fact that he just popped up in my room in the middle of the night after ignoring me for the last five months was less than ideal.

But *damn*, I missed him.

My heart, racing from being violently awoken, amped up again at the way he looked.

I had always been envious of his skin, because it looked tan year-round and never got acne. His mom had named him after the sun god, for godssake. He was pale now. His eyes were wild. He looked totally on edge.

I wondered if he was holding right now. Being under twenty-one, our kind weren't supposed to be able to throw magic. All *magikalia* could gather it from our surroundings, but if you didn't have an outlet, it could make you crazy holding all that power inside you. Magic ate you up, trying to get out. That was exactly how my ex-best friend looked right now.

"Why are you here?" I asked, afraid that he'd just walk out. I dropped my gaze to his chest.

He had on one of those sweatshirts that, first of all, nobody had been seen wearing since 1997, with the cinched cuffs and bottom hem. And secondly, had this corny image advertising a ranch in Montana, with a white horse, mid-gallop, and a river of stars behind it. I never could be sure if Apollo wore these types of things to be ironic or if he genuinely liked them. Whatever the reason, his clothing hardly fit the badass-musician vibe he'd been grasping at since his dad got him a mini Fender Squire when we were seven.

The thing about Apollo was that he never stopped moving. He always had to be wagging his leg back and forth, or tapping his fingers, or playing a guitar while you were trying to have a conversation with him.

Right now, he was very still as he stood next to my dresser, five feet away.

"I need you to come with me."

His voice was quiet and lethal. The way he was looking at me right now made me cold. Maybe it had just been too long since I'd seen him here in my room, so close we could speak.

"What is going on?" I asked.

"Please, Jonah. I don't play this card often, but I'm really going to need you to hold the questions."

He played that card exactly never, since we didn't talk anymore.

"Okay, just let me get—"

"We have to leave now."

"Okay. I just have to—"

He growled. Literally. I think my name was somewhere in there.

I was afraid he would wake up my parents, or worse, the baby, or even worse than that, one of my nosy siblings—specifically Maddie, two years older than me—who would have too many questions about what Apollo was doing here. Then she would pause. Then she would add almost a full minute later, '*in the middle of the night.*'

I grabbed my phone, keys, and baseball bat from behind the door for good measure. I wasn't sure what we were going into, but I had never seen Apollo look that afraid.

Apollo's bug was not the kind of car you sneak out in. He didn't seem to care as we drove through the neighborhoods we used to wander together. Once we got on the highway, I couldn't keep silent anymore.

"What are we doing?"

"You would never believe me."

"Must be pretty bad for you to call a cease-fire."

His hands tightened on the wheel. "Jonah." He turned his head like he was going to say 'you're the one that stopped talking to me.' I wasn't ready to talk about any of that, so I didn't push for more.

He had his sweatshirt sleeves pushed up. I could see the tendons shifting under his skin. I watched him in the passing glow of the street lights and neon signs, his concentrated face, his dark eyelashes and strung out eyes.

A memory flashed in my sleep-fuzz brain: Apollo and his dad working on this car, Apollo taking in the dubious glance I flicked at it, assuring me it would work—eventually—and me handing him tools, assuring him I believed him—not really. There were a lot of days spent like that, just hanging out at his house or him at mine, days I tried not to think about anymore. I didn't like to think about things like that, because . . . well, because it wasn't an efficient use of my time, as my Dad would say.

"Is this going to be very long, because—" My stomach growled.

Apollo looked at me like I was revolting

"I'm starving," I said.

"You woke up like two minutes ago," he said. I wasn't used to this quiet, withdrawn Apollo.

I hadn't known Apollo to be a cold person. Everything about him had always run hot—his temper, his beliefs, his passions. I felt my face get hot and turned away. I swear, I never got philosophical like this unless I was woken up at an ungodly hour before getting ten hours of sleep at minimum.

"Besides," he said, "All the late-night places are closed."

"Not Jack in the Box," I said, coughing into my fist.

More of those memories I shouldn't be thinking about swam to the surface of my mind: Apollo and I playing Risk with my family, listening to his dad, Jack, lecture about the difference between a condenser and dynamic mic, us staying up until four a.m., binging Stranger Things or Twilight Zone since catching Mom watching an episode once. We spent more time tossing curly fries in the air and trying to catch them in our mouths than watching. We'd already seen all the episodes anyway.

I closed my eyes, leaning my head back. City lights lit up the back of my eyelids. The handle of my bat knocked against my knee.

I thought about anything I could so I wouldn't think about how we used to be. How we weren't anymore.

Bottom of the ninth. One of ours on third waiting for me to hit the home run. The crack of the bat against the ball. A white horse, mid-gallop. Fall. Coffee. Cheeseburgers. Garlic Fries.

Trying to distract myself was just making me hungrier.

"Sorry for waking you up," he said. "I didn't know who else . . ."

That's what I'd been waiting to hear. I sat up, pretending I wasn't tired. "It's fine."

We passed dirt lots featuring rusted irrigation pumps, water silos, rickety step platforms that sat in the middle of nothing, leading up to nowhere. There were darker shadows of power lines against the bruise-blue sky.

I could feel my heart throbbing against my chest. I started to sweat.

He stared hard at the road. I knew his eyes were probably bloodshot. They had been for months. His jaw was clenched. I looked for the other signs of holding.

"I'm glad you came to me," I said, and immediately wished I hadn't. If this were some sort of punishment for what happened between us, I'd sound like an idiot. I hoped Apollo wouldn't be that cruel, but I didn't really know him anymore.

Then again, he couldn't possibly have planned for this tension pulling all of his limbs, even his magic, because if I could feel it, so could he. I could almost taste it, metallic and sizzling between us.

"See? I'm not so sure you're going to be saying that in a minute."

He turned then, into Orville Orchards just outside of San Alvarez. We were on a dirt road that the agriculture vehicles used. The abandoned Miller house was somewhere out there.

"I hope to god I was seeing shit earlier . . ." he said before cutting the lights and letting off the gas.

"This isn't exactly the best vehicle for Incognito," I said, painfully aware that I sounded like know-it-all Maddie.

He looked at me and put his finger to his lips.

I closed my mouth and followed his stare out the windshield. I noticed the shadow about five hundred yards away. Inside the tree rows, something, some *creature*, moved like an animal. My fingers found the end of my bat.

It *moved* like an animal but had the form of a man. Like a rabid man-animal, high on bath salts. Like Edward Norton fighting Tyler in Fight Club. You know, *after* the twist. It reminded me of seeing my neighbor's dog attack a stray Chihuahua when I was a kid, the way it shook the smaller dog around like a toy.

A breeze came through the cracked windows. In fact, it was strange that Apollo didn't have a cigarette out. He almost always smoked while driving. I'd gotten so used to catching the residual scent of Camels on my clothes, turning around in my seat in class, or reaching to open my locker.

The thing stopped moving. Neither of us breathed. It was looking our way. It was impossible that I could see its features in detail from this distance at night, but I could swear its eyes flashed like a cat's when it locked on us. My heart literally stopped.

It stood up. I could feel Apollo's heart kick up as if it were mine. Then, whatever this thing was came at us.

Everything happened fast. Apollo flipping the key in the ignition and pounding the clutch, then brake, shift, ease off clutch, gas. We were moving backwards, but as I stared at that *thing*, it didn't look like we were moving at all. Because even though we were going thirty through the orchard, it had to be moving at least that fast.

We flew out of the trees on the other side, and as the car spun around onto the road, we lost track of the beast.

Apollo got the bug up to forty-five and the odometer was still rising. He was shifting manically. As we flew down the country road, I finally gasped in a breath, looking out the back window.

When I turned back around, there it was in the middle of the road. A blackness so large that it blotted out what little light the moon gave.

One of us took a religious figure's name in vain.

Instead of slamming on the brakes, like any other person would do, Apollo hit the gas harder. I braced for impact.

It felt exactly like plowing into a mountain.

The metal crushing around our legs, the glass shattering. I shut my eyes to the shards. I could feel every part of my body pummeled by the impact. Twisted metal sliced my leg as a wave of glass rained on us, but I couldn't process any pain. I reached over for Apollo, grasping his leg when I found it.

I thought of hitting that home run at the end of the last season.

I'd never felt like I had the advantage in baseball being a magikalis. But that day, I did. I'd wanted to win so badly, and with the score where it was, I knew I had to make this the one.

I'd seen the ball coming at me like I was holding the hands of the clock in place. I looked at the bat and moved it an inch. And when I hit the ball, the bat broke in my hands, wood splinters flying everywhere. I felt like one of the greats. The impact was slowed down like that moment.

A sound boomed on the empty country road. Had that thing jumped on top of the car?

A stream of blood ran a rivulet from Apollo's hairline. The cold air slid in through the shattered windshield. It was too still out there.

The figure seemed to drop from the sky then, trying to rip Apollo from the car. I scrambled for my seat belt, but my legs were trapped. All my nerves started screaming at once.

I had to get Apollo.

If we died, our parents would have no idea what happened. There would only be some drops of Apollo's blood left behind—*blood.*

Apollo screamed in agony as the thing tried to wrench him out, making his legs bend the wrong way.

"*No*!" I screamed.

The car released our legs as the warmth of magic poured through my body. The creature had vanished.

Our kind's blood has a scent the *vampiria* call the blood song, which makes them lose control. Turns them into . . . well, *this*.

Madness from the blood song. That had to be what was wrong with this thing. If that small amount of blood was enough to do this to one of their kind, no wonder the Bureau kept our movement restricted. Our borders existed just as much for them as they did us.

The vampiris was lying on the road. I had put it there with the magic Apollo and I pulled from the same well. It was sparkling through me now, begging to be released again.

My door was stuck. I leaned back with my head against Apollo's shoulder and kicked. It flew open with a groan. I ran around to Apollo's side, laying my bat on the ground and got him out.

"Okay, Jonah?" he asked as I sat him against the side of the car.

I just pulled his concussed ass out of the car, and he was asking if I was okay?

I grabbed my bat and walked over to the vampiris.

It looked smaller like this, crumpled on the ground. I'd done that with the sheer, brute force of my magic. The sheer, brute force being around Apollo gave me.

I used my bat to push it until it flopped onto its back, leaving a glistening stamp on the asphalt, darker than the night. He was covered with blood. You see so much on TV and in games that it doesn't really bother you, in theory. But seeing so much of it and knowing it had previously been in another living thing's body—and the *smell*—sensitized me to it. Its face was lined with all these black veins. And I could see underneath the almost black blood that it was all bloated and red. It had looked sapien from afar, but up close, it made me sick.

I jumped when I noticed its eyes. Open. The pupils almost swallowed them whole save two thin rings of iris—blue or green, it was hard to tell. The eyes looked right at me, aware, while the body laid inert. Had I paralyzed it?

I glanced back at Apollo, and a force barreled into my chest. I landed on my back, and the vampiris pulled my ankles. That's when I smelled it: blood. I'd gotten some of Apollo's on me.

It was opening its mouth. It was definitely a vampiris. Maybe it smelled us on the wind back in the orchard.

I gripped my bat with both fists and swung it back.

The contact with its skull cracked through the air like a pop of static electricity. All I could see was it trying to rip Apollo out of the car, its face as it pulled me toward it. I kept hitting it, wood and bone colliding. Something jerked me back by my sweater, the neck tightening around my throat. I started to swing the bat around.

Apollo.

I stopped, breath scraping in and out of my throat. It felt like there were knives in my lungs.

"We need to burn it," he said. Blood streaked his cheeks like war paint where he'd tried to rub it out of his eyes.

He was right. We couldn't leave any evidence. "Okay."

He pulled out his lighter and kneeled, putting the flame to its clothes. I crouched down beside him and saw just how filthy the clothing was. The knees of the pants were worn out, just like all the hems of the shirt. Strange, given *vampiria's* whole control fetish. Not to mention being a creature with an acute sense of smell.

I put my fingertips to the flame. A spark crawled into my hand, spitting and turning, growing. I carried it to the other end of the body, letting it loose. I second-guessed myself as soon as the flame devoured its kindling.

"Are you sure it was . . . ?" I wanted reassurance. I really hoped we hadn't just killed some mental patient with an NBA vertical jump.

"I'm sure."

As he stared down at the pyre, Apollo's skin seemed to absorb the flickering, orange light and glowed in the heat, while his hair swallowed the night.

We stood there, waiting until it completely turned to ash. The fire burned fast. It was easy to forget what they were before: sapien, one chromosome apart from us, before they turned. This one had a life, maybe even was lucky enough to have a family that loved him. A best friend who missed him.

I stared down at the ashes and bones—femur, jaw, and skull scattered as though a dog had tossed them down after picking them clean. While it was good that we hadn't killed a sapien, it was not reassuring that we had just taken out a vampiris. They weren't supposed to be in any areas where *magikalia* lived. So why had this one been at the border of our territory?

Were there more?

"You okay?" he asked.

"We can't tell anyone," I said, unable to look away from it. We'd killed it, so the clan didn't need to know. If we did tell them . . . "They'll know what we are."

I should have been fine with the idea of being separated from Apollo, since we hadn't been talking for months, but the idea of it, after seeing him nearly be *devoured*, made me sick. It made me feel like we'd wasted so much time fighting over something stupid.

He stepped closer to me, and all the magic in me flared.

"Come on," he said.

I followed him back to the bug.

"I see you got most of it back to its original shape," Apollo said, seeing where I'd blasted it out after the collision.

"Trying to save your ass," I said, voice shaking as I shivered.

He looked grave. This thing had taken all the fight out of him. "Help me with the rest of it?"

I steeled myself for the charge I would feel when we touched. The latent magic that woke up and unfolded when we were around each other and burst into life like it was hit with a defibrillator as soon as we made contact.

Right about now, I understood why the elders stigmatized Kindreds, why they feared the bond of our magic. It was because of this. Because of what we could do together.

I put my hand on his shoulder and let it fill me up. It felt like the good feeling in your head the second before a sneeze, like a wet dream, like sticking a fork into a light socket—I would know. I had actually done that.

I held on to that feeling inside of me like a flame devouring oxygen.

3

Jonah

We'd both been magically active for a few years now, and we never talked about why we'd stopped being friends—mostly because we never talked anymore, full stop. So I'd say we were pretty good at keeping secrets. Which was good, because if we breathed word of this, we wouldn't see each other again until we turned twenty-one at least. Not to mention the trouble we could get in for using our illegal magic to *kill* a vampiris. The echo of what we'd done tonight felt like thick bile rising up my throat.

After the dazed drive to my house, neither of us moved. When we were a good distance from the borderland, we'd stopped and used an old bottle of water to clean off the blood. Apollo still had a streak of it underneath his eyebrow. I couldn't look away from it.

"What were you even doing out there?" I asked, my throat raw.

He shrugged. "Thinking."

Apollo liked driving, but to go as far as the borderland? I decided not to push it. He looked like he was getting lockjaw already, and I hadn't even asked the most important questions.

"How did that . . . thing not notice you before?"

He frowned, tapped his thumb against the steering wheel.

He cleared his throat before speaking. "I think it was . . . feeding. What we saw was the after-dinner show."

I took a shuddering breath. Nightmare fuel. Once, I'd snuck into the living room to watch Insidious. I couldn't sleep for weeks.

"Why did you come to me?" I asked.

I knew the answer to this question, but I needed to hear it, after everything that had happened tonight, after the last six months of radio silence.

That finally got his attention.

"Really, Jonah?"

Okay. He was pissed.

"Please say it," I said. It was so quiet, he probably wouldn't have even heard me begging for him to say it, except that he was staring at my mouth.

He sighed a shaking breath. "I couldn't do anything without you. I needed you. Happy?"

"Yes. I mean, kind of? Not really."

That was the thing about us. It was great and all, being able to use our magic before we were twenty-one, but neither of us could throw unless we were close to each other. It only took being in the same block to feel it rearing up in my chest. It was completely addicting.

It terrified me.

Underage Kindreds were supposed to come forward. The Bureau forbade them from spending unchaperoned time together, because Kindred younglings were thought to be wildcards, and given what we'd just done, they were kind of right. Our kind just don't have magic like that before they turn twenty-one.

On your twenty-first birthday, the clan helps you throw for the first time. They kind of crack the magic out of you, like an egg. It's a whole thing. Apollo and I already shared our first throw, alone, completely by accident. Too afraid of being separated, we never told anyone. I had wondered if it felt that powerful and uncontrollable for the rest of our kind when they came of age. I know it did for Apollo. He told me I made him feel out of control.

Our magic had the same effect on me. We had to be damn near touching, but when we did, magic roared through me like a waterfall without a spigot to turn it off. I could still hear the rushing in my ears from all that we'd used tonight.

"What if there are more like this one?"

"You want me to sleep in your bed with you?"

"I'm serious."

"I don't know," he said, the derision gone from his voice. "We'll get some sleep and reconvene tomorrow. We all know you need your beauty rest," he sounded detached. Defeated. Maybe emptied out, because he'd been holding magic all summer while I'd fantasized about throwing it the whole time.

I wanted to touch him. I wanted to feel it one more time.

I didn't want to think about where he'd be now if he'd been out there by himself.

"It is tomorrow," I said.

He tapped the steering wheel. "I'll see you in a few hours."

He was dismissing me. Cool.

I really hoped he didn't go back to pretending I didn't exist. I thought about bringing up the Jack in the Box he promised me, so we'd have more time. Instead, I clicked the buckle to release my belt, but it wouldn't come loose.

"You're a mess, Jonah." He reached over, brushing my hand to release the belt. The charge ran up my arm and into my chest.

I stumbled out, barely shutting the door before Apollo peeled off.

I turned to the house, checking my phone. It was almost six. Dad didn't have work today, but Mom might be up with my baby sister Joss. I'd have to be quiet to avoid an Inquisition.

I went straight to my room in the basement. I kicked off my shoes and stripped down to my boxers. On second thought, I got some shorts from my drawer, just in case an ex-best friend caught me unawares for a covert mission in the middle of my REM cycle again.

Before getting in bed, I saw the picture of Apollo and I that I'd hid behind a baseball trophy was in the middle of my dresser now. We were laughing at something. Maddie had taken it. She had told me she hardly ever saw me so at ease and happy before. Which was honestly surprising, given all the dumb shit I always had to talk Apollo out of. Maddie gave it to me in a frame that Christmas.

I'd moved the picture behind my trophy after our falling out. Apollo must have moved it. I wondered if he still had it saved on his phone from when he'd asked Maddie to send it to him. I thought about tipping it face down but left it standing there.

Sunday School taught us about what we were. Here in San Alvarez, our clan met in an old records building that had been condemned by the sapiens in the 50s until our clan repurposed it.

There was the lingering smell of old paper from the records that used to line the shelves. An unmanned desk sat at the center of the main hall, like that episode of Twilight Zone where the guy with amnesia walks around an abandoned town.

I found Apollo leaning on the mezzanine railing. The cut on his head was tucked just within his hairline. Though I'd come out of it scrape-free, I felt like I'd been hit by a truck. We could hide away the physical damage from that night. The rest was a different story. I remembered thinking for a moment that night that I might never see his smirk again.

He still didn't look at me as I came up beside him.

It had been easier to talk when danger necessitated it, when the night felt like a viciously tangled dream and nightmare. Today, we were back in a weird place.

"Why are we even fighting, Apollo?" I asked, tired of the silent treatment.

I knew what had started it, but I didn't get why we stopped being friends over a drunk kiss. It would make more sense, us fighting, if I hadn't kissed him back, if I'd gotten mad, but it didn't bother me. I think the problem was that I'm not gay. I'm dating Courtney now, and sometimes I wonder what she would look like naked. Ergo, not gay. That's why I thought the best course of action was to pretend the kiss never happened. But after our last big fight, we'd both shut down the lines of communication, so obviously, not my smartest move. I just wanted him back.

"I'm sorry, okay?" I said.

The atrium on the opposite wall poured sunlight over him. Apollo was made for the light. It was easier to pretend everything was okay in the dark, when I couldn't see the contrast of the sun slanting through the dark hair over his forehead. Or the sharp angles of his cheekbones and jaw, and the dangerous corners of his mouth.

"It was a stupid mistake," I said. "Can we talk about what we're going to do now?"

He clenched his fists before pushing off the railing and walking away.

I crossed my arms, pressing my hands into my ribs, so that I didn't hit something.

I found my family in the meeting room. Apollo and I used to sit by each other during the meetings, our families on either side of us. Now, he was far enough away to make a point.

I hated this. Getting him back just to have him walk away from me again. I glanced at him and saw his normally-slouching back rigid. He was staring down at Graham Jones, our clan leader, and I realized I'd missed whatever Graham had said.

"I shouldn't think I would need to remind any member of this clan that the borderlands are our first recourse of protection. Without them, we are at war for our every breath. Please respect them."

Had someone sensed the fingerprint we left with our magic? Maybe the clan or the Bureau had some kind of spell that let them know when someone stumbled too close, like a spider with its web.

Graham went on about more ordinary things like fundraising and the unanimous vote to preserve the plot of land where the clan performed the twenty-first birthday ritual. I was too much of a nervous wreck to focus on any of it.

Maddie and I went out to the car to wait for Mom and Dad to get the other kids. In the parking lot, we passed a group of a couple elders and some younglings.

"Jonah and Maddie Clarke!" Cody Iver called out to us. "The Bureau son and daughter could do wonders for the cause."

Up until this last summer, the first summer Apollo and I hadn't spent every waking minute together and I didn't have my magic at the ready, I hadn't thought much of Cody Iver.

The entire clan had been there for Cody's 21st birthday, where he'd been provoked to release his magic for the first time. Only, Cody Iver didn't throw a spark that day. He just stood there, waiting for a flood that didn't come. I was always sort of waiting for this to happen, for someone to be a dud. Up until freshman year, when Apollo and I learned we were Kindred, I feared that would be me.

Cody's magic did eventually erupt, a few months later, but I remembered having to crouch from the secondhand nausea or relief, hand to the earth so I didn't fell over. Apollo's fingers had been cool and reassuring on the back of my neck as spots danced in the corner of my vision. I'd had no idea what the comfort of his touch had meant then.

A breath passed as birds sung in the trees around the parking lot. Being likened to my by-the-book dad, who worked for the Bureau, after doing what we'd done was less than ideal.

"What cause?"

Talbot Erikson, who had been quietly watching, blocked Cody from my line of sight. Okay. Not weird at all.

I could still hear the others' voices fighting for dominance in a conversation that made no sense to me.

"—new head of research—"

"—trying to find a way to help others."

"She wants a world where our species can live side by side."

I had no idea who they were talking about, but I hoped to all that was holy they weren't talking about *vampiria* and us living side by side. If they'd ever run for their lives from one, there's no way they could see that as a good thing.

A few parking spaces away, Apollo and Quinn Young watched the group.

"Did Talbot harp about all that at the club?" she asked him.

"No." He flicked a glance our way, uncrossing his arms.

Quinn threw an arm around him before joining her parents. Apollo ducked into his bug, leaving a trail of condensation from his exhaust pipe as he left the parking lot.

"What are they talking about?" I asked Maddie, nodding at Cody's group.

Maddie kicked the tire of our Tahoe. "They're pro-cure. Who knows."

"Pro-what?" I asked.

Why had Apollo been so interested in them?

"God, you're so clueless. The movement to find a cure so *vampiria* won't be driven insane by our blood?"

I was only half listening, because I was still seeing the burning vampiris. Every time I thought about it, I got wound up.

We almost died.

We *killed* a vampiris.

Apollo still hates me.

"Why would they want that?" I tracked the growing distance between me and Apollo.

"You're hopeless."

First, I was a mess. Now, I was hopeless. I was batting a thousand.

"*What?*" I asked. Sometimes getting Maddie to answer questions was like prying your own fingernails up.

Dad looked pissed as he walked up, passing Joss to Mom. As she strapped Joss in, Dad's knuckles turned white over the top of the driver's side door. He was listening to Cody and Talbot's group.

Maddie glanced at Dad, straightening one of her curls between two fingers, before saying, "It's a radical stance. They think curing *vampiria's* blood lust for us would be this harmonious, diplomatic achievement. But if *vampiria* got themselves all nice and immune to the blood song and called off the treaty, we'd still be at risk to a species stronger than us with exactly zero moral misgivings about feeding from the living."

"Now's not the time to discuss this," said Dad, as he got in. I glanced at Miles and Macy, who looked fine. Maddie turned to stare out the window.

Dad often had to deal directly with the *vampiria* (thank god for video calls). Dad knew better than anyone that the treaty depended on the one weakness *vampiria* had to us.

As Dad backed out of the space, Mom took off her belt, sliding to the middle of the seat. She kissed his neck before laying her head on his shoulder.

"Put your seatbelt back on," he said.

4

Jonah

We used to ride to school together every day. And even though we battled and took down a rabid vampiris together last night, here I was, walking to school alone.

As soon as I arrived, I tore off my jacket. I leaned my head against the inside of my locker door. As soon as I closed my eyes, I saw the vampiris, eyes rolled back in its head. What had we done?

Something touched my back. I about jumped out of this realm.

Courtney.

She had a concerned look on her face as she pulled her hair behind her ear.

"I think I just fell asleep while standing here," I said.

"You okay?" she asked.

I really wasn't.

"Just tired." I smiled at her. I hated making her worry, and apparently, I was just this walking worry-inducing mess. Who wants to be that guy?

"You?" I asked.

"I'm fine, babe." Her smile was uncertain.

She reached up to smooth my hair down, then hooked her hand around my neck and pulled me into a hug. She smelled like vanilla and something sweet and floral. I wanted to fall into her and take a nap here on the floor by the lockers.

"Hey! Clarke!"

Brixton, from the baseball team, slapped my shoulder on his way by. I tried not to wince. I had fallen on it wrong, out at Orville's.

"You look beat, dude. Stay up cramming for that Wilshire exam? Make sure you get at least passing for the team's sake."

I slammed my locker shut.

"Why are you mad?" Courtney asked.

"I finished studying for that physics test three days ago. *I'm* the one with straight A's, but everyone assumes I'm this big, dumb jock." It would be easier to pretend to be the dumb jock and live up to everyone's expectations if I didn't experience nuclear meltdown when people brutalized the English language.

"They just don't know the real you like I do."

She leaned in to kiss me again. Her tongue surprised me. I enjoyed kissing my girlfriend, and I enjoyed partaking in French kissing. But not right in the hall.

"Personal space, Mr. Clarke," said my math teacher, Mrs. Hudson, as she walked by.

After school, I was in a mood. As I threw turkey and mustard on bread to fight the hanger, someone knocked on our door. I inhaled half the sandwich before coming out of the kitchen to see Macy answering the door.

I felt myself gathering before I realized why my magic was all pinging inside me excitedly.

"How many times have I told you not to answer the door yourself?" I asked Macy. "Come get one of us."

She dead-faced me. "It's just Apollo."

I jerked the door open. He certainly looked like he'd gotten plenty of sleep while skipping the first half of the school day.

"Great," I said, "now you want to talk to me."

Maddie ran past me as I walked back to the kitchen.

"Apollo!" Her voice was ridiculously girly.

Before disappearing down into the basement, I saw her jumping into his arms. He had this stupid grin on his face.

Wonder when they'd become best friends.

My phone buzzed in my pocket with a text from Mom.

Don't forget about the dishwasher.

If our magic worked like bippity-boppity-boo, I wouldn't be wasting precious time on chores. I could be napping and reactively ignoring my ex-best friend instead of unloading the dishwasher. Unfortunately, it doesn't work like that.

Besides, no one in my family knew what Apollo and I were, that were both able to use magic while underage. I'd almost told Maddie so many times. Despite being two years older, extremely annoying, and having skipped a grade, we were close.

I tried to hurry with the dishes so I could go down to my room and lock the door behind me. Maddie appeared in the doorway. She was doing that thing where she's got her arms crossed and her hip out to one side, because she just knows everything and weren't you a douche for making her explain.

"You're being an ass," she said.

"I'm sure he'll be happy to tell you why. I didn't start it."

She dropped her voice and came up beside me. "This is your chance to finish it."

"Maybe I'm tired of always being the bigger person."

"What other situation, ever, have you had to be the bigger person?"

I willed something, anything to come to mind. I know there had been something—"Look, Maddie, I can't just pull every situation out of my ass to appease you."

She put up her hand, palm out. I thought she might say something profound. She did do that once in a while.

"Your anger is not with me, young Padawan."

I pushed past her to the basement.

I wasn't *hoping* to be followed. I wanted to be left alone. But when I heard the lock unclick, I threw myself on my bed. The door opened and closed.

"You're not supposed to do that," I said through my teeth, annoyed that he'd risk using our magic where any one of my family could notice.

No response.

I flipped onto my stomach, clenching my pillow so I didn't throw it at him. He looked around as though he forgot what the Clarke family basement/my room looked like. Then again, it had been a while since he'd seen it in the daylight.

"If you hate me so much," I said, "why did you bring me into this?"

"You know why."

I hated that he didn't argue. I sat up, leaning back against the wall.

"I'm just having a little trouble wrapping my mind around the scenario in which you saw that and thought, *oh, you know what? Jonah and I can handle this.* I mean, I'm flattered, and hey, we're alive, but why didn't you just go tell someone? Then we wouldn't be walking around like fugitives."

He took a couple steps back toward my dresser and sat on the floor. He drew his knees up and draped his arms over them.

I hated his untouchably green, ice chip eyes. I hated his sharp mouth. I hated that he was so closed off to me now.

"It wasn't really a thought process kind of moment. It was just: stop this thing or it attacks the clan; get Jonah, or die trying to stop this thing alone."

"Why not leave it? It was out at the boundary. No one is out there."

"Except whatever it was already eating," he said in an even voice.

He was right, but I couldn't let it go. "I don't know what exactly I would have done, in your place. But I wouldn't have dragged you into it and flipped into asshole mode on you."

Apollo's smile was tired and lazy. "Just because you saved my life, doesn't mean things can go back to the way they were, Jonah."

Yeah, apparently, if he was content to smile at me in private and ignore me in public.

"I didn't say I wanted that," I snapped. "And I didn't save your life."

"No?" he asked, raising his eyebrows. "Throwing the vampiris away from me? Reversing the bug's damage to get me out? Almost hitting that thing's head off its body? What would you say it was?"

"Wasn't really a thought process kind of moment," I said, mocking him. He didn't deserve the peace offering, but I think he needed it. Like I had needed to hear him that night.

I was helpless without you.

His eyes swiveled to me. The silence was full of understanding. I was about to ruin it.

"So, were you just using me?"

"What?" His voice had kind of an edge.

"What am I supposed to think? You've been ignoring me ever since."

He stood up without using his arms for leverage.

He was strong for someone so . . . angular. You could see my strength. Apollo's strength showed in maybe something deeper than that. Grim determination probably.

He leaned down so that his eyes were level with mine. His inky brown hair looked like an orgy of ancient Greeks splayed on fainting couches. His mouth had always seemed girly to me. Pink and shaped very symmetrically. I watched it form a small circle, like a kiss.

"You are an idiot," he said, and hit me on the top of the head with a hardback book I didn't see him grab. Then he walked out.

I didn't move to catch it as it fell. I didn't do anything, just tried not to feel sorry for myself. A few tears leaked out anyway.

5

Apollo

"What are you doing here?" asked Quinn.

I jumped and rolled out of the hammock onto my knees.

I hadn't planned to drive to Quinn's after leaving Jonah's house. It just happened, the giant oak tree waving in greeting from blocks away.

"You don't look great," said Quinn.

"You know, I've been playing with my color palette. I must be getting it all wrong." I dusted my pants off as I stood.

"What's going on, buddy?"

"I had to get out, you know?"

Quinn nodded. Crossed her arms. "Anything happen with your new Elder friend? I didn't see you at school." She got jealous when anyone left her behind for someone else. I could totally relate.

"*Nada*." I itched for a cigarette, but it pissed her parents off. I tapped a beat on the pack through my pocket.

"Oh, come *on*! There was a distinct bubble around the two of you, warning off other viable mates." She snorted. She always laughed at her own jokes, even if no one else did.

I forced a smile. "Yeah, guess it was all mine. Want to go out?"

She looked as though going out two times in a seven-day period was overdoing it. But that had been *last week*.

"I'm staying home tonight," she said. "Dad says you can come in."

I tried not to feel like a stray dog. Quinn's parents were totally fine with me crashing on the couch. That's just how the clan worked. Blood was blood.

"Come on. We could pool our Monopoly assets. I'll let you have Baltic and Mediterranean."

I loved my purple properties, but I didn't want to interrupt their family time. Also, I had a headache, so a Young family game night was out of the question.

I begged off and checked my phone before starting the bug.

Mom: *Leftovers in the fridge if you're hungry when you get home.*

She was never too inconvenienced by my absence.

And then, Jonah: *Can you please just talk to me?*

It was weird seeing a text from him. The last one in our conversation was me congratulating him on his new baby sister, Jocelyn, months ago, right after our blow out. I hadn't received an answer. I wondered how long he would have ignored me if I hadn't shown up at his house the other night.

The last few months had been a kind of self-imposed torture—a withdrawal period. I could have just bit my tongue and acted unbothered by the whole thing, which is basically what Jonah did. (Let me just point out here that I don't make it a habit to base my behavior on the example of Jonah.)

I know it's not the best idea to kiss your more-than-likely-straight best friend. But I had to. That night, I had to know.

We'd been up late, mainlining Stranger Things on Netflix. Friday nights were always my favorite because of the weekend looming ahead of us. *Us*, because it was always a given Jonah and I would be hanging out.

The lights had been off, and the TV was low because my parents were sleeping. We were chugging Sprite mixed with Jack Daniel's and popping Skittles. We were also sharing a blanket, because it was a rainy night, and we had the window open cause otherwise Jonah would get too hot. We were on the floor, with our backs against the couch in my room.

Our sugar-alcohol rush was losing gas. I had thought we were close to falling asleep when Jonah's gravelly voice broke through the dark.

"Do you think what we're doing is wrong?"

I hadn't been sure what he meant, but I was sure it had to be different than what I was thinking because we weren't even *doing* anything.

"What are we doing?"

"You know, Apollo." He suddenly looked wide awake, unblinking. I wondered if he was drunk.

My buzz had mostly worn off. "Do I?"

He finally looked away and scoffed, tossing his hand back to hit me. I grabbed it before I could stop myself and held the back of his hand to my chest. He looked at me again. Then I kissed him.

I knew, I fucking *knew* that moment would change everything. I wouldn't be able to take it back. But I didn't stop.

I expected him to push me away.

He didn't. Everything in my body lit up like a Christmas tree, because he kissed me back. Jonah Clarke, who I had been best friends with since my first memories, for whom I had come to feel more than friendship some time freshman year (who made sure I knew to say 'for whom'), who I was ridiculously, savagely in love with, was kissing me back. I was so happy, because straight guys didn't kiss other guys like this.

I almost felt bad for ignoring him. Turns out, he'd just been placating me, giving me a taste of what it could be like, before completely writing it off as nothing. Oh, correction. Before writing it off as a 'stupid mistake'.

I shouldn't have thought anything of it. He was drunk. Jonah always wanted to give, to comfort. Maybe that was part of being in a big family like his. Though I'd taken care to never let my stare linger, never acknowledge things a platonic best friend wouldn't acknowledge, maybe he had known how I felt and just wanted to make me happy. He was always trying to make everyone else happy to the point that it was nauseating.

Whatever his reason, apparently I wasn't supposed to interpret it the way I did, as his sober-sounding voice told me as soon as we'd *finished kissing*: 'I'm not gay.'

My mouth still tingled from his forceful kiss that told me he wanted this as much as I did. But, then, he *literally* told me he didn't.

I lived and breathed those three words for weeks. The scene played over and over in my head, on my lips and tongue. I was embarrassed and ashamed, and I hated that my best friend, who I'd always felt completely comfortable around, could make me feel dirty about who I was, like I'd taken advantage of the situation and somehow inflicted my gayness onto him.

Since our fight the next day about it, with his affronted puppy dog eyes saying 'What did I do?'—God, he could be such a martyr—and the way he'd completely shut down after I told him off, I hadn't been able to bring myself to let go of my magic.

Holding for that long was inadvisable to say the least; it made you feel sick, kind of woozy and heavy like a sodden sponge. But holding became compulsive.

Normally, we trickled out what we could when we were near each other. Instead, I held mine in like I hugged my pillow to the hole in my chest for the next month straight. My mom had checked on me every day, didn't 'give me my space.'

Those four days of fever sleep showed me what it must have been like for Jonah to have nightmares that made him wake up screaming. But the time after our fight showed me what it was like to love someone you couldn't have. That's what I did, because I'm an expert at self-destruction.

Even now, six months after I fucked everything up, I couldn't bring myself to admit that maybe he just was not gay. I had already known that I was, but I'd never felt *that* kissing anyone else. Hadn't he felt it too?

My phone pinged. Think of the devil.

Jonah: *We have to be on the same side here, Apollo.*

Getting me to say I needed him when I woke him up to come with me had been a power play. I could tell he thought of it as an 'I forgive you.' So not the case.

The look on his face when I showed up at his house twisted a thorn under my rib though. I hated hurting him.

Even when he was hurting me worse.

I looked up Quinn's street. Quiet, peaceful. The club waited with shiny distraction.

Oblivious Jonah went right on.

Jonah: *With my Dad's job, we can't just pretend nothing happened.*

I knew his dad worked for the Bureau and that his mom taught at Sunday School. I hated that he felt the need to remind me. It reaffirmed that we'd grown apart, that he thought I could forget something like where he came from and the people who raised him.

Jonah: *We used our magic to kill a vampiris.*

I put him out of his misery.

Me: *I remember.*

What *were* we going to do?

Jonah: *I can't close my eyes without seeing it.*

My chest tightened. I pressed back against the headrest.

Whenever he used to spend the night at my house, he'd throw himself around in his sheets, guttural sounds escaping his throat. Used to be, when he'd been having a night terror, I'd lean over the bed and guide him with my breathing. If that didn't calm him down, I'd touch him. I'd run my hand through his hair. Or just barely touch his chest—always shirtless because he was too hot when he slept. I'd feel the calm leaking out of me and into him. He'd always wake up in the morning as though nothing had happened. Maybe you had to be good at forgetting things to come back from dreams that did that to you.

Now, I imagined his low, gravelly voice over the phone with Courtney as *she* calmed him down from his nightmares.

Me: *I'm sorry.*

And I meant it. I can't say that I wished I wouldn't have come to him, because I would be dead. That's how Kindreds worked. And I couldn't *not* go back out there, despite his claims from the hypothetical moral high ground.

Jonah always had this image of how he wanted things to be, thought they should be, and he refused to stray.

Jonah: *We need to deal with this together.*

I wondered if he'd read any of the book I'd hit him over the head with.

I hadn't liked reading until Jonah had introduced me to it. Lending me his books like they held the secrets to the universe. Goosebumps when we were in sixth grade. Then *Hatchet*, *The Lion, the Witch, and the Wardrobe*—the magic of which made me extremely self-conscious during the endless stretch of months it took me to read it—*Bridge to Terabithia.* I thought of Jesse and Leslie in *Bridge to Terabithia* and how it all turned out for them.

I agree, I wrote back.

Back at Purple Haze, I weaved through the crowd, looking for Talbot. I guess I wanted to check on him after everything that had happened at Orville's, before and after he'd left me alone. I forced myself not to dwell on my assumptions about him hitting on me. I had read the entire situation wrong, which was turning out to be my brand apparently.

I was about to head out back to smoke, when a woman came up to me.

Her chestnut skin looked rough, like she'd picked up a pack of Marlboros when she was five and never looked back. I guess I couldn't talk, but at least I'd waited until my teens. Her tight hot pink dress indicated that she didn't shop at stores for her age.

She fluffed her dark hair; it looked like a life-long habit. I hadn't really come out to be hit on by old chicks.

"Apollo? Apollo Tormey?"

"Maybe," I said, shoving my hands in my pockets.

"They told me about your scar," she said in an accent, touching the cheek below her left eye, opposite the side my scar was on.

Not necessarily a cool story. I'd fallen off the couch when I was a baby and hit the corner of the coffee table. Looked badass though.

"I'm Lupita," she said. "You know Junior?"

I glared at her. I knew enough about Junior's mom to know that she left when he was a kid and they'd reconnected recently.

"Have you seen him?" she asked.

"Yeah."

"We were supposed to meet up yesterday. He never showed."

"Okay."

She looked at me like I was being a turd. Fair.

"Can you tell him I was looking for him? I'm at the Rosington."

Why would someone who threw her kid away like trash suddenly start keeping tabs on him in his *twenties*? Was it that easy for sapiens? To only love when it was convenient for them?

"Sure. Yeah. I'll tell him." I didn't know if Junior would laugh or cry when I told him. He rarely did anything between. Even two decades after his father left, he still always joked, 'you ever met a Junior who didn't have a Senior?' He obviously still felt some type of way about being abandoned by his parents.

I went outside and opened my conversation with Junior. He hadn't said anything after my distracted text back on Saturday.

Hey, I texted. *Your mom is looking for you.*

I lit my cigarette and picked my phone back up, smiling.

This is not a test, I wrote. *Or a 'your mom' joke. I guess you missed your date with her?*

I expected to see him responding. He never once let me down over the summer while I was recovering. After a minute passed, I called him but it went to voicemail. He didn't have a personalized message. I hung up, knowing he wouldn't listen to a voicemail anyway.

After only a few hours of sleep, my mom summoned me back to the world of the living. I opened my eyes to her standing in the doorway of my room, the hallway light on behind her. I put my pillow over my face.

"What?" I moaned.

"We have an emergency meeting with the clan before school today."

Anxiety turned into a rock in my gut. I took the pillow off to gauge her expression. It gave away nothing. "Okay," I said, suddenly wide awake.

"Do you want me to do an aura-cleanse before we go?" she asked.

Getting smudged was Zarina Tormey's version of wiping your feet on the floor mat when you walk through the door.

"I'm good."

When I finished gathering my clean clothes for a shower, she didn't move out of my doorway.

"Nice reply last night, by the way" she said.

I grunted, about to move past her, trying to hide how worried I was about this sudden meeting.

She put her hand on my chest and wrinkled her nose. "Were you imbibing?"

"No."

"You know I don't mind giving you your independence—God knows my parents kept me on a short leash, and look where that got me. Knocked up at twenty-one—but you need to pick up the phone if you're going to be gone all night."

To be fair, I *had* picked my phone up. And checked my socials. "Noted."

After my shower, the smell of bacon lured me to the kitchen. I couldn't remember the last time I'd eaten. My stomach had been in knots since the orchard. And being around Jonah again. That too.

Dad glanced over when I leaned against the counter, waiting for food as he cooked.

"Hey, Stranger," he said.

"Greetings, Earthling."

He frowned at the bacon. I could start a YouTube channel about how to be a disappointment to your father in under five syllables.

Mom was such an advocate of my freedom to "find" and "express" myself that she didn't worry about me too much. Dad definitely worried more, but, not being like us, he seemed almost afraid of me, this foreign species, his gay son. Music was the only language we spoke fluently to one another.

"No potatoes?" I asked through a bite of bacon, scooping eggs with chiles onto my plate.

"Ingrate."

He pretended to joust me with the fork, but I danced out of his reach, mouth full and laughing.

He took his plate and disappeared into his studio, so I ate breakfast alone. This way, I didn't have to pretend like I was interested in whatever Mom would be talking about—chakras or aura imaging. I didn't have to listen to Dad talk about stuff I cared about—music—while all the other things I cared about—things embedded in my atomic make up—weren't even worthy of a footnote.

I wondered if the real point of parents was to make you feel more alone.

Except for Jonah's parents. They were full of love. They had enough for each other, all their kids, and even me. I could see why Jonah looked to their relationship as a model. Maybe that's why he chose Courtney. Then again, I guess I didn't really know what the hell he was thinking, since I never gave him a chance to explain.

I'm not gay.
That should be enough, right?
Why did it feel like it wasn't?

There was a specific feeling when you walk into the old records building for Sunday School, like the building scented you, made sure you belonged. Usually, when it bid me welcome, my whole body warmed in relaxation, like entering a separate world from the outside that completely accepted us. Entering it now, for the second time in the span of a few days, it felt like it was condemning me. I moved quickly over the threshold, sure I might catch fire.

I nodded at Danish, who stood at the door. I don't even remember how he got that nickname. Probably ate so many Danishes he got sick. The guy loved food to a fault.

It always felt weird leaving my dad behind for these meetings, like forgetting my phone or wallet.

Going in, I didn't know what to expect. After shooting Jonah a text this morning—*do you know what this is about?*—all I'd gotten in response was, *no clue.* Less than a paragraph reply meant he was probably shitting himself. And I got it. If this was about us, his dad was going to disown him.

Mom and I walked through the entry hall to the main chamber at the back. The ceilings were towering and arched, with columns lining either side of the center walkway.

There were a lot of old places in San Alvarez, but the records building reminded me of our heritage, reminded me that we had been here as longer than any of these old buildings.

At the end of the main hall was a round chamber, doors lining the whole thing. The center door was the conference room, where the Elders and the older kids like Jonah, Maddie, and I, joined the clan meetings. Before these meetings commenced, the teachers, like Jonah's mom, Isabel, took their groups of younger kids to the other rooms at the end of the hall. The teachers got the gist of the meeting before the rest of the clan arrived. Since this was an emergency meeting, it looked like most of the youngest kids had been left home with a babysitter. Except for Jonah's little siblings. Baby Joss was in Isabel's lap, and the twins sat like a couple of stone-faced statues barring entrance to a church.

The conference room was this epic amphitheater. There was a circular little space for the speaker to stand. I imagined trials happening in this room, a defendant standing down in that little circle, pleading his case to a hundred unseeing eyes.

Everyone gathered on the top level, behind the balcony railing, swarming like vultures around the food and drink. I was picking through the faces and voices, but when Jonah and I locked eyes, I turned away.

Talbot. That's who I should be looking for.

Relief flooded through me when I saw him. I left Mom with the elders and went over to him near the coffee dispenser. Fortunately for me, there were donut holes and little square napkins laid out beside it. These meetings reeked of a support group.

I watched him for a moment before saying hi and popping a donut hole into my mouth.

He glanced at me like he had no idea who I was.

Ouch. I was about to slouch away.

"Apollo." He said my name like a disappointed elder who didn't have time for me and my youngling woes, a very different person from the one he had been flirting with me at the bar. I had the same moment of dissonance I'd had then. How was this the guy who'd brought a bottle of Patron? Who'd looked *nervous*?

"How are you?" he asked, taking a drink of his coffee—black, I could smell it—and looking around over the top of his disposable lid.

"Oh, exhausted, a bit edgy. The uszh," I said.

As Jonah watched us, I popped another donut hole.

"Did you end up finding what you were looking for the other night?" I asked.

Driving back from Orville's that night, I swore I'd seen his car and another, thankfully parked far from the action. He'd had no problem finding someone else. Why had he invited me out there if he hadn't been into it though? I swallowed against the tightening in my throat. Whatever.

Talbot's eyes widened, and I swear I could see a blush climbing up his neck. Maybe he was shocked that I knew his game.

Then he lifted his chin and walked away.

Okay then.

Strange that Talbot had thought I was a wolf, I remembered as I sat with my mom. Weird that he had never linked me to her. But then, I used to sit with Jonah and his family all the time.

Also, there was the distinct possibility that he hadn't even noticed me before that night.

"First order of business," said Graham, laying his hands on the podium. There were no papers for him to read from. He splayed out his fingers like he was grounding himself. "There is concern that Gilberto Sanchez, known by his friends as Junior, might be missing."

The words hit me slowly, like I was underwater.

I slipped out my phone and opened our texts, expecting to see him jab back at my your mom comment. But he hadn't answered. I went up to our conversation from Saturday, after leaving Purple Haze. His last message had been *on my way.*

What if he'd come after me, worried about me going out to the borderlands? Or that Talbot might steal my virtue—*he's not the type you bring home to ma.* He'd been high, too.

When I'd come across it alone, the vampiris had been feeding. The sugar from the donuts rose up my throat. *No.* I'd seen Junior an hour before. I rubbed my chest, trying to reassure myself. Wolves were always missing, but they're always here or there.

"We, of course," Graham went on, "pride ourselves in being what we are. We are special. But too often, we forget that we're still humans at the base of it and just as susceptible to weakness, fatigue, and mental affliction. It is only when bad things happen that we're reminded we must always be on our guard.

"Even those who linger on the outer edges of this clan are still *magikalia.* They are still family. And we don't leave family alone to fend for themselves."

The only way our clan would know anything about the whereabouts of one of the wolves was if someone had brought it up them. Had Junior's mom gone to them?

I looked over at Jonah, sitting straight and proper between his dad and Maddie. He looked tired.

Everything was hazy when I turned back to Graham. I couldn't stop hearing those words. *There is concern.*

Gilberto Sanchez.

Missing.

I wanted to stand up tell them 'his name is Junior.'

There is concern. It sounded like the opposite of concerned. And here I was, trying to get Talbot to look at me while Junior was missing.

I needed a little more than '*there is concern.*'

I made it to the restroom just in time for the donut holes to come back up.

6
Apollo

After the meeting, I drove out to the orchards instead of going straight to school. For some reason, it was easier to stomach this incredibly stupid idea in the day. I didn't want to think about the possibility that Junior had skipped out on me or about the clan's "concern" anymore.

Driving out to Orville's Orchards at night, you only saw the trees and whatever your own fears were manifesting in shadows. In the day, it looked like a forgotten post-apocalyptic world.

Either way, the sight of the orange trees gnawed a hole in my stomach.

I passed the place where I had seen Talbot's car parked a few hundred yards down from where Jonah and I killed the vampiris. I remembered worrying for a flash that Talbot could get hurt, even though we'd eliminated the threat. Didn't matter. His blank face at the meeting clearly advertised his dumb, happy ignorance to everything I'd been through after he'd left me alone on the shoulder near the treeline.

The abandoned farmhouse jutted up in my peripheral. It was the only sign that anything may have once inhabited this no man's land.

I kept driving, just a little farther ahead. I had to see the scene in the light. Was it as bad as I remembered?

Worse.

There were three vehicles parked on the side of the road, close to where everything had gone down. People in Hazmat suits gathered around the back of an open van. A woman in a suit, hair almost as blonde as her skin was white, stared into the trees while she talked on the phone. She turned as I drove past, locking onto me.

She was one of them. I could feel it, same as Saturday night.

While the one we had killed was pure animal, this one was pure control.

Her eyes followed me until I couldn't see her anymore.

The face of the vampiris as it came through the bug's shattered windshield had been twisted with its single objective of swallowing me whole. I had thought their kind were supposed to detain them when they went ape-shit.

"You're a little late, guys," I said just to feel less alone.

In PE, Jonah dribbled the ball like nothing had happened, like Junior wasn't potentially missing. He had no idea that I'd been running with the wolves while we'd been on the outs. It was disorienting to think that he didn't know that entire part of my life.

As everyone headed to the locker room after class, I slumped down on the empty basketball court.

"Feeling okay, Tormey?" Mrs. Trowbridge nudged my shoe on the way past. Some of the kids called her Mrs. Troll Bridge, but I always thought she was nice. I nodded, and she disappeared into the gym.

I closed my eyes, pulling the heat from the pavement, the echoes of plays and stomping feet, soaking in the magic from all of that energy.

Then I felt it, probably because I was closing my eyes, concentrating on magic—I felt him. He came out of the locker room, dressed already. He probably didn't shower. Using the showers in the locker room embarrassed him. Probably why his socks were the worst smelling socks on this side of the equator.

His girlfriend waited for him by the gate. Courtney Christie. The Girl With Two First Names. Steadfast. Safe.

Instead of going through the gate with her, he stopped. I thought he was going to look back at me. Instead, he started gasping, breath wheezing in his throat. I could hear it from here. I scrambled to my feet, watching. I'd never seen him go off like this, in the day, while he was wide awake.

I'd been having my own nightmares about monsters. Now add to that a woman flaring like a film burn on the backs of my eyelids.

I thought about going over there, then knew that I couldn't. I would just remind him of what happened. All I wanted to do was drag him back into this nightmare with me, because he was my 'on' switch.

He had Courtney now. She was good for him.

She knelt down in front of him. I assumed she was helping him follow her breathing. When they hugged, that was my cue to go.

Inside the gym, I hit the lockers until Jonah got far enough away that the circuit of our magic snapped. I dropped my head against the metal.

"We should have had you hit them from the inside to get all the dents out."

I looked up to find Danny Matthews. He was the best pitcher on the baseball team. He also wasn't wearing a shirt, and his generous athleticism showed. Just, if we're observing all the facts.

"You okay, man?" he asked.

"Yeah," I said.

He sat down on the bench with me. I couldn't stand when people assumed you weren't telling the truth when you said you were fine. I definitely wasn't, but still.

"You're Jonah's friend, right?" he asked.

"Yeah."

He leaned forward, elbows on his knees, deltoids tensing. In it for the long haul. Fantastic.

"I get it. My girlfriend—my ex—dumped me for Dickson, on the football team."

I sat up. Did he know? How could he possibly . . .

"I saw you watching the two of them. Courtney, right?" he said, like she was this magnanimous creature of unearthly beauty.

"Ha! If only it were that simple."

He furrowed his brow. Then it went up. High. "Oh. Oh! That does make things . . . more complicated."

Moments like this, watching Danny's perception of me shift were always kind of disorienting. It was surprising he hadn't already heard from the gossip mill—I'd been out since I was twelve. And it was also irritating that knowing what gender I was attracted to could make someone need to shift their perception of me.

Danny rubbed his hand along the back of his close-cut hair. "My mom says it's better to talk about these things?" He said it like a question, like he didn't really want to be asking about my feelings. "She's a psychologist." He said it like an apology.

"Doesn't it bother you? Knowing that . . ." I couldn't even finish it. What if I was wrong and he still didn't get it?

"That you're gay? Nah. Why should it bother me?"

"Well, it shouldn't. But there's a whole history supporting the fact that it does bother a lot of people."

"Not me. Can't help who you love, right?"

"If I could, I wouldn't be trying to steal the locker's lunch money," I said, making him laugh.

I didn't bother showering, mostly because I didn't want Danny to think I was coming onto him. But I did turn the water on hot and light a cigarette.

Funny how there was magic in even that, in igniting the lighter and taking a drag. It was everywhere. I just had to be aware of it and I could dip right in it. Why would anyone ever want to let all of that warm magic out of their grasp?

7

Jonah

When I was ten, we drove out of state to visit a friend of Mom and Dad's from college. Maddie and I decided to play hide-and-go-seek. Because it was an old house, we didn't think we'd ever exhaust all the crazy hiding places.

I knew Maddie didn't like going into dark places, so when I found the cellar storm doors outside, I was already claiming my victory. I closed the heavy wooden door after me with a *thunk*. From the top stair, I pressed my face to the strip of light between the warped wooden doors and waited. Eventually I got bored staring out from that small crack, and frankly, I started to get a little freaked out looking at the woods at the edge of the property. I kept telling myself if I just stayed down here long enough, I would be the all-time champ. I laughed, thinking of Maddie's face when I won. But the echo of my voice and the stirring of dust made me suddenly aware of my surroundings.

I hadn't looked behind me before closing the doors. I had no idea what was in all that darkness. And it was *dark*. I couldn't even see my hand unless I moved it to the shaft of light. I decided I would olly-olly-oxen free—or maybe just sneak out and find a new hiding place—but when I pushed on the door, it didn't budge. Maybe it was just stuck, or locked somehow. So I kept pushing, and pushing, and then throwing my body against it.

I panicked. What if no one ever found me? What if I starved down here?

I reached out, instinctively, with magic. Nothing had happened, of course. I wouldn't throw with Apollo until I was fifteen, and besides he had been thousands of miles away back in California—we'd called each other almost every day that week.

Without any hope of my magic saving me, I screamed until I didn't have a voice and beat the door until my hand bled.

I don't even remember being found. Later, Maddie told me I'd been lost for three hours.

That was when my night terrors started. That's what Dax, the therapist I'd seen at the time, called the dreams I had that woke me up in a cold sweat, with a throat scorched from screaming. We never played hide-and-go-seek again.

For a while, I snuck into her room to sleep on the floor, but that made her worry about me even more, so I stopped. I felt guilty. It had been my fault, my stupid idea to hide down there—though it had turned out to the best hiding place in the history of our games. Just saying.

Today at school had been the first time I'd ever freaked out like that during the day. All because I'd seen some stupid red paint spilled on the ground. At least with my night terrors, I was unconscious for most of it. When I was sleeping through them, I wasn't aware of every breath squeezed through a closing airway, every tremor and jerk, trying to get away from something that wasn't there. But there, in the middle of school, in broad daylight, I could feel people staring. Courtney was staring.

Worse, I was looking right at her, and I still couldn't stop. She had to get me to follow her breathing like a child.

"Are we going to talk about what happened today?" Courtney asked as she pulled up in front of my house.

I looked out the window. M&M's super soakers were still in the yard from the end of summer. "There's nothing to talk about."

"People always say that when there's plenty to talk about."

"I freaked out. I feel like an idiot. That's it."

"You shouldn't feel like an idiot."

I rolled my eyes. "And yet . . ."

"You can tell me what upset you."

"I can't."

And then this realization: I wanted to talk to Apollo.

"I'm okay. Let's just forget about it."

"If that's what you want." Courtney was always saying that. Why did it always have to be what I wanted? Why did she have to be so agreeable? Why was I annoyed by that right now?

"Do you still want me to come in?" she asked.

I forced my face to relax. "Of course."

When we walked in the door, Mom came out of the hallway.

"Good. You're here. I have to go now. Jocelyn has a bottle in the fridge for when she wakes up. Give her some peas if she gets hungry again." She handed me the baby monitor. "Why are you looking at me like you don't remember talking about this?"

"I—"

"Jonah, I told you this morning, I have that emergency faculty meeting."

I glanced at Courtney, still standing by the door, gripping the strap to her messenger bag over her chest.

"Yep." With everything that had happened that day, I'd forgotten.

"Thanks, babe. I'll see you in a couple hours. You staying for dinner, Courtney?" Mom asked as she lifted her hair out of her collar.

"Uh—"

"It's okay. We'll make plenty." Then she was gone.

I looked at Jocelyn in her crib on the monitor. She slept on her stomach with her butt in the air. Just seeing her in there, sleeping peacefully, made me feel calmer.

"I'm sorry," I said, looking for the slight movement of Joss's breathing. "She asked me this morning. I forgot. You can leave if you want." Maybe I'd be able to catch a nap while Jocelyn was still asleep.

"No. I'll stay with you," she said.

I felt like a jerk. Courtney had been the one with me earlier, talking me through my attack.

"I can study in the living room while you feed her. Why wouldn't she ask your older sister, though?"

I looked at her like she was crazy. "She's working on her thesis. She isn't really a human right now."

"You're just trying to make everyone happy."

"And failing miserably."

"I'm happy. I'm with the nicest guy in the world."

"Right," I said with a watery smile.

I laid down on the couch while Courtney set everything up on the coffee table. I put my arm over my eyes.

"You're not going to do homework?" she asked.

"I—"

A cry from the monitor broke me off. "Nope."

After changing Jocelyn's diaper, I put her in her bouncer in the living room to make her bottle. I listened to Courtney talking to her as the bottle warmer steamed, Joss's manic giggle making me smile.

"Hey," said Maddie, making me drop the bottle.

"Could you not sneak up on people like that?" I snapped.

"Sorry." She opened the cupboard and got out a mug.

I could feel her staring at me as I got the bottle out of the sink.

"What's with you?" she asked.

"Nothing. Just tired." I was so tired. Ever since the night in the orchard, I hadn't been able to get a proper night of sleep. I kept seeing it, over and over when I closed my eyes. "We're supposed to be studying for the Holcomb exam on *Cat's Eye*, and I forgot Mom asked me to watch Joss."

"Ooh, that one's tough."

"Yeah." I tested the milk on my arm as I walked past.

Maddie took it. "Listen, I've just had a breakthrough. I'll get Jocelyn. Go do your thing."

I paused, not sure what to do. I felt bad that my very illegal issues were interrupting her studies. But at the same time . . . bed.

"Thanks," I said.

"Your house reminds me of warm French toast," Courtney said as we walked back to my room.

"How so?"

After a quick check for anything embarrassing, I stuffed all my dirty socks and underwear in my hamper and pushed it over to the side of the room with the washer and dryer.

Given that my room was also the basement, someone could come down here any minute. While most guys would probably be disheartened by the fact that they could get interrupted with their girlfriend at any moment, the thought gave me comfort.

Courtney had always kind of intimidated me. She'd had other boyfriends before. The scariest part was she liked me the most.

"It's just so full of love and happy chaos."

I snorted. "Happy chaos. That's one way to put it,"

"They all love you so much. It's like being in a house full of like-minded people. So really, it's just an ego boost for me."

I wanted kiss her smile and throw up at the same time—not in her mouth. It's just that we never talked about Love.

I saw the book that Apollo had thumped me on the head with on the ground and picked it up, glancing at the cover. The word 'Kindreds' was right there in bold letters and my heart panicked in my chest. I deposited it on the top shelf in my closet.

Courtney was lying on my bed when I turned around. She was pretty. No, she was beautiful. I'd always loved long hair, and hers was long and golden brown, spread out around her like a mermaid in water.

"Come here," she said.

"Was this your plan all along? Pretend to study until you get to my room?"

She stretched on my bed, smiling suggestively. I glanced at the door before crawling on top of her. It felt good. Dangerous.

I always felt on the verge of losing her. Ever since we got together, I'd run my fingers through her hair and think that she could slip through my hands just like that, at any moment. Maybe it was post-traumatic stress after Apollo or something. When your best friend says every mean thing he could think about you—*ignorant, coward, homophobe*—knowing he felt they were true, maybe you kind of started believing it too. But things had been easier since Apollo had ditched me, hadn't they?

Apollo was like a George R. R. Martin novel. He was complicated. Infuriatingly layered. I was like a middle grade book. Simple. Straightforward. But I wasn't thinking about Apollo right now.

I pulled back from Courtney. "We really should study. I am so far behind in this book."

"You didn't like it?" she asked, undeterred by me putting on the brakes.

"I liked it . . . kind of," I hedged. "The chronology is disorienting."

"She gives you hints when she's talking as her younger self versus her adult self though," she said like she would make me love it as much as she apparently did. It bothered me. Maybe I just wasn't into it.

I sat up on the edge of the bed, picking up my copy. Courtney settled on her stomach beside me with her notebook.

"We're supposed to be looking at the motifs," she said. "What have you noticed so far?"

I noticed that I wanted to lay down and pull my pillow over my head. I was saved from answering by the door flying open. Apollo came down the stairs, my bat dangling from his hand.

His eyes darted to the space between me and Courtney. "I need to talk to Jonah."

I don't know why I was so relieved he hadn't come in a couple of moments before.

"Interesting, given that you haven't answered any of my texts." I'd been messaging him since the meeting this morning.

He looked struck. "Sorry."

"Why do you have a bat?" asked Courtney.

"I borrowed it from your boy toy here. I was practicing my swing."

He leaned it against my dresser and crossed his arms.

Courtney stood. "Well," she said.

Could she feel, like I could, that Apollo wanted her to disappear?

"I'll let you guys catch up. Talk to you tomorrow, Jay."

She leaned over and kissed me. It felt insensitive to touch her in front of Apollo, so I held my hand along the curtain of her hair instead. It felt like water.

She smiled at Apollo as she walked out. He dug one out for her in return, from the nether reaches of his soul, I was sure. It came off a little toothy.

"Jay?" he said as soon as the door closed.

"What?"

"Nothing. Just didn't know anyone would need a nickname for a two syllable name."

"I call her Court sometimes."

"Even better," Apollo said, sarcastically. "Move over."

I swallowed. "Why?"

"You're infuriating, Jay."

He spread something out on the bed next to me. I moved over to make room.

"A map? Where did you even get that?" I tilted my head to see it better.

"Geography Room," he said.

"You stole from the *Records Building*?"

Unbothered, he plopped on my bed, one of his legs folded under him, his knee bumping mine.

"I didn't know you had panic attacks in the day too," he said, his voice quiet.

I looked at him, then away. "I don't. Or I never have before." I shut my eyes and dug my hands through my hair, growling. "It was just *paint*, red paint on the ground, and I had to go and have a breakdown."

"Hey," he said. "Breakdowns are underrated. They should be enjoyed at the very least annually." His crooked grin was irritating and contagious.

"Let me guess. Yours was at that Khalid concert?"

He looked down, slipping a finger underneath the leather band on his wrist. He pulled out the pick, then pushed it back inside. "No. May."

Heart panicking again. "Apollo."

He pulled me down on the bed with him, the map crackling under us. My skin tingled where his hand still rested on my arm.

Every sleepover came back to me, talking into the morning, laughing until we couldn't breathe, being just like this without all of the other stuff taking up room.

The door opened before I could ask what he was doing.

"Good to see you again, Madeline," said Apollo.

"Whaaaat are you . . . ?" she began, like we were in here *doing things.*

My face went atomic.

Apollo pointed up at my Star Wars poster on the ceiling. "Admiring."

She laughed, and Apollo winked, right over me like I wasn't here.

"Never mind," she sang, closing the door.

"If I knew it would be that easy to get her to leave, I'd keep you in my bed all the time." As soon as I said it, I blushed. He stared up at me with eyes as clear as water, hands folded on his chest.

Then he vaulted off the bed. "I just realized you and Courtney have probably done it here. Ugh!"

I laughed, trying to sound casual. "We haven't . . ."

"Oh? Is the Sanctimonious One waiting for marriage?"

"Actually, I think she might want to," I said. I don't even know what kind of reaction I was looking for.

"I meant you," he said, turning to my dresser.

"Oh." Would he notice I kept the picture of us in front? It was probably good he had no idea how often I looked at the ones in my phone.

"Don't you want to? With Courtney?" He frowned at a stack of books on my dresser.

I tried to remember what I had up there. Probably that novel about a videogame scavenger hunt, one of the later Hunger Games, maybe the anthology for English.

"I—yeah, I think. But it always feels . . . awkward when we get past a certain point."

He raised his eyebrow.

"Have you?" I swallowed. "Done it before?"

"No."

"Really?" I folded my hands over my stomach, turning my head to watch him as he took catalog of my room. Literally nothing had changed, but sometimes Apollo saw things I didn't.

"What?" he asked. "Is that so unbelievable?"

"I thought you'd lost your virginity when we were like twelve."

"What do you think I am, some kind of man whore?" he asked, laughing.

"You always acted like . . ."

"Like what?"

"Like you knew things."

He grinned. "I do know things."

I sat up, annoyed for some reason. "Then why haven't you?"

"Same reason. Awkward past a certain point."

Hearing that he had about as much experience as me was reassuring. "Is that normal?" I meant with him being gay. Like, was that a normal thing for gay guys.

"Is anything about us normal, Jonah?"

He didn't get what I meant.

"I guess not," I said.

"You're wrinkling the map."

"You made me," I said, sitting up, grateful for the change of subject.

He sat beside me again and took a breath. "We might have a problem. So, remember where we killed it?"

His eyes were fevered. I wonder when he'd last released his magic. I hoped it was more recently than what we'd used to fight the vampiris and put the bug back together.

I nodded. "Orville Orchards."

"Genius! Someone get him the Nobel Peace prize!"

I glared at him then looked closer at the map. "I guess we were about here. Why?"

"That's what I thought too. There was someone out there this morning."

I closed my eyes and took a deep breath, so I wouldn't pop off. "Why would you go out there alone after hearing Junior is missing?"

His eyes snapped up to mine. "You know who he is?"

"Saw your Instagram." Fortunately, he had no way of knowing I'd stalked his Insta posts all summer.

He looked down at his phone. "Yeah. He's a good friend."

As opposed to me. A bad friend. I cleared my throat. "It's normal for the wolves to disappear all the time, isn't it?"

"Have you ever heard of the clan taking an interest in one of them? They don't even acknowledge their existence half the time. And he hasn't been answering. Look," he said, turning his phone to me.

" '*Por dios*'?"

"No," said Apollo, rolling his eyes. "Look. He said he was on his way, then he just drops off."

I scanned the texts. "Has he posted anything new?"

"The last thing he'd posted was a picture of him and his girlfriend, earlier that night." He showed it to me.

I stared at a threadbare part of the rug. "What did he mean by 'he's not the type you bring home'?"

"He saw me leave the club with Talbot."

"Talbot Erikson? The elder?"

Apollo kept his focus on the map, like he didn't want to answer.

So I answered for him. "He has to be at least five years older than you!"

"So?"

When I'd asked him what he'd been doing out there, he didn't say anything about Talbot. "You lied to me." We had always told each other everything. Lying wasn't even a possibility between us. That's why everything he'd said when we fought hit so hard.

"Right. And if I told you I was out there trying to scam on someone—I just didn't think that was info you needed."

"I guess not," I said.

He looked back at me like I was ridiculous for being mad. He sighed, scrubbing his hand through his hair, curly and thick on top, cut closer on the sides.

"This morning, there was a woman out at our spot. And other people in these, like, Hazmat suits."

Every exhausted muscle felt like it had been shot with an epinephrine pin.

He took a deep breath. "I'm pretty sure she was vampiris."

Goosebumps raised along my back, body reacting to the threat that wasn't even present. "What?"

"Jonah," he said, catching my eyes. He was trying to catch me before I spiraled, but it was too late.

I leaned forward, pushing my fingers through my hair. "What the fuck?"

"Yeah." Apollo laid back on my bed again. "We run into that vampiris, then Junior goes missing, and now this lady poking around out there. It can't be a coincidence."

"It definitely can be," I argued.

"We killed it, right? But what if it's not over?"

"It is if we let it go."

"You don't believe that. The day I'm more heroic than Jonah Jeremy Clarke is the day you burst into flames."

I hated that everyone felt like they had the right to decide who I was. I was not a hero. "Maybe Talbot saw something."

"Would you get over it?"

"What!"

"He didn't."

"How do you know? Have you talked to him?"

Apollo's jaw tensed. "I know he didn't see anything," he said. "He left too quickly."

"Why?"

"Because I misread the situation, apparently," he snapped.

I kept a lid on my relief. "So, what, you think Junior might have followed you out there?"

"I don't know. Maybe I should retrace his steps."

"You can't do anything alone, Apollo," I said, practically vibrating with anger. "If his steps lead us out there, what then?"

He gave me a look.

I literally recoiled. "We almost died out there! You would have. You almost became that thing's dinner until I—"

"Well, now it's dead, isn't it?"

"And what if we run into that woman? You shouldn't have even put yourself in that situation to begin with! To go back could be . . . suicide," I said. "Or worse, we could get caught, Apollo. You know we left a fingerprint."

"I need to make sure."

It was stupid. It was rash. It was just like Apollo. "No," I said.

"'No' what?"

"No offense, but you're being stupid about this. It's reckless"

"How is that not offensive? And you chose to come with me that night."

"Only to—" I cut myself off. *To be with you. To make sure someone's watching out for you.*

"I just need to know he's alright."

"Then we find another way."

Apollo threw his legs off the side of my bed and stood up. "Let me know when you're ready to step up to the plate, Jay." Then he was gone.

When he left, I fell back on my bed where it smelled like him—like fresh herbs and clean aloe. It was such a familiar smell that I almost cried. It might have been easy for him to run around, breaking the rules, but I already felt like I was betraying Dad for keeping the fact that we were Kindred secret. And now we'd done this huge thing that I had to keep inside every day. All this pressure was building, and there was nowhere for it to go.

8

Apollo

Downtown San Alvarez had fine lines everywhere. Between two buildings on 2nd Street, I moved from well-to-do, blue collar businesses into pawnshop territory with grimy gold lettering. Crossing Edison, I'd gone from the lower middle class, Starbucks-gulping neighborhood into homeless territory marked with shoplifted shopping carts.

I turned between a cash advance place and a bail bondsman. The bricks on the loan building displayed an illegible graffiti message. I touched the paint and felt the hatred behind it. Everything has a kind of magic to it.

The place between these two buildings felt like a pocket in time. The high walls on either side of me amplified noises from far away. A few blocks over, a dog viciously barked. The Amtrack was rolling into the station over on N. Palm Street.

The alley poured me into a crumbled parking lot, pavement the color of rain clouds. I kicked a chunk of asphalt that skittered away. An abandoned building sat at the end of the lot. It was the color of bile that ends up in the toilet when there's nothing left in your stomach but your body keeps trying to turn itself inside out. I kind of always felt like that. That's why I pulled magic from the Range Rover that barely missed me as I jogged across the street, why I ran my fingers down an electrical pole, wood splintering off into my calluses. I sucked all that thick, sweet magic straight into my blood.

I'd been here once with Junior. He'd come to stash his money. I wondered about someone finding the cash and taking it. He assured me no one had found it in the three years he'd lived there.

"And besides," he'd said cheerily, winking at me, "if it goes missing this time around, I'll know exactly who to track down."

He had done this before, disappeared and came back from Mexico a month later, but his mom would have no idea about that since she had only been back in his life for like two seconds. If his money was gone, then I could stop worrying about him.

I jumped up, clutching the first rung of the rusted ladder to the roof. As I climbed, my body screamed in betrayal. I should have been in school or sleeping. I should have been throwing to balance how much I'd been gathering. At the very least, I should have been at home, playing video games, eating vast amounts of Bugles, and not falling through a second-floor broken window of an abandoned warehouse.

It didn't look like anyone was home, which was a good thing for me because I hadn't thought that far ahead. The kind of people Junior ran with probably wouldn't be too keen on some kid skulking through their digs. I scanned the bundles of stained bedding strewn in the corners and the shadows in the far ends of the floor anyway. Just to be safe.

I made my way to Junior's hiding place, toeing aside bedding and discarded clothing. I might have been able to do a locating spell to trace his last location if I could find something he valued.

I pulled off the outlet cover over an uneven hole I'd seen him shove his beefy hand into. I reached in, giving half a mind to black widows, or worse, rats. I cringed at myself for thinking in Jonah logic.

I felt the edges of his stack, bills fanned out, heart dropping.

So, he hadn't taken his money. Not an ideal scenario. Maybe he'd return to find it missing and come looking for me. Too bad money passed through too many hands to make it good for a locating spell. He valued it enough.

I divvied up the stack between my pockets. I assured myself one more time that no one had seen me. Last thing I needed was getting jumped for Junior's *feria*, only to be jumped by Junior when he found out I didn't have it.

On the way back to my car a few blocks away, I couldn't shake the feeling of being watched. I made an unplanned stop at the street seer's shop.

It's not like I was actually starting to believe in this stuff. Maybe I just hoped to catch a break. Didn't mean I was giving into the whispers from the elusive *Other Side* my mother communed with.

Gertie, the street seer, was a friend of my mom's and older than my parents. Maybe as old as my grandparents? She wasn't a typical witch in a cottage though, but I was only sixty percent sure she didn't eat children. She was covered in tattoos, her white hair in dreads, and she filled out an A-shirt with more assertion than I did.

A tinkling chime sounded as I entered. There were trinkets everywhere—crystals, tarot cards, rune stones while books on grief, reincarnation, and latent psychic powers populated the shelves.

"Apollo," said Gertie, leaning on the counter where she took people's cash in exchange for parlor tricks.

She pushed off the counter with those impressive biceps, all business. "The streets have been whispering your name at night."

She came around the counter to flip the 'open' sign and crack the deadbolt into place.

"I've been waiting for you."

Of course she would say something like this. It was stock seerism.

"I'm looking for someone." I looked around the shop as though Junior might pop out, waving a copy of *Eat, Pray, Love* at me.

"Come with me," she said.

Her combat boots crossed the ancient carpet that was almost black with grime.

"Keep an eye on the place, Dot!" she called, I presumed, to the homeless person curled fetal between the shelves. "A regular," Gertie explained.

She cranked the doorknob of a swollen wooden door and shouldered her way through. A blast of reeking air hit me in the face. We were in the alley behind Gertie's Gifts—see what she did there?

The strip of grey daylight above us was like a faraway dream. Gertie pointed over to a black mark on the pot-holed asphalt. It looked like the site of a small, contained explosion. I was about to ask her whether someone had spontaneously combusted in her alley, but she swung herself into the dumpster.

"Sorry, just gotta find something that's not mine in here," she said after some shuffling. "Aha!" She popped up, pulling herself over the side of the bin with a bag in tow.

She walked over to me, jutting the hand that wasn't holding the bag in my direction. She had a knife. I jumped back.

"Calm down, Sunshine."

Wasn't she just clever, I thought, a little pleased with the nickname despite myself.

She jerked her head at the bag. "You gotta rip it open."

I took the knife and stabbed the blade in with grim satisfaction. I pulled down like I was gutting a bloated, white fish.

Trash spilled out. Gertie took her knife back, flipping it closed with one hand and slipping it into her pocket. Her arms tensed, tattoos shivering, as she shook the remainder of the bag's contents onto the ground around my feet: Fast food wrappers, 40 oz bottles, packaging for raw hamburger, shriveled lemon wedges, a child's Transformers notebook—probably a dealer's ledger—wristbands from the strip, like the people who'd cut them off had meandered over here to eat a chicken shawarma sammie afterward. She ripped the remains of the bag open and the last few things exploded at my feet. Pulling a Parliament from her baggy jeans, she lit it as she walked around me, never looking away from the garbage. I wanted to light one too, but then I would seem nervous. Or at least, I would be admitting to myself that I was.

"Interesting," Gertie said.

I fought not to roll my eyes as trash juices pooled around my Pumas.

"I am getting two things here. Like two fates are . . . intertwined?"

I told my heart to calm the fuck down.

She looked up at me, her cigarette out to her side. "Does that make sense?"

"Sure."

She said something under her breath, still focused on the trash.

"What?" I asked.

"The one who lies to himself will lose what he loves most." She wasn't looking at me but through me as she spoke. I turned around, wondering if there was more trash back there whispering the secrets of the universe.

Her eyes flashed back to me from yonder middle distance, then flicked down to the Styrofoam, plastic, and paper modern art installment.

"Hold on. There's something else here." She got down on her knees and started moving the trash around with her hands like a regular psychic moves cards over the table. She picked up a can, its aluminum lid jagged and hanging on by a thread. It reflected sunlight into my eyes. I closed them. When I opened them again, she was looking up at me, the can still in her hand.

"Death in darkness. Or . . . lost in the darkness, he finds death."

I didn't want to hear anything about death or darkness while I was looking for my friend. I wanted to kick the can out of her hand.

"I kind of feel like I should tell you I don't believe in any of this stuff," I said.

She stood up, chucking the can into the dumpster, as though it hadn't just delivered that foreboding tidbit. Like it was just trash. Which it was. But if this was her trade, shouldn't she be a little more reverent?

"That's okay," she said and picked up more trash.

I wasn't sure if she was done with her 'reading.'

"My job is not to convince anyone, or explain how I see the things I do. I just see them."

"That would be a tough job. To be a seer and to have to convince people it was all true."

"Exactly," she said, not catching my sarcasm. "I just don't have the time or the fortitude to deal with that part of it."

When she finished picking up the trash and started walking back inside, I took that as the end. I followed her back to the front and dug out a couple twenties from Junior's stack, writing a mental IOU. I was about to walk out the front door when her voice stopped me.

"You're disappointed."

I shrugged. I was being shitty. She was probably so used to people acting like skeptical assholes.

"Sometimes a token makes people feel like they got more out of it."

My heart hammered like I'd just chugged a quad shot. "Whatever."

She flicked her fingers like she was throwing something. She widened her eyes toward my chest. I looked down. A playing card stuck to my shirt like a wind held it there. Ace of spades. Edges worn soft and bent, with flecks of . . . blood?

"A souvenir from my prediction feels very passé to me, but if it means more business . . ."

"I'll be sure to tell all my friends," I said, holding up the card. "Was the blood really necessary?"

"Blood?" She looked startled. She came around the counter to look at the card. "Must have gotten some paint on it." She licked her finger and scrubbed it against the corner of the card as I held the other end. It was just as awkward as it sounds.

But the blood didn't come off.

After the fat lot of good Gertie's Gifts did me, I decided to make a pit stop before school the next morning. Junior's last text burned against my thigh as I walked up to the Rosington. *On my way.*

I'd never been into the Rosington, but one didn't need to go into the Rosington to know what it's about.

The desk clerk peered at me through the smudged door as I put my cigarette out and tossed it in the trash. I pushed inside, no clue as to whether Junior had his mom's last name or his dad's.

"Lupita?" I tried.

"No. Greg," said the clerk.

I smiled in a way that any human organism would be able to identify as sarcastic.

"No. I'm looking for a woman. Lupita. About ye high, dark hair, dark eyes, petite Latina, obvious smoker? Any of this ringing a bell?"

"We can't give out information about our lodgers."

"The thing is, Greg, Lupita told me to come find her. It's about her missing son. I'm sure, if you just give her a ring there, she'll want to talk to me."

I wasn't sure if it would work, but it seemed like the right moment to do it. I held up a twenty between my fingers. Greg took it, picking up the phone.

I justified dipping into Junior's cash as a penalty for not telling me he was ditching the city for a few days.

I leaned on the counter, reminded of the bruise on my arm from where the vampiris had grabbed me to pull me out of the car. I had thought my arm was going to snap. This morning, it had been yellow with blooms of purple and grey. The blooms perfectly matched where the vampiris's fingers dug into my skin.

Your almost-death kind of haunts you after something like that.

But here I was, alive, because Jonah had saved me, put his neck on the line—worse, his magic. Still I wondered what it would be like, to vanish without a trace.

Greg hung up the phone. "Ms. Navarro says you may go to her room. 46."

Lupita opened the door after one rap. I'd almost knocked on her forehead. It's a good thing I didn't because it might have shattered. She was the same woman who'd walked up to me at the club, but she definitely looked more tired.

"I need something of Junior's." It was a long shot that she would even have anything after splitting. "Something recent."

It was a test. Tell me you love your son without telling me you love your son.

She opened the door wider for me, already lighting a cigarette. She held one out to me. I took it. Hey, I'm not going to turn down free smokes. Even when on official business.

"The Elders already came and did a locating spell," she said.

"Not like the one I'm going to do."

A personal connection could amplify whatever spell you were doing tenfold.

"You?"

So she knew I was underage. I had to tread carefully.

"I know people. Junior knew people who would want to help."

It was a reminder that I knew Junior better than she did. Why was she so worried after years of only casual encounters with her son? Junior had made his own way since he was ten and hardly ever mentioned her.

I didn't feel so different from him. Once, I found a small wooden box containing letters between my parents. Mom's parents forbade her from seeing my dad, so they wrote letters during that time. There was one letter, from her to Dad, where she'd been apologizing for being pregnant. I figured, at some point, they'd decided they didn't want kids, and I was an accident. I wondered if the reason they'd decided not to have kids was because Dad was scared I would be magikalis like Mom. Gay as a bonus. Lo and behold, Apollo Reid Tormey does not disappoint.

"Besides," I said. "If they'd found him, we'd know, wouldn't we?"

Silver bangles and big hoop earrings were scattered on the desk like a tithe to cross a bridge in a fairy tale. Her black boots slouched under the chair. She seemed vulnerable, smaller somehow than at Purple Haze.

She rummaged through some grocery bags she had on a chair.

"This is all I have."

I didn't recognize it at first. It was bundled up and looked like it was about a century old. When I took it, I realized it was just the material: alpaca. I unfolded it. A dark grey poncho shot through with lighter strands and two bands of red, black, and white striping down either side.

I rubbed it between my fingers, trying to taste its history.

"This what they used?" I asked.

She gave me something between a nod and a shrug. "You think you can find him?"

I dropped the poncho to my side. "Why did you come to me in the first place?"

"They—the wolves, they told me that you would know. That he watched over you like a brother."

I dropped my head, feeling undeserving. I almost asked her not to say anything to the elders, but I knew her dealings with them were probably done until he was found. We exchanged numbers and I started toward the door.

"I didn't want to leave him, you know," she said.

"You didn't have to," I argued.

"You couldn't understand," she said. "You're a child."

I nodded. That was how I understood just fine.

9

Apollo

My phone vibrated when I pulled into the school parking lot.

Jonah: *Why aren't you in school?*

Was he afraid I'd gone off to look for Junior on my own? I'd be seeing him in PE, so I didn't answer.

In the locker room, I couldn't not look at him. He was literally right next to me, our shoulders bumping as we tied our shoes.

After we'd kissed, I wouldn't look at him. Since then, I'd done my best to erase Jonah from my life. Now, I had to learn to be around him again with my heart believing we were still the same.

The rest of class played soccer while Quinn and I opted to run the mile. It wasn't long before we slowed to a walk.

I was dead weight.

"What's going on with you?" she asked. "Aside from your star-crossed lovers scenario with your bestie."

I immediately bristled. "Nothing."

"'Nothing' doesn't have you looking like this."

It seemed everyone was asking me this lately. The only difference I noticed in my reflection was the murky pond water green of my tired eyes.

"The whole clan is worried about him, you know," she said, her voice as soft as the pale inside of her arm.

Junior. She was talking about Junior.

"Not like I am."

She raised her brows, waiting.

"The clan worries because they're obligated to be worried about him. 'Blood is blood' and all that. Would you even know he existed if not for me?"

"That's not fair, Apollo."

I could tell I'd pissed her off. Maybe if I isolated myself, no one else would get hurt when I went supernova. I shrugged. "Is what it is."

"Asshole." She ran past me toward the field where the others were still playing.

Needless to say, she wasn't waiting for me after class. I sat by myself at one of the tables on the quad. I didn't mind because I had a huge headache on top of feeling bad for snapping at her. Apparently, I did a bang up job of attacking people who didn't deserve it.

A cardboard tray clattered next to me, a hot dog flying out of it, the dog and bun separating. Cue stomach and chest in my personal space. I looked up, expecting to find Jonah.

It was Danny Matthews. Shirt on this time.

"Hey," he said.

"Hey." I nodded to the disassembled hot dog. "You dropped your wiener."

He picked it up and put it back in the bun, bringing it to his face for closer examination. He blew on it before taking a bite.

"You realize that would have gotten approximately negative twelve percent of the germs off?"

"Builds immunities, right?" he said before taking a bite.

I laughed. "Don't you sit with the team?"

I didn't look to see if Jonah was with them. He used to sit with me most of the time, unless they had a game. Now if he wasn't sitting with them, you could bet he was off carrying Courtney Christie's lunch for her.

"I do, but Jayden used to sit with us. And . . . you know. Still too fresh," Danny said through another mouthful. It kind of reminded me of eating with Jonah.

I couldn't help it. I looked over at the team's table. Jonah was staring back at me.

Danny bumped his shoulder into mine. "We could be jilted lovers together."

I looked down at my cheese pizza in its cellophane wrapper. Maybe, sometimes, it helps to have somebody just as pathetic as you trying to make you feel better.

After stashing Junior's poncho in my room, I found my mom in the spare room she used as her makeshift office. Office was a loose term for all the *brujería* that went on in there.

The windows were covered with sheer emerald scarves. Mom stood at the hutch between them, mixing her oils. I used to love coming here when I was younger, touching everything I could get away with and just watching her. Now that I was older, I steered clear. It felt like she would somehow be able to divine the imbalance of my chakras just by my being in the room.

"You missed class today."

Yep, there it is.

"After I already let you stay out part of the day yesterday."

I twisted the small bottles so that all the labels faced out. "Is that really what the education administrators are focusing on? They didn't call to tell you I killed it in third period when we discussed electro and magnetic fields?"

"Apollo."

"See? No recognition."

"Where were you? And don't say 'here,'" she said, holding up her hand. I closed my mouth. "Your father was home while I was at the shop. You left at your normal time."

"I was going to go to school, but I wasn't feeling well. So I went down to the beach for a while, then siphoned Starbucks' wireless." It didn't even surprise me how easily the lie came.

She looked at me like she was waiting for more. I figured my story was pretty complete, so I wasn't sure what she wanted.

"Is it happening again?"

"What?" I asked, genuinely confused.

She turned back to her oils, biting her lip like she was about to cry. I fell into a state of emergency. What was I missing here? I just skipped a little school. I'd done that before. Then I remembered. When I couldn't get out of bed after fighting with Jonah, I had told her holding magic was the only thing that made me feel better. She admitted that she'd gotten hooked on holding when she'd been younger, which went against what the clan tried to beat into our heads: holding was not hereditary; it was a choice. Even before we're able to throw, the clan shows us other ways to let it go.

Sometimes there wasn't a choice. I held magic as close as possible, to fill all the holes at the bottom of my boat letting in water.

When M&M were just starting to walk and get into things all over the house, I remembered Isabel telling Jonah's dad that she'd read that babies had zero impulse control so Tom would go easy on them. That even though they knew they shouldn't do something because they understood when they were being told not to, the impulse was too overpowering. That's exactly what holding magic felt like.

"You have to be careful, Baby."

"Mom." I really didn't need her worrying about this.

"You think I wouldn't know when my own son is gathering? Your aura is muddy."

"Ha! That's a compliment at this point."

I wanted to shrink back out of her gaze, because even as the lies tumbled off my lips, I knew the whole cycle was starting again. It felt like I'd never really climbed off the hamster wheel.

"I know what magic feels like," she said. "I know what your magic, in particular, smells like, my love," she said, sticking a label onto the vial she'd been filling: "Vanilla & Lavender for Tranquility".

"How?" I felt a knot form in my throat. I wanted to climb into my bed and feel the backs of her warm, dry fingers on my cheek, light as feathers.

"Like . . ." She smacked her lips.

I laughed.

"Don't. You'll distract me." She put down the bottle and ran her fingers through my hair.

I closed my eyes as an obligatory, "Mom," escaped.

"Like huckleberry honey," she said. "Like stargazer lilies and wet stone." She broke away with a gentle slap to my arm. "Like sugar, and spice, and most things that are nice." It was moments like this, her swiping a tear away and lifting her chin, when I could almost forget about that letter I'd found, her apology for me growing inside of her. "Make sure to open your hands and let it pour out every so often, okay? You'll get used to doing it automatically."

"Did you have to do that?"

She avoided my gaze, moving the essential oils unnecessarily. "I did. It's second nature now."

I crossed my arms, leaning against the hutch beside her, closing my eyes to the clinking.

"You and Jonah are hanging out again?" Her attempt at a casual tone was cringeworthy.

"Yeah."

"It's okay to hold some cards close to your chest, Apollo."

I was trying.

"Does he have anything to do with this?" Mom had loved Jonah until our falling out.

'This' referring to me holding.

"No." I focused on the dried herbs laid out on the desk. This was all my own drama. I cleared my throat. "Jonah's good for me."

One had to wonder how true that was when I found myself on the ground outside his window in the middle of the night.

Even though he was asleep, I put my hand to the wall. Dew seeped into my sweatpants and then the thermals I had underneath. I was so cold. I lit a cigarette just to be able to feel something and got to work.

I pulled out my pocket knife Dad had given me, more for emergency defense than any hope of cutting anything. I carved a circle into the dirt of the empty flowerbed. I pulled a baggie from my pocket and spread its contents into the indent of the circle. An hour of meticulous work stared up at me like an empty eye. A circle was the most powerful symbol there was. What better way to find something than to put a circle around it?

I picked up the poncho and ripped a loose thread off. I put it in my mouth, tasting dirt and the echo of some familiar spice that I couldn't name. I put the thread in the circle and lit the powder with my lighter.

The tiny fire exploded and died down to a smolder. I lit the thread too and put my face close, inhaling.

For magic to really work, you had to take it inside of you.

The spell jerked my stomach. I scrambled to my feet. My eyes were open, but I couldn't see the night or the street in front of Jonah's house anymore, as familiar as my own street.

Faint images knitted together.

The taste of salt in my mouth, like the ocean. So strong, I almost gagged. Junior in his mother's arms at the beach.

As a little boy, wearing the poncho. The worship of his dad, who'd left him, woven into every thread. That taste is stronger than the salt, heavier. But then . . . nothing.

I shake my head. No. That can't be it. Why would his mother give this to me if he didn't use the damn thing?

Because she didn't know him.

But then, there's Junior's Dad. I thought I had seen his face in his mother's, but he was his father's clone. He wore the poncho and carried an army sack on his shoulder, walking out the door. But he stopped, dropped his bag to the ground and pulled the poncho off. He folded it, and laid it over the back of a chair before leaving.

Junior, when he was about my age, crying into it.

First his dad, then his mom. How could anyone walk out on a kid? Why was loving so hard for people to do?

The only difference between Junior and I was that my parents kept me. My good ole dad stuck around. What good had that done me? I was still hopelessly in love with my best friend and probably a stone's throw from an Edgar Allan Poe fate the way I was going. Only instead of absinthe and opium, I'd end up face down in a gutter, consumed by my own magic.

10

Jonah

I woke up, feeling like there was a cinderblock on my chest.

In my dream, I had been alone—an anomaly for me, really—only it wasn't dark like it usually was when I'm having a nightmare. I was walking through white. Snow maybe. It went on forever, in all directions. I had been looking for Apollo.

I threw off the sheet my mom must have covered me with. I hated when she did that. Like, I sleep in my boxers and her coming into my room to cover me up was not cool.

When I was finally able to move, I noticed it. Every part of me buzzed with our magic. I sat up and looked around, wondering if he snuck in here, but I was alone. I checked my phone. Nothing. Then I smelled smoke, the same smoke I associated with riding in Apollo's bug or hanging out on the pier or his T-shirts when I borrowed them.

I jerked the curtain back and looked out the basement window. I always had it open (though Dad complained about heating the neighborhood). But the street was quiet. Empty.

I punched my pillow and tried to get comfortable. There was no way I was falling back asleep though. I was hungry or thirsty or something. I went to my closet and dug through the clothes I'd thrown in when Courtney came over. I needed my sweats, because even if it was five in the morning, it was not advisable to go prowling around the house in your underwear at any hour when you had four other siblings, specifically when two of them would point and say something devastatingly intelligent like, 'eeeeewwwwwww'.

I hit my elbow on the closet door frame, as I jerked my pants on. I cursed as something fell on my head.

The book Apollo left me, *A History of Kindreds*. I tossed it on my dresser on my way to the kitchen for a glass of milk.

I wanted to ask him why he was missing school. I hated not feeling needed. It was selfish, but I kind of expected Apollo to be this brooding, solitary figure without me. He wasn't. He was with Quinn all the time and Danny now too. So I did the mature thing and threw myself into assignments; I ran the mile if he decided to play whatever sport Trowbridge assigned; I tried not to look at him at lunch, wondering all the while why we couldn't sit together again.

After getting back into bed, I couldn't stop seeing the words on the cover of that book he'd given me. Had other Kindreds kept their bond secret from their clan? Or was it so shameful as to be left out of the official history? Were there other Kindreds who were best friends? It's not like this stuff was recommended reading for younglings.

The first time Kindreds were mentioned in Sunday School, we hadn't known what we could do yet. It was almost a mythical idea. Sometimes two people could be joined by their magic. It would be stronger when they were close. They may even be able to throw before they turned twenty-one. As all of us kids fantasized about being able to use our magic before we became boring adults who lived by strict rules, the teacher Ms. Lowell explained that if we thought we might be a Kindred, we were required by the laws of the clan to come forward.

I remember wondering why such a special bond was so scary to the Elders. When Apollo and I realized we were Kindred, my primary concern was keeping it secret because Ms. Lowell had said Kindreds were often in love. I was afraid of what people would think. After seeing Apollo almost die, after seeing what he was doing to himself now—and for how long?—that was the least of my concerns.

I picked up the book. An inscription was written inside:

Thanks for saving my life
-Apollo

I turned to the first page.

> "Kindred *magikalia* seem to be the most unfairly judged and fettered of our kind. They live in fear of coming forward and many of them never do for the harsh restrictions they expect to be placed upon them. But to stifle that which makes them Kindred is to stifle that which makes them *magikalia*."

That made me feel even more justified in keeping the vampiris a secret.

I flipped through the pages, stopping on the story of Abraham "Bram" Perron and Renaud Phillippe Deschamps. Bram had come forward to their clan about their bond and they were forced to separate, forbidden to go near each other for fear that they'd have access to their magic at too early an age. When separation wasn't feasible, Kindreds were kept from using their magic with a strong binding spell. There was no doubt, any magikalis would use their power if they could. It was our nature, unless we actively resisted it by holding onto it.

Holding was an anomaly. I thought about Apollo's sleepless eyes, the dark circles around them. I hated the idea of either punishment. Lose my magic, or lose Apollo . . . again. Our strained relationship was still better than that prospect.

The separation seemed to have caused depression in Perron and Deschamps though, and even manic behavior in Deschamps. They broke their clan-sanctioned segregation and were eventually found, years later, living together as a couple.

I closed the book and covered the word Kindred with my hand.

There it was again. The snap of our magic, exactly what comes after a rubber band pulled taut. My knees went gooey and I definitely smelled smoke.

Damn it, Apollo.

I stuffed my feet into my Nikes and shoved my arms into my jacket on the way out.

He slouched by the basement window, a cigarette burned to the filter, dangling between his fingers. In front of him, the remnants of a spell. I hated the idea of him using me to access our magic and do this on his own.

I wanted to help him do what he thought was right, but I couldn't betray my dad or my family again. Apollo and I already had too many secrets.

"Hey," I said.

He looked up. "Jonah?"

"Yeah," I said like 'duh'. "You're right outside my window. I could feel you."

His eyes tripped down my body. I shifted from one foot to the other under his gaze. Pretty sure he saw I wasn't wearing socks.

"What are you doing?" I asked.

"Locating spell. Didn't work."

I had every right to be pissed at him for siphoning magic from me without permission, creating a fingerprint right outside my damn window, but he looked even worse than usual, slumped there like he didn't have the strength to hold himself upright.

When I helped him up, I pulled him into a hug. He seemed surprised, but I held tight. Then he latched onto me, fingers clawing against the back of my jacket. All my jealousy and frustration with him suddenly seemed petty.

"Come inside," I said. "Get some sleep."

"Can we just drive?"

His breath sent goosebumps over my neck. I pulled back, but he wouldn't look at me. I didn't know if I'd ever fully understand what he was going through, but I would have done anything in that moment to make him happy again.

I looked at the house—no lights on. "Fine, but we're going to Jack in the Box. You need to eat something. And you still owe me."

He nodded.

We both stopped at the passenger door.

"I can't drive right now," he said.

"Are you drinking?" I asked.

"No. That spell wiped me. Can you just . . ."

"What? You know I can't drive stick." Even the idea made me break out in a cold sweat.

"I'll show you how. Please, Jonah."

"Okay, okay." I would have given him anything he asked for in that small voice.

It was surreal seeing him sit in the passenger seat of his own car . . . that I would be driving.

It would be fine. I'd seen him do this a thousand times.

Apollo reached over with the keys. I started the bug.

So far so good.

When he took my wrist, I jumped.

"You're going to keep this hand on the gearshift," he said.

And even though I knew about the clutch, he told me to keep my foot by it all the time, to engage it when shifting. I'd always thought it was very adult-like, his ability to drive stick. I did not feel ready for it.

"To get going, don't release the clutch. You want to feather the gas a little."

When I finally got to fourth gear, we left the neighborhood behind and found ourselves in downtown. In the silence, I counted the passing columns of white light. When we came to a red light, I noticed how it shaded underneath the angle of Apollo's jaw, how the shift to green made shadows from the veins in his hands.

"Okay, let off the gas, and press the clutch all the way in," Apollo said as we slowed down to pull into the Jack in the Box parking lot.

"You and Junior got really close these past few months," I said, chest aching for some reason.

"Yeah."

The bug stalled in the parking lot, which of course made me forget everything I'd just learned.

"Screw this. I'm going in." Despite my bluster, I carefully parked.

I hadn't grabbed my own keys or wallet when I left the house, so I came back to the car. Before I said a word, Apollo held out his wallet.

"Yep. Thanks," I said.

After I got our food, we laid on the bug's hood. He laid there with his hands on his chest while I unwrapped my burger.

"I got you everything I got for me—"

He put his hand on my arm. "Jack in the Box isn't going to have any food left!"

"Shut up," I said.

I put his burger on his chest, but he didn't move to eat.

"I've seen you put away two foot-long subs and a two liter of Coke. You're going to eat all that," I told him.

"Yes, Dad."

He didn't even have to ask me to keep driving when we crumpled our wrappers and stuffed them into the bag.

Getting out of the parking lot was just as awkward as pulling into it. But again, except for instructing me every so often, Apollo lapsed into silence, indifferent to the bug's appeals.

I took the freeway back to my house, which was a mistake. While merging on hadn't been that bad, getting off was stressful.

"Just calm down and feel the car. It tells you what it wants." He paused. "Listen with our magic."

Something clicked right away. I felt like my fingers themselves were guiding the movements of the engine. I pulled off from a red light, trying to fluidly shift the way I'd seen him do so many times.

I was starting to see why Apollo loved driving so much, why we'd done it so often together. It was actually enjoyable when I wasn't getting cramps in my hands from clenching the wheel and gearshift so tight.

"It's kind of hot seeing you all concentrated on not killing my car."

I messed up the shift, gears grinding. Apollo laughed. We used to joke with each other like that all time, but I couldn't laugh it off now.

"Want to listen to music?" I asked, face still burning.

He didn't answer, so I left it off.

He picked up a Patron bottle from under the seats and appraised it.

"Why do you have that in her?" My mind was going to every worst case scenario, specifically the one where I left the house in the middle of the night—*again*—without my license to drive around with a bottle of liquor in the car.

"Talbot," he said. "A consolation prize, the gentleman."

I couldn't tell how he felt about that; Talbot had obviously rejected him, but Apollo was hard to read. Frankly, I thought it was pretty irresponsible and gross of Talbot.

I pulled over down the street from my house. "Tell me how to help you."

"You can't."

"Come inside."

"No. I didn't mean to wake you up."

"Then I'll just sleep out here with you."

That got him out of the car.

I used our magic to unlock the front door without thinking about it. I guess that happens once you start breaking rules.

Apollo followed me down to the basement and sat on my bed.

"You want something to sleep in?" I asked.

"I'm fine," he said.

I peeled off my jacket and threw it in the closet, grabbing a hoodie. I tossed it to him, remembering how he'd woken me up Saturday night.

As he tugged it on, I took off my shirt and decided to leave my sweats on.

"You don't have to keep your clothes on," he said. "I promise I'll be good."

"Ha ha," I said, but the suggestion tugged low inside me.

He scooted to the inside of the bed. I laid down on the outside and pulled the blanket over him. He looked exhausted.

"Are you going to plug in your light?" he asked.

Apollo was the only one who knew about the nightlight I plugged in after everyone went to bed.

"I don't need it. Not with you here."

I watched his face slowly relax.

When I woke up for school in the morning, he was gone.

School was the same as the day before. Despite seeing him through that low last night, he was back to tiptoeing around me.

I was beginning to understand Apollo was one person in the day and a completely different one at night, and the terms of our friendship reflected this. I wanted to be there for him when he needed me but it would kill me to get half of him all the time.

With this being my last year of high school and things with Apollo since the orchard, I hadn't hung out with Miles and Macy at all, and I couldn't remember the last time I'd let Jocelyn chase me around. Maddie and I used to talk nightly, one of us going into the other's room and laying down to discuss our days, like a patient and psychologist. We hadn't done that in ages. Maybe that's why I was so tense all the time.

We piled into the living room to watch a movie after dinner, Joss in her bouncer, M&M on the floor in a pillow fort. Mom and Dad were on the loveseat and Maddie and I on the couch. She was laying down taking up two thirds of it and had her legs on me.

I kept watching Dad. He traced his jawline with his thumb as he stared at the screen, his other arm around Mom. I wondered if he was distracted thinking about Junior.

Earlier, he'd found me sitting outside not doing anything. Not scrolling or hitting my punching bag, just staring at the jet trails in the sky. When he had settled down next to me, I tried not to sweat.

"I know it must be difficult for you right now," he'd said, "with that wolf missing. To be what we are with all this power waiting inside of you, unable to do anything with it."

I nodded, swallowing. Here I was, a liar, while he carried the weight of the world.

Dad had always been my ideal of what a strong member of the clan should look like, how they should act. I aspired to be that one day, but his shoes seemed impossible to fill.

I couldn't betray him. But I also couldn't abandon Apollo to deal with this on his own, no matter how much I didn't agree. I wondered if my dad would understand that some rules had to be broken.

My idle pity party came to an end on Saturday when I went to say goodnight. Mom was feeding Jocelyn a snack, but I'd just say goodnight on my way back through the kitchen. Even though M&M were playing a video game and Maddie was probably still awake, I figured I'd hole up in the basement and read *Cat's Eye* until I passed out. Because I would pass out reading that book.

The door to my parents' room was slightly open. Dad was in a Bureau meeting. Odd that it was so late.

"If the *vampiria* are crossing into our territory and attacking these wolves, they've rendered the treaty void."

My blood rushed to my head. This is what Mom's emergency staff meeting was about. This was why the Bureau was having a meeting at 9:30 at night.

Was Junior's disappearance somehow related to the one we'd killed?

I got out my phone to text Apollo as I came into the kitchen.

"Can you finish feeding her?" asked Mom. "I want to switch over the laundry before you go to bed."

I took the container of strawberry-banana from her.

"Mind if I go out for a while?" I asked, guilty as hell.

"Where?" she asked, walking to my door as I sat down in front of Joss. She flapped her hands on her tray, impatient for her next bite.

"Apollo's."

"Back no later than eleven, okay?"

"Of course." I shot a text to Apollo, telling him we needed to talk.

My phone started playing "Fade to Black," one of Apollo's favorite songs.

There was loud music in the background when I answered.

"I'm feeding my sister," I said, weirdly jealous he was out doing anything that involved loud music. "That's why I texted."

"Do you want me to hang up and text?" he asked, his voice quiet despite whatever rager he was at.

"No. It's fine." It was annoying how flustered I was, but it bothered me he was living his life like I didn't belong in it. "Where are you?"

"Purple Haze."

"I'll be there in a minute." I slipped my phone back in my pocket, juggling Joss's food.

"I heard Apollo came over the other day," said Mom, coming back up from the basement.

"Doesn't mean we're back to normal." I scooped some dribbling strawberry and banana from Jocelyn's chin. "Things actually seem worse."

"Why?"

"It's hard to explain."

"You might be making it more complicated than it is, babe."

I waited for an explanation, but she raised her brows before wiping off Joss's face and picking her up.

"Be good," she sang, walking back to her room.

I'd already failed that request.

11

Apollo

We stood in a circle down on the beach, feeling the hole where Junior should be. My eyes burned against the light from the bonfire. The wolves were holding a vigil for him. I didn't see how dropping some joints around a dollar store prayer candle would bring him back home.

I was the only one who knew where he might have gone. I broke free from the group, sick to my stomach—this was getting worse. Even with nothing in there.

Jade followed me under the pier.

I breathed in salt, heavy on the mist. It reminded me of Junior's memory from the locating spell.

"Lupita told me you came for something of his," said Jade, from beside one of the other pillars.

So he'd been close enough to his mom that he'd introduced her to Jade. That stung. I'd been latching onto Quinn and Junior like buoys in a storm all summer, but I hadn't been anyone's first choice.

"Didn't work," I said, swallowing the failure creeping up the back of my throat.

"Could you try to find him with this?"

I could just make out its shape in the light of the restaurant on the pier, the smell of battered shrimp beckoning my painfully empty stomach. A ring. A prized possession, or in this case, a token of a disappearing man's love.

I took it, feeling its weight between my fingers. Her eyes were big and hopeful.

I still believed he was out there. But why did she?

"At what point do you accept he's gone?" I asked.

I wanted her to hurt like I did. It was selfish. She didn't owe me anything. And what the hell did I think Junior owed me? To not disappear off the face of the planet, for one, leaving everyone scrambling, even the clan elders who usually acted like the wolves don't exist. The decency not to go from invisible to revered.

She stared at the waves coming up between the pillars of the pier, sparkling in the moon's light.

"I don't think that point exists for me," she said.

Dimples appeared on each side of her mouth as her lips pressed together in worry. This is what it looked like when loving another person was easy, what it looked like when losing them was hard.

I wanted people around me. I wanted to be surrounded with lights and movement and heat and magic seeping into my bones. I texted Quinn.

"I *am* an asshole," I said when she showed up at the club. "I'm sorry."

She pinched my cheek and gently slapped it, then we hugged it out. That was how easy it was for us. I almost cried.

Danny texted me to ask what I was doing. Then he showed up too.

I had the ring on a chain around my neck, but for now, I was soaking in the atmosphere. My blood sang its songs. I imagined the magic seeping into every cell. I felt like I could fly. Surely this, people congregating, dancing, laughing and happy would summon Junior. I sent him a text.

Me: *Partying at your spot. Miss you.*

I imagined what Jonah was doing. He was probably reading A Series of Unfortunate Events with the twins or helping put Joss to bed or he and Maddie were having their nightly therapy session.

My heart ached. Lately, all I did was want things I couldn't have.

My phone buzzed and my heart pounded at the sight of the ID.

Jonah: *We need to talk ASAP.*

For one panicked moment, I worried I'd somehow performed a Call spell just thinking about him. I called instead of texting him back. Of course that pissed him off. But he was coming.

Danny joined Quinn and I, dancing. I think he smoked something at some point, because his eyes, which were usually alert and penetrating—damn observation skills—were sleepy looking. Relaxed. We all laughed at his ridiculous moves when I felt Jonah walk through the door.

I saw him through the flashes of light, alternating green, then blue, then purple on his face. Seeing him be the golden boy at school was different than seeing him drive my bug, intense and determined.

But seeing him here, in my environment, for me, was seeing him with whole new eyes.

When he found me, his face relaxed a little and he almost smiled. Almost.

He stopped in front of me. We stood there in the middle of the club, people bumping and brushing against us as they moved in time to the techno thumps. Danny and Quinn came over.

The surprise on Jonah's face was pretty obvious. "What's he doing here?"

Danny laughed. "Nice to see you too, bro."

"Just didn't know you guys hung out," Jonah said, shoving his hands in his pockets, drawing his shoulders up. I didn't care if he was uncomfortable. And I was very curious to hear what he had to say.

"Hey, Quinn. We need to talk," he told me.

"But first, anyone?" asked Danny, waving a joint he'd produced out of thin air.

I watched Jonah process this, his stern expression an exact duplicate of his dad's.

"What the hell, Apollo?" he yelled to be heard over the music. Or maybe just to yell at me.

I'm a horrible influence apparently. Don't let me around your children. Especially those who can make choices for themselves.

"Dude brought his own weed," I said.

"It could affect his place on the team," Jonah argued.

He still thought this was somehow my fault. Sounded about right.

"Only if someone told," I said, appealing to logic instead.

Jonah glared at me, smoke practically coming out of his nostrils. His eyes looked like the eyes of those celebration dragons being gallivanted down the streets in China. He looked pissed off and ridiculous.

I got closer to him, so I wouldn't have to yell.

"I really hope you didn't just come to accuse me of inebriating your teammate."

He saw Junior's ring against my chest.

"Can we talk? Now?" he asked, voice cracking.

I followed him to the bathroom.

The door closed behind me and Jonah went forward, checking under the two stalls for feet. I lit up a cigarette to have something to do with my hands. I hadn't expected to see him tonight, so I was wearing his hoodie. I wondered if he noticed.

Satisfied the place was empty, he went to the sink and leaned back against the counter.

I stopped in front of him. It was a small space between Jonah and the wall. The music thumped the entire bathroom, the walls, the door, even the faucet rattled.

"You have to stop doing this if we're going to be able to accomplish anything," he said.

I took a drag, glaring down at the floor between our shoes. "Doing what? Trying to forget that it would be more convenient for everyone if I just disappeared like Junior? Or trying to have a good time?"

His face fell. Did he remember me showing him the letter about my mom regretting me?

"Danny's a big boy," I said. "He can take care of himself, Jay."

I didn't mean to use his girlfriend's dumb nickname. Suddenly, he felt like a stranger, our differences so stark under the pink-tinted fluorescent light.

He rushed me. I was back against the opposite wall, and Jonah was pressed against me. I think I hit my head. Still had my cigarette though. For a second, I thought he might kiss me, and I had to threaten my brain with bodily harm to shut up. *Stop*, I told myself. *You can't love him anymore. He will burn you up.*

"Stop," he said, grabbing his hoodie. "Stop trying to push me away."

Lot of good that did. I was the opposite of scared.

I cleared my throat. "Point taken."

He backed off, grabbed my hand instead. No, my wrist. He lifted it, the cigarette trailing a smoke signal—SOS—as his fingers traced the tendons in my wrist. He brought my hand to his face and took a drag of my cigarette. I'd never seen anything quite so hot. Still don't recommend smoking, but seeing Jonah lose control took me back to days splashing in the waves at the beach before collapsing on the shore together, sea water drying on our skin.

He released me and backed up against the sink again. He gripped the edge of the counter.

"Mom had an emergency meeting with the other teachers the other day when you came by. Then my dad was on a meeting last night at like nine, talking about the *vampiria* potentially attacking the wolves and voiding the treaty."

"I told you it felt connected."

He scowled at me. "Is now really the time for I told you so?"

His scowl fell when I stepped closer. I put my hand on his shoulder. "Jonah, it's always the time for I told you so."

I put out my cigarette under the faucet behind him and threw it in the trash.

"Let's get on with it," I said.

"What?"

"You'll see."

We found Danny and Quinn dancing near each other but not really with each other.

"We have to go," I told Quinn.

She looked at me before flicking her eyes to Danny. "Really?"

"Sorry. I'll text you later."

Jonah gripped my shoulder as I weaved us back to the bar.

"Can I have the salt?" I asked the bartender.

I poured a small mountain in the center of a napkin as the bartender grumbled about charging me if I kept wasting it. I drew all the corners of the napkin together, twisting it.

As we walked out, I sucked in as much of the magic as I could, a heady mixture of adrenaline, sweat, high hopes, and crashing disappointment. It all compacted in the center of my chest and filled the hole right up.

"What are we doing?" Jonah asked.

I went to the bug. He jerked the door open, getting in after me.

"Apollo, I have to be back by eleven."

"You will. Promise."

I laid the napkin on my knee, started unwrapping it as Jonah watched.

"That book," he said. "*A History of Kindreds.* Where'd you get it?"

My stomach dislodged and floated at the mention of my very romantic gesture. "Maddie helped me find it."

He turned on me. "You told Maddie about us?"

"No," I said slowly. "I told Maddie I was interested in reading more about Kindreds."

"You shouldn't have done that. Maddie's smart."

"I know she's smart," I said. She answered my algebra and pre-calc questions, day or night. "But she wouldn't ever think you'd keep something like that from her."

"I've been keeping a lot of secrets," he said.

My heart pounded loudly in the quiet. I knew all the secrets he'd been keeping from everyone, so why would he say that? Unless he had new ones. It had been a long time since we'd been like this, talking, not quite as easily as we used to, but within the same six foot radius.

I took the chain from around my neck and slipped the ring off.

"Help me with this, and then I promise we'll get you home on time," I said.

"Whose is that?" he asked about the ring.

"Junior gave it to his girlfriend. She gave it to me."

I put the ring in my mouth. Jonah's mouth fell open. He and Maddie had exactly similar looks of disgust.

"What?" I laughed.

"That's disgusting," he said, looking away. "You have no idea where it's been."

I shrugged. "Magic can be disgusting."

I dipped it in the salt and put it back in my mouth again. I tasted metal and the sea. I immediately felt the pull without any type of incantation. I tasted sweet bread and mildew. Yes, there was Junior. I could smell orange blossoms, water on dirt. I could taste . . . pain. I could taste blood.

That didn't seem right.

"Another locating spell," he said. "What makes you think it will work this time?"

"This means more to him than what I used before," I said, the ring sitting in the palm of my hand. "You should do it too."

"What? Why?"

"You're the unbiased party here. You don't really care, so it might be clearer for you."

"I care."

I dipped the ring, wet from my mouth, in the salt and held it out to him.

Here I was, asking him to break yet another rule. *Come on. Let's dig ourselves in a little deeper.*

He took the ring. He glanced at me, embarrassed, before putting it into his mouth.

He pulled it from his mouth, salt gone, and handed it back to me. He closed his eyes and sat back.

"Fuck," he said.

The magic had this kind of intense pull behind your belly button that felt just on the edge of good. A magikalis doing what we were designed to do.

"Yep."

I slipped the ring back on the chain and put it around my neck.

"Apollo," he said, taking a breath.

I knew what was coming.

"It's leading to Orville's," he said.

"That's what I'm getting too." I felt numb all over. I still couldn't be sure if I trusted it, but magic didn't lie. Any misinterpretations were all user error.

The ring could have just led us to one of the places Junior had been. Or . . . it could have led us to the last place he was alive. I shivered.

"Take my jacket if you're cold."

I wanted to say yes. *Pipe dream. Pipe dream.*

"We'll make a plan?" I asked, fully expecting him to shut that down. "I understand I'm asking you to risk everything. I know it's horrible, because your dreams—"

"Fuck my dreams! I don't care about that. I care—"

He abruptly started jerking around in his seat, nearly giving me a heart attack. I realized he was taking off his jacket.

"Here."

"I'm not—"

He reached over for my hand, holding it up between us. "You're freezing."

Of course I was compared to him. He was as hot as a supernova. Sometimes I wondered when I threw magic, if I wasn't drawing some from him, from his heat.

"Thanks." I slipped it on.

He sat back in just his thermal.

I didn't feel high off the magic, like I did earlier. It was waning. You had to re-up it, just like any other fix.

He looked at me and put his hand on the door.

"I'll see you tomorrow?"

"Yeah," I said.

He lingered a moment longer than necessary. I waited, not allowing myself to hope for a damn thing. Then I realized.

"Your jacket," I said, reaching to take it off.

"I just gave it to you," he laughed quietly, and my heart wrenched. "I'll get it tomorrow." He opened the door, looking back again. "'Night, Apollo."

I forced a smile. It was always easier being with Jonah than away from him.

I followed him home. At a red light, he texted me. He was definitely using voice to text. He never broke any rules.

Except the once.

Jonah: *You didn't have to follow me.*

I wanted to, I sent back. I almost deleted it. Just three little words.

Since the night he made it crystal clear he didn't want me, since the night at Orville's and he was there when I needed him, no questions asked, I was terrified I would say something damning. Something that would repulse him. Something that would make me lose him again. Or lose him forever.

I watched from across the street as he pulled into his driveway. As he walked up to the house, I felt him release, a quick open and close of his hands at his sides. The interior of the bug began to heat up. Just enough to be completely comfortable with his jacket too. I smirked.

Me: *That was risky.*

I didn't know if other *magikalia* could feel it when they released near one another the way we could feel each other. I drank the richness of his magic right off the air, like thick, steamed milk in a latte, sweet with a deep, almost burnt flavor. Closing my eyes, I let it shudder through my body.

Jonah: *Probably.*

I could almost see the afterglow on his face, the dopey smile.

Jonah: *I had to though. And why not make up for your broken heater while I'm at it?*

I knew I should release too. But I held it in, basking in the heat Jonah had left me with, and drove home.

12

Jonah

Dad was tense and snapping at everyone.

Miles, stop shaking your leg.

Macy, sit in your seat right.

Jonah. Slow down. This isn't a mess hall.

Maddie and I locked eyes across the table. She had tried to talk to me earlier this morning, before I'd even woke up. I snapped and threw a paperback in her direction.

Mom brought up Jocelyn's six-month appointment tomorrow, which seemed to take some of the heat off the rest of us.

I pulled my phone out and put it on my lap, swiping a text to Apollo.

"Mom, Jonah's sexting with his girlfriend," said Miles.

I glared at him with the full force of my betrayal.

Dad set down his fork. "Miles. That's inappropriate. Where did you hear that language?"

Miles shrugged. That was his thing lately. "School."

"Well, your classmates may be allowed to throw around words like that, but you are not. Room."

Miles pushed back from the table, another shrug barely contained, and shot me a dead-faced look. I hoped I wasn't that moody when I was his age.

"Jonah, are you using your phone at this table?" asked Dad, looking right into my soul.

"No. I mean yes, I was just texting Apollo. I wasn't—"

"Jonah," said Dad, putting up his hand like he was halting a barrage of dirty details. "You know the rules."

"I know," I said, getting up with our empty plates and taking them to the sink.

After cleaning the kitchen until it sparkled, Maddie followed me to my room. "I need to talk to you," she said. Her eyes looked like she'd just drank an entire pot of coffee.

"No." I walked past her, closing my door behind me. I landed on my bed, planning to have a long think about last night. Something changed with Apollo and I. Something for the better.

My door opened.

"What do you want?" I moaned. I just wanted to lay here and think about the awkwardness of my relationships in peace.

"Give me one good reason not to tell Mom and Dad that you can access your magic already."

I sat up, hitting my head on the bookshelf Apollo had helped me mount above my bed; I'd gotten FOMO after seeing it on a bookstagrammer's feed.

"What?" I asked, rubbing my head. There was no point in evading though. Maddie was a dog with a bone when she had an idea, that metaphorical dog being Cujo.

"I saw you last night when you came home," she said.

That's what I get for being a responsible magikalis who throws after gathering.

"Why didn't you say anything?" she asked.

There was a flash of something in her face that she immediately shuttered. Apollo had said Maddie would never think I'd keep something like this from her. Maybe my secret had hurt her.

"I've been trying to talk to you since this morning, if you would recall. But Ali Hazelwood had other plans."

"I don't own any Ali Hazelwood!" I said a little hysterically. I had *one*.

"Besides, it was just a hypothesis, but now that you've confirmed . . ."

I rolled my eyes, but my heart was racing.

"Also, I didn't want to attack you about it," she said, her voice a little softer.

"What do you call this?" I asked.

She ignored that. "You've been acting weird."

"Me? You're the one running into Apollo's arms the second he starts talking to me again." Evasive maneuvers weren't going to work.

Were they?

She tilted her head. "Again. Thank you for confirming my hypotheses."

"What?"

"Nothing. Just call your boyfriend. Tell him to get over here."

"Apollo isn't—he's not my—"

"If you can throw, that means he's your Kindred. And I have a proposition for you both."

I had left the door unlocked for him, wondering whether he would just come in like he used to.

Joss screeched like a pterodactyl when he let himself in, appearing in the kitchen.

"Hey," I said, but it sounded hoarse. Clearing my throat, I opened my mouth to say something else, but my mind went blank. "Sleep okay?" was what came out.

He almost smiled. "Nice and toasty." He set my jacket on one of the dining room chairs.

"Thanks. Hungry?" I was stalling.

"I'm good. Where is everyone?"

"Their rooms. Mom and Dad went to the store." Joss turned away from her next bite. "She's never like this. Except of course today, when I'm feeding her."

She stared open-mouthed at Apollo. Sometimes I was speechless when I looked at Apollo too.

"So, this is baby Joss." He took her sticky hand.

"You've never met her?" No. Of course they hadn't. We hadn't been talking since right before she was born. I hated the reminder that I'd been exiled from his life.

"I mean, I've seen her at the meetings. Can I feed her?"

I let him sit down. With Apollo feeding her, she ate her food like it was the best thing in the world, making happy nom noises. Where were *my* happy nom noises?

I crossed my arms as a defense against the adorable scene in front of me.

"Does your dad have any beer?" he asked.

"What?"

"You need to chill."

"How did you do that?" I asked as he scraped the last of the bananas out of the container for an all too eager Joss.

He shrugged as she took her last bite. "Maybe it has something to do with me not being an uptight—"

I groaned.

He watched as I cleaned her up and got her out of the high chair. She was oddly quiet, clinging to me as I took her back to Mom and Dad's room. Probably watching Apollo as he followed us. When I put her in her crib, she immediately scrambled up and started crying. I turned the monitor to her crib and shut the door, as she started really going.

"Why's she crying?"

"She doesn't want to take a nap."

"Should we get her back up?"

I almost laughed at how stressed he looked. "You can't go back into the lair once you've put the beast down."

"It can't be as bad as that," he said, still craning his head back toward the room as we walked down the hallway.

"You think what she's doing now is bad? No. You have to let her cry herself out. She'll be passed out in ten minutes, tops."

Knowing what I had to tell him when we returned to the kitchen, I thought maybe he was right about needing to chill. I pulled out a Coors. I'd have to drink it fast before Maddie finished with her advisor meeting.

I leaned on the counter and Apollo took post at my side.

"I wasn't serious," he said as I chugged the last couple drinks.

"It was a good idea," I said, belching. "Already feel like a million bucks."

"Lightweight."

"I can still take you," I said, then realized how quiet it was. "Listen." I pointed to the baby monitor. "She's asleep."

He looked closer at how she slept with her butt in the air, smiling. "That's adorable."

"Agreed. Come on." I gathered the monitor and crushed the can, shoving it into the recycling bin before we went downstairs.

"Jesus, Jonah."

"Right?" I said, closing the door behind us and leaning against it. "I've never done that before."

"I can kind of tell," he said.

My giddiness faded at the sight of him standing in the middle of my room, arms crossed and waiting.

I sat on the bed. The only way to get this out was to just rip off the band-aid. "Maddie knows about us."

His expression didn't change. Was he listening?

"Knows what about us?" he asked.

"She saw me throw last night."

"Okay?"

"How are you not freaking out about this?" He probably wasn't freaking out because out of the two of us, Apollo was definitely Maddie's favorite, and he wouldn't face the brunt for keeping this secret.

"Makes sense your genius sister found out."

"You do realize this puts a kink in our plans to follow the ring."

"What am I supposed to do? Go around chugging beers and yelling at people?"

"I'm sorry," I said, lowering my voice. "You told me to drink the beer."

"Are you going to do everything I tell you to do, Jonah?" he asked, sitting beside me.

"I pretty much already have, haven't I?"

"Don't do that," he said. "You know I needed you. Why do you keep making me say it? I needed you, and I still need you, Jonah."

I sat down beside him. "We'll find him."

13

Apollo

For an insane moment, I thought he might touch me. He cleared his throat.

The basement door opened. We looked to find Maddie's pale, heart-shaped face swimming in a mess of dark hair and thick hoodie. She shut the door behind her, and faced us with her hands in her hoodie pocket.

Judging by her pursed lips and high eyebrows, she had us by our balls.

I gave her my best smile. "Hey, Maddie."

"Don't 'hey, Maddie' me, batting your pretty eyes. I know if he's throwing, you are too."

"You think my eyes are pretty?" I asked.

Jonah groaned and stood up.

"What are you guys up to?" she asked.

"We're not up to anything," said Jonah.

Subtlety at its height, right there.

"I told you I saw you sneaking back late. And I found the bloody shirt in the hamper."

"You went through my clothes?" Jonah's face twisted into a grimace. Everything seemed exaggerated by the beer.

"It will benefit everyone for you tell me what you're up to."

"No," we both intoned.

"Okay." She walked to the door, affecting a grave countenance. "Wonder if Mom and Dad are home yet. They'll want to hear this together."

"Stop!" Jonah put his hand on the door. "Damn, Maddie." He ran his hand through his hair, looking about ready to pull it out.

We locked eyes over her head. He turned away, looking defeated.

I told her about the last time I'd seen Junior, at Purple Haze, and Quinn and the wolves. Talbot coming up to talk to me.

"Talbot Erikson?" she interrupted.

Jonah turned away, busying himself with organizing his book collection.

I was self-conscious about this part, but I wanted to make it clear that the only reason I'd gone out there with him was that I thought he'd been interested.

"Just tell her, Apollo. Get it over with."

Because I apparently did everything Jonah tells me to do—wait, stay, roll over, et al—I told her about finding the vampiris when it had been feeding and how I brought Jonah back with me. "We tried outrunning it in the bug."

She crossed her arms. "You can't be serious."

I shook my head. "We wrecked into it."

"I freaked out when it went for Apollo," Jonah said, swallowing. "I used magic to throw it away from him."

I realized then, for him to use that kind of power, without even thinking about it, he must have been terrified. I was terrified when I woke up outside the car to see the thing about to swallow Jonah whole like a python.

I could practically see the calculations happening in Maddie's eyes.

"Jonah," Maddie said, shaking her head. "This is bad."

"Yeah. You're telling me."

"Anyway," I said. "We killed it."

"You *what*? Mom and Dad are going to freak!"

"No," Jonah said. "They're not, because you're not going to say a word. I can't believe we brought you into this." He thumped his head back against his dresser.

"She's a big girl, Jonah," I said.

"That's your favorite answer for everything," he said.

I touched my nose, immune to his snark.

"I brought myself into it," she said. "Besides, I meant when they inevitably find out. There's no way you can keep this up, keep hiding how much you need each other until you turn twenty-one."

"What are we supposed to do?" asked Jonah.

"I get it. I don't want you to be separated either," she said, a little quieter. "Not when . . ." She didn't have to finish.

Not when we'd just started to be friends again.

Not when I was clearly in love with him. It would kill me to be separated against our will.

I loved her for understanding why we'd carried this secret for so long.

"How did you do it?" she asked.

Jonah picked at a thread on his jeans. "Burned it."

"After running it over," I said.

"Damn," she said.

"Yep. That's about where we're at," I said.

Jonah cut me a look. "We're going out there again to look for clues. So if you'll just—"

"Clues?" she said. "It's dead, right?"

I remembered the ashes in Jonah's hair that night. "Very." I told her about seeing the vampiris and her cronies sniffing around the next day.

We had touched something that should have been untouchable. And we left the shattered pieces behind for anyone to find, and this development worried Maddie as much as it did us.

We heard the front door open.

"Mom and Dad are back," Maddie said, but she didn't move. "You're sure the woman was vampiris?" she asked me, her voice lowered.

I nodded. "I could feel it."

"What'd she look like?"

"I don't know. Kind of severe but put together. Like a hot but strict teacher."

"Can you give me something a little less objectifying and abstract?"

"She was slim. Super blonde hair, like, white, like Elsa white, hair. It was short, wavy. Kind of a 60's style, I guess. She had a suit on too."

"Much better," said Maddie.

"Why does it matter what she looks like?" Jonah asked, on edge again.

"We need to find out what she was doing there and if you guys are in danger."

"Junior," I said. "The guy that's missing. I think he might have followed me out there." My throat was tight, and all the guilt I hadn't been letting myself think about was a song I couldn't get out of my head.

Maddie opened her mouth, confused. "I thought it was—"

"Gilberto Sanchez," Jonah said, tossing a bouncy ball.

He didn't realize the effect that had on me. He'd never even met Junior, but he remembered his name from the meeting.

I opened my conversation with Junior and handed her my phone. "He sent me that when I left. And then, when Jonah and I were leaving, there were a couple cars. Talbot's and another one." Junior must have been pretty spot on about Talbot being a player.

"So Talbot was there when all this was happening?"

"He was parked a ways down from where we took it down. We didn't see him or anything. I just assumed he brought someone else out there. But then, we did a Locator spell on a ring his girlfriend gave us—"

"Talbot?" interrupted Maddie, still reading on my phone.

"No, Junior."

Jonah was looking at me like I'd said too much.

"What?" I asked. "We may as well tell her everything," I said.

I tried not to feel miserable as she took screenshots and texted them to herself. She handed it back and shoved her hands in her hoodie pocket. "You guys absolutely cannot go back," she said.

"We have to," said Jonah.

Don't get me wrong, I was glad to have him in my corner but someone needed to get him a massage certificate or something.

"If something happens to Junior, because of me," I said slowly. I couldn't even finish.

She glanced between the two of us, then she blew a sigh up at her loose hair.

"Fine. But I'm going too. I want to make sure you don't do anything stupid, but mostly to be able to say 'I told you so' if you die."

"No," said Jonah. "Absolutely not."

"Let her," I said, knowing he was going to kill me for this.

"Are you out of your mind?" asked Jonah.

I opened my mouth.

"Never mind. Don't answer that," he said.

"She could help us," I said.

"You know I could, Jonah," said Maddie.

"You didn't see this thing!" he hissed, trying to keep it down so Tom and Isabel didn't hear.

She calmly looked him in the eye. "It doesn't matter. I'm coming. And we should go now, during the day."

We all shivered.

"Fine," Jonah relented. "Go tell Mom we're going to Apollo's to—"

"Watch Netflix," I said, not taking my eyes off Jonah as he looked at me. The last time he'd been at my house, watching Netflix, I'd kissed him. Before I went down my spiral of worrying whether I'd forced him into something he hadn't wanted to do, I broke the connection.

"Yeah, movies." He reached out for her arm as she passed. "You should bring a weapon," he said almost apologetically.

I looked at Jonah after she'd left. "Well, that went well."

"Is that my sweater?" he asked.

Grinning, I ducked past him out the door.

"Let the record show, I've never done anything like this before," Maddie said as she climbed in the backseat.

"I seem to be having that effect on people today," I deadpanned.

"Oh?" she said, raising her eyebrows at me in the mirror, then looking at Jonah. "Is that why my brother smelled like a stale dive bar before noon?"

"God," Jonah said faintly, putting his head in his hand.

"Madeline Ruth Clarke. Do you charge me with getting your brother drunk?"

"Did you get my brother drunk?"

"He needed to relax. And I didn't do anything but plant the seed in his head. I could never convince him to do anything he doesn't want to do."

"I'm sitting right here," Jonah said.

I looked back at Maddie, ignoring his pointed stare. "Did you bring enough accessories?"

She had her laptop bag strapped across her, a pocket knife clipped onto her pocket, and something in a case around her wrist. She passed us bottled water and Chex Mix in baggies.

I held up my baggie to Jonah. "Quaint."

"There's nothing wrong with preparation," she said.

Jonah made a face at me. I lit a cigarette after we got a safe distance from their house.

"There's a charge on your car," said Maddie. "When you said you wrecked into the vampiris, I didn't realize you literally crashed your car."

"Yeah." I moved my hand along the wheel.

"And you . . . repaired it with magic?" She sounded like she was trying to work it all out. And honestly, even though it was terrifying to have it all out in the open with someone who didn't have a stake in this, it felt good to have Maddie on board. It felt like we were making headway, like we were a little closer to finding him.

"We did what we had to do," said Jonah.

As we passed the first row of orange trees to Orville's, Maddie sat forward, grabbing onto our chairs. "This is the edge of clan territory."

"Yes," I said, using the abandoned farmhouse as a marker in these identical rows. I turned the bug into the trees when I saw it.

"Where?" she asked when I parked.

I pointed to the clearing across the way.

"What was it doing when you first saw it? Explain exactly."

I told her it had been feeding and how it had been acting unusual when I came back with Jonah.

"So do you guys ever pay attention in Sunday school? Or do you just throw paper airplanes at each other and play footsie? You're the future of our clan, for god's sake—"

"*JUST*! Get to the point, Maddie," Jonah said, nearly popping the head rest of his seat off.

"*Vampiria* don't go flailing themselves around like rabid dogs. They blend in better with society than our kind do."

I doubted that after seeing the woman in the suit. The only place she was blending in was a fairytale about a murderous ice queen.

"They draw their prey in, while our species warns sapiens away to protect us from discovery."

"Right. When it went for Apollo, all crazy, he'd been bleeding," Jonah said, eyes going to the scab hidden in my hairline. "It made me think of what they call the blood song."

"Exactly. Maybe it was somehow exposed to our kind's blood before you'd shown up."

I thought about how Jonah looked that day at school when he saw the paint and thought it was blood. That's how I felt right now. Like I needed to put my head between my knees or something. I could feel sweat running down the sides of my face.

"What's wrong, Apollo?" asked Maddie.

I shook my head.

"He thinks Junior might have . . . crossed paths with it," said Jonah gently. "But the timing would have to match up to, like, the hour for that to be possible. You said you'd just seen Junior, before you met Talbot out here."

His gaze was the gentlest I'd seen all day.

"That wasn't him," he said. "Otherwise, this is all kind of pointless."

"It isn't," Maddie said. "It does involve the entire clan's safety, but it's difficult for you two to see past your bubble, I know."

Jonah looked out the window. But she was right, and here I was putting them both in harm's way.

"Come on. Let's look around, so we can get out of here," said Jonah.

I wanted to grab his arm, keep him close, protect them both. But I followed as he got out. Junior, who'd kept my head above water all summer, was missing. The ring had led us here. We couldn't turn back now.

Before she could get a limb out, Jonah closed Maddie's door.

She rolled down the window. "What the hell, Jonah? Let me out."

"No. You're completely helpless out here."

"No different than in here," she said.

"We'll put a Protection on the car," Jonah said.

I went over to him, and it was like fireworks on the right side of my body. It was like our magic knew we needed it, and it was rolling awake. I didn't want to touch him. I was afraid I wouldn't let go.

"Do you even know how to do a Protection?" Maddie asked.

"Your doubt in us," I said. "It hurts." I put my hand over my heart. "Right here."

"I'm sure we can figure it out," growled Jonah.

Maddie crossed her arms. "I feel better."

Jonah put a hand on my shoulder. My knees almost gave out when his hungry power barreled into me. Did he have more than I did, because he didn't hold onto it? Was he a better environment for the magic, because he wasn't selfish about it? Or did it come crashing into me because his magic hungered for mine. Just like my magic hungered for his?

I put a hand on his shoulder and imagined weaving a grid of protection, growing it until it got big enough to cover the car. It manifested in front of us, a gauzy, shimmering wall, lengthening to three times our height until we guided it over the bug.

"That's pretty awesome," said Maddie. "But this is exactly why they keep Kindred separate."

"I told you she'd figure it out with the book," Jonah said. "Text if you see anything."

We got to the road. My heart pounded like I'd gone too many nights of holding instead of sleeping. I remembered the copper smell of the vampiris as he had tried pulling me out of the bug. I remembered being very aware that my bones were hollow, that the right amount of pressure could snap them like twigs. I'd been staring death down.

Jonah touched my arm. "We shouldn't stray far from the car. We can't outrun them if we run across another."

I grabbed his hand. His startled look made me roll my eyes. "If we're touching, we can."

We called our magic up again for Incognito. Then we stepped onto the road. It was still far from that clearing, but everything in me wanted to run. We walked along to the area where it happened. But there was nothing.

"Those Hazmat guys probably scrubbed it all away," Jonah said.

That's when I realized I had been looking for the oil spill of that thing's blood. I shivered. It still felt like that thing was here. I could smell his hair burning.

"We should go back," he said. "There's nothing out here."

We couldn't go back empty-handed. I walked forward and felt the weight of Jonah's arm as he followed.

There was something in the grass on the side of the road closest to the clearing. I kneeled down, pulling my hand from his to pick it up.

"What is it?" he whispered.

"It's cloth," I said. It was so faded, it had blended in with the dirt embankment.

"Let me see."

I handed it to him, and his nostrils flared.

"I think this is part of the shirt it was wearing," I said. "Remember its clothes?"

"Yeah. They looked torn and gross. Like he'd been wearing them for a while."

I took it back, brushing Jonah's hand for the intoxicating buzz.

"It wouldn't make sense to do another Locator spell," he said.

He was right. That would just lead us here.

"A Discernment could show us if it has any link to Junior," I said.

Discernments were tricky magic because you used them to basically read the present like foretelling the future.

I felt like retching the entire way to the car. We were at a dead end until we could do this complicated spell.

"Maddie, what the—" Jonah asked as cellophane crumpled in the back. He looked back at her. "Are you eating Twinkies?"

"I stress-eat, Jonah!"

"You gave us Chex Mix and you have Twinkies?" I asked, but Jonah wasn't fooled by my joke.

I could feel his eyes burning trails into my skin as I started up the bug.

"Did you guys see anything?" asked Maddie.

I gave what we found to Jonah to get back on the road. I half-expected it to turn to ash in our hands.

I checked my mirrors, marveling at how normal the day had seemed. The temperature was perfect and the trees were lazy in the afternoon sun.

But it had felt too quiet. Too perfect. Maybe it was just knowing what the trees had seen a couple weeks ago.

Maddie took our find from Jonah. "What is this?"

"We were going to try a Discernment on it," I said.

"You know how?" she asked, shocked.

"I thought I could talk to one of the wolves."

"You have to be careful, so they don't suspect you're going to do it yourself," Maddie said, passing the cloth back up to me. I kept it in my hand.

"Half of them think I'm older anyway."

"Well don't talk to them without me."

"Maddie," Jonah argued.

"Don't you dare tell me it's not safe when you guys are taking all the risks! What do I have to lose?"

Everything. She had everything to lose. They both did, and it was my fault.

As I pulled up to their house, Maddie leaned forward.

"Guess bringing this was overkill," she said as blue electricity zapped loudly in her hand.

Jonah and I both jumped away.

"Mom and Dad gave it to me when I started university. For all those nights staying late at the library I guess," she said, casing it back up.

Jonah shook his head. I stared at the space between us where the blue arc had lit up.

"See you tomorrow, Apollo," she said and got out.

Jonah didn't move to leave.

"How do you feel?" he asked.

"How am I supposed to feel, Jonah?"

"I just mean—are you alright? After throwing?"

Sometimes it blew my mind how well Jonah could read me. I felt empty after pooling our magic together for the Protection and the Incognito. "I'm fine. Great."

"You don't have to do that with me."

"I'm not doing anything with you, Jonah," I said, facing the road.

"Whatever," he said, reaching for the handle.

"Hey."

He turned back, exasperated. I held out the faded scrap.

I wanted him to know that I wouldn't make a move without him.

14
Jonah

I was getting coffee when I felt Apollo walk into the records building. Something nervous fluttered in my stomach.

His mom, Zarine, stopped to talk to my parents. I could hear him say 'hi' to Maddie on his way over.

He looked startled by the attention when I smiled at him. Or maybe by the upsurge of the buzzing that began the moment he walked in. I know he felt it too. When he got closer, my brain was pure white noise. My fingertips itched to touch him. I had always wondered if that was typical of Kindred. Or was it just because he was my best friend?

"Hey," he said.

"Get some food. Good stuff today."

He crossed his arms. "Not that hungry."

"Apollo." I got closer, tilting my head so only he would hear me. "Don't make me lecture you. Eat."

"We've just made up, and you're already going there?"

"Yes," I said, forcing a paper plate to his chest, giddy that he'd admitted we were friends again. "*Eat.*"

"Christ! Fine."

Apollo loaded up his plate, popping food into his mouth as he went. I popped a cream cheese tart in my mouth, moaning around it. "Did you get any of these little tarts?"

"No."

"They were over here. They must have run out."

"Ran out? You took them all. Give me one of yours."

I held it out to him, waiting for him to take it. It was a purely physical reaction when I felt his mouth glance off my fingers, like being socked in the stomach. I snapped my head at him, but his eyes were closed.

"You're right. That *is* good," he said.

I swallowed, not that hungry anymore.

We all sat down together like we used to. I wondered what Apollo had told Zarine all those months they sat away from us. Mom and Dad only asked once before realizing even his name was a no fly zone.

Beside me, Apollo seemed like he was trying to take up the least amount of space as possible. I settled back in my seat, my shoulder pressed against his.

From his podium at the bottom of the room, Graham finally got to what we'd been waiting for. "I am sorry to say that there are no updates on the status of Gilberto Sanchez. The clan is doing everything they can."

Had they even gotten as far as us? Did they know, for instance, that Junior had gone out at Orville's where a vampiris had been losing its mind?

"In the meantime," said Graham. "Everyone will be participating in defense lessons."

My stomach knotted. Apollo's breath came faster as his arm tightened against mine. If they were making a move like this, that meant the clan was on high alert; they didn't think that Junior was just being a wolf. I watched Apollo out of the corner of my eye, but he'd always had an epic poker face.

Younglings didn't have to take defensives after seventeen, but Graham wanted to be sure we refreshed ourselves on it, 'in light of recent events.' The language seemed cold.

They herded us to the training rooms, less like the school's weight room and more like a martial arts institute. It was all bare walls and padded floor. We focused on using our magic to enhance our physical prowess, but the clan also taught us to fight without using any magic at all. Despite the treaty and the lack of any conflict with *vampiria* for decades, we had to 'Be ready for any enemy'. This precaution was also because of our negative effect on most sapiens.

We were divided into age groups. Maddie, Apollo, and I were put with those around Talbot's age. Talbot looked superior, arms crossed over his chest, as though he was better than all of this training. I knew I could take him. My nerves twitched, itching to prove it.

Maddie paired with another girl about her age, but she kept looking over at me. I raised my eyebrows at her. *What?*

I saw Quinn and expected to see Apollo nearby, but she was talking to who I thought was her dad.

"Partner?" Apollo's voice in my ear made me jump.

"Why'd you sneak up on me?"

"Be ready for any enemy," he said, looking as though it was the most obvious answer.

I laughed, pulling my jacket off and tossing it out of the way.

"Alright, everyone," said the defense instructor. "We'll start with some basics. You're free to go farther if you're comfortable. We're just brushing up here, making sure everyone has the same tools at their disposal."

I stopped listening when Apollo pulled off my hoodie and the long-sleeve he had on underneath. In his white A-shirt, it was obvious he'd gotten thinner. His layers had been hiding it and quick, careful glances in the locker room hadn't painted the full picture.

He noticed me looking and seemed like he'd bolt at any moment. I met his unreal green eyes. I hoped he knew that he could come to me for anything. That I'd take all of this away from him to be able to see him relaxed and zoning out on guitar for hours or skipping from place to place, like he was a coiled spring. I could see now that he didn't have the strength for any of that. I hadn't seen him that weightless since . . . since we kissed.

I hadn't even realized the instructions were finished before Apollo butted his shoulder into my stomach. I reached over his back, grabbing his waist, and we circled like that, our strengths almost cancelling each other out. Apollo was strong, despite how thin he was. I dodged around him, temporarily letting go, before getting him in a headlock.

He melted out of my grip and was suddenly against my back. My head was forced back by the rock-hard tendons in his forearm pressed to my throat. I reached up to grip his arm, but he forced it tighter. I was just thinking that maybe his thin form had been an advantage in that move, when his hand trailed down one of my arms to my bicep, laying his fingers there. I wasn't sure if my sputtering was for lack of oxygen or the shock of his touch.

He was so close to my ear, I could feel his breath, hot in contrast to his cool arms. "Apollo, one. Jonah, zero."

I broke away from him. I could feel the sweat at my hairline.

"Again," I said.

Our defense instructor, Steve, commended our work.

I watched Apollo's feet as he came at my waist again. I wouldn't make the same mistake of going too low. I let him barrel into me, hardly moving with the attack.

"You're not thinking clearly, Tormey. You know that I'm better—" I pushed back, knocking him off balance. "At *force*."

He fell on his back. I threw myself on top of him, knees holding his arms down.

He looked startled for a moment, then flicked his gaze down to my legs straddling him.

I scrambled up, reaching out to help him up, ignoring the heat creeping up my neck. He tilted his head with that look again, like he knew things. Then his eyes moved past me, and he nodded over my shoulder. Face still hot, I turned to find Maddie talking to Talbot.

"Think she's lecturing him about the irresponsibility of inviting you to Orville's?" I asked.

"No clue."

I ducked to pick up my jacket and tossed him his shirt and hoodie.

As we all reconvened in the lobby area, Graham spoke up to get everyone's attention.

"Thank you for humoring me today. But I believe precautionary measures are wise. Be safe, and honor thy brother."

The saying was archaic, but it functioned as a greeting and a farewell in one. It meant that your clansmen were your brothers. Magic was as deep as family.

Apollo turned and walked outside.

"Honor thy brother," many of the elders mumbled back.

Zarine was talking with my parents as I headed for the doors. She glanced at me and at the door. Her look was clear: *Well? Go after him.* After letting Dad know I'd catch a ride with Apollo, I found him off to the side of the building, smoking by one of the trees.

"I can't believe this," he said, watching the clan mill out of the records building. "They're not doing *anything*!"

"Apollo, calm down." I successfully distracted him by stealing a drag of his cigarette after looking around. I could hear Maddie's voice in my head: *Those are death sticks, Jonah! Don't be an ignoramus*! Dad would kill me. Mom would find a way to resurrect me just to kill me again.

"They're working on it." I watched the smoke come out in puffs around my words.

The taste of it was different than how it smelled on him or the way it smelled whenever he lit one with a match. That was in my top five smells. Right up there with coffee, Mom's spinach-cheese quiche, and the exhaust of the bug when it first started up in the morning.

He plucked the cigarette from my hand. "I don't care if they're done. We're not."

"Okay. We'll go back to Orville's."

He looked at me weird.

"What?" I asked.

"Don't talk to me like that."

"Like what?"

"Like I'm a ticking bomb."

"I'm not. But you're stressing me out. So can you just—"

Before I could even ask, he turned the filter of his cigarette toward me. Did our Kindred bond let him feel me hankering for it? I took another drag.

"Let's go see the wolves about the Discernment tonight."

I tried to blow rings. Nothing resembling rings came out. "Of course." For once, I was saying exactly what I thought. Like hell I would let him do that kind of complex magic without me.

"Think Maddie's still on?"

I almost rolled my eyes out of habit but remembered that she hadn't changed the way she'd treated us when she found out. It was actually nice to have her on our side.

My phone buzzed. I forgot I'd turned it on silent. I fished it out.

Courtney.

Apollo took his cigarette back as I answered, kicking at the saturated ground.

"I'm going to fail calculus," she said.

"What? Why?"

"I can't figure out the stupid homework for tomorrow. And if I don't get this, then I don't get any of the chapters that follow, and then I fail. If I fail, my parents are going to flip, Jay. And you're like a math genius. So really, it will be all your fault." I knew she was joking, but still.

"You're not going to fail." I turned away from Apollo even though he could hear every word. I could guess he was probably pretty annoyed. Here we were talking about the fate of one of our clan and my girlfriend pops in to talk about her calculus grade.

"Can I come by with the homework? I promise I'll make it up to you." I felt my face heat up. Even though she didn't mean anything like *that* by it—and what kind of perv was I for even thinking that she could possibly mean *that* by it?

"Sure."

"Thank you, Jonah. Thank you, thank you, thank you! I'll be there in an hour."

"You're welcome." I laughed, but it sounded more like I was being strangled.

I hung up, turning back to Apollo.

"We can still go after," I said.

"Nah," he said, clearly pissed off. "Don't worry about it."

"Apollo—"

"Do your thing, Jay." He walked off toward the parking lot. And then he was gone.

Of course he was mad. It looked like I was choosing Courtney over him. Which I wasn't, not really.

I thought of that line between his eyebrows when I got off the phone, deeper than it used to be, before we stopped hanging out. I thought about his mouth around my fingers and his instigating in defense. I thought about how skinny he was under that thermal.

I tossed my phone between my hands.

He needed to know I was there for him, now more than ever.

I'll text you when she leaves, I wrote. *We'll go after.*

I didn't get an answer.

At home, I went straight to the punching bag. It had been a birthday gift from my parents. It was for training, but more often than not, I used it to exhaust myself into a stupor until I stopped thinking.

Mom opened the sliding glass door. I held a hand on the bag to steady it.

"Your girlfriend's here."

I followed her inside, but she stopped at the door, turning back to me. "It's a school night."

"I know. No later than nine."

"And . . ."

"Door open. I know," I huffed. "We're just going to work on calculus, Mom." I hated having to explain these things.

She smiled. "You're such a good boy, Jonah."

What did that mean? Did bad boys want to close their bedroom door when their girlfriends came over? I followed her inside to find Courtney standing by the door, looking gorgeous. Yes, they definitely did.

"There's some leftovers if you're hungry, Courtney," Mom said, before picking up Joss from her baby gate corral.

"Thanks, Mrs. Clarke. I may take you up on that. But first." She turned to me. "Help!"

She actually looked worried, which I'm sure was unnecessary. Courtney usually figured things out pretty quick. After I helped her work out a few kinks with the homework, she'd take the rest home to do it herself. She was that control freak that did all the work in groups, not trusting anyone else to it. That's kind of how we started dating. We'd fought over who would take the brunt of a group research assignment in English.

She followed me to my room, discarding her messenger bag, scarf, and jacket. She dug her book out of her bag in a frenzy, and stopped, looking at me.

"Why are you all sweaty?" she asked, as though she'd just really noticed me. I thought about how I knew Apollo's temperature at any given moment.

"I was training," I said. It wasn't exactly a lie. Hitting the bag helped beef up my swing for games.

"Oh." She laid her text book on my bed and pointed at the open page. "That. That right *freaking* there! What is that?!"

I sat down and picked up the book, resting my elbows on my knees.

Binomials. "I can't really explain this without doing one for you," I said.

"Whatever you got to do. Please, just work your magic."

I took her offered notebook and pen. I wrote out the problem and solved it, explaining my process to her step by step. I couldn't take full credit; I'd gone to Maddie many an afternoon, clueless as to where to start or whether I'd gone the right direction.

Courtney tried the next one.

"I knew you'd get it right away," I said, leaning over her shoulder. "You worry too much."

It definitely felt dramatic with everything I should have been focusing on instead of binomials.

"Jonah Clarke says I worry too much," she muttered, erasing a mistake. When she fixed it, she sat back and smiled at me. "Thank you."

"Glad I could help."

"I'm sorry. I came over here and unloaded all my crazy on you." She shut her math book.

"Why are you sorry?" I said. I guess I should have denied the crazy unloading bit.

She looked at me. "You seem stressed."

"I guess. A little maybe."

"Want to talk about it?"

"Talking requires thinking, and I really don't want to think about anything right now," I said, laying back with a sigh.

She laid down on her side. She ran her fingers through my sweaty hair.

"You can tell me anything. You know that, right?"

"Why?" I asked, drawing it out, feeling something tighten in my gut.

"I just felt like you needed to hear it. Can I tell you something?"

I looked at her.

"You look really hot right now."

"I'm cooling down now," I said, embarrassed by how sweaty I was.

"No," she said. Then her hair was in my face as she straddled me. "I don't mean temperature, Jonah."

"Oh," I said, my hands going to her hips for lack of anywhere less awkward.

She kissed me. I kissed her back, wondering if I tasted like cigarettes still. Like Apollo.

I kissed her harder.

"Thank you," she whispered.

"For what?" I said, reaching up to feel her hair.

Not thinking was nice.

"For helping me. For always being so good." She leaned down to kiss me again.

The word 'good' repeated in my head.

You're such a good boy, Jonah.

It felt like a challenge. I dived into her, well, as much as I could while being pinned under her. An image came into my head unbidden: Apollo underneath me on the mat.

I opened my mouth, gripping Courtney's hips, and moved a little against her in a way that we've *never* done.

When she moved back against me, I suddenly felt sick.

"Stop," I said. "We have to stop."

I pushed her off.

"You started it," she said, slipping her hand under my shirt. Her warm fingers slid under the waistband of my pants. I gasped a breath, leaning back.

Don't be a good boy, I told myself.

I closed my eyes but saw the wrong thing again.

I grabbed her hand. "No, really." I was panicking. "We can't," I said, gesturing to my door—'to remain open at all times'.

She looked at me, her perfect hair perfectly messed up, her lips swollen from my harsh kisses.

I sat up and put my hand on her face. "I want to. I do. But we can't."

"Okay," she said. "It is kind of a bad idea, with your parents here and all."

"Exactly."

"I'm sorry."

"Don't be sorry. I liked it."

"Promise?"

I kissed her again, soft this time. "Okay?"

She nodded. "I'm embarrassed now."

"Don't be," I said.

She smiled, glancing up at me.

"I just don't trust myself to stop." I hated lying to her.

She bit her lip. "I should head out."

"I'll walk you."

We emerged from the basement and I thanked every god that is and ever was that none of my siblings were present. Even better, my parents were in their room.

We walked out into the chilly air. Under the white sun, I stood by her car, useless hands in my pockets.

She put her hand on my chest and stood up to kiss me. "See you tomorrow."

I smiled down at her, suddenly exhausted. "Yeah."

I watched her drive away, feeling like an asshole.

I wasn't lying about everything. I did like it. So what the hell was wrong with me?

15

Apollo

The bare trees looked like skeletons against the colorless sky. Sitting in the driveway before heading to school, it made me sad that I'd missed my favorite season as the leaves died in flame-colored explosions before their descent. I looked away from the branches, so exposed to the cold.

It seemed I functioned better on fumes, because a full night's sleep did nothing for me. Or maybe the wishful dreams I'd had all night of holding hands with and kissing Jonah was what made me feel like I weighed a thousand tons. And instead of telling me he's not gay, he says he wants more.

I felt guilty and embarrassed for how I acted yesterday. It's not like he could let his sapien girlfriend know what we were doing and why he didn't have time to help her maintain her GPA. Really, we could have gone later, but I'd been too jealous.

Me: *Need a ride?*

Waiting for his response, my stomach felt as light as if I'd missed a step; there was the possibility that he could decide I was too much trouble. What stake did he have in this? Would he still care if we were separated?

Jonah: *No. Mom is taking me on her way to the records building.*

His mom usually didn't go to the records building this early. What did this mean after the defense lessons yesterday? Things felt like they were spinning out of our control.

I opened my text with Junior. We hadn't gone a day without talking since June when I'd shown up at Purple Haze in full blown self-destructive mode and he'd lured me in with his kindness and jokes. His friendship. My last message sat unread. That was probably the worst part. They weren't even read. If they had been, it would be easier to believe he'd just gotten bored of hanging out with me.

Jonah: *Lockers?*

Part of me wanted to make him squirm, but it would be like trying to play catch with a brick wall.

Me: *See you there.*

I turned on the bug and let each injection of the cylinders wake me up. I grabbed it all, tasting as I consumed it. The light, burn, and drag of my cigarette. The sun evaporating the morning dew. The grind and percolating of coffee beans.

I felt Jonah as soon as I got to school. We'd gotten our lockers assigned to us earlier in the year. Same row, just seven apart. When we were that close, the live wire between us started to spark and it was impossible to forget his presence.

He was there now, and I could see he felt me too.

"Here." I held out the coffee I stopped to get for him (four creams, eight sugars).

We used to leave for school early sometimes, so he could get some. Back when riding together every day was a given.

He stared at the coffee in my hand.

His hair was cowlicked, like he hadn't gotten time to style it (Jonah's version of "styling" was to swipe a handful of gel through it, and poof, gorgeous). He looked like he hadn't slept well.

"I know you've been sleeping shitty." I tried not to look at his overheated pink cheeks, like he'd just rolled out of bed. More like he was burning up in that sweater in here. "Which is pretty much my fault, so . . . would you just take it?"

"Thank you." He took a drink and leaned his head against the lockers. He held up the cup. "It's been eighty-four years."

I laughed despite myself.

That was another thing about Jonah: when he loved something, you knew it. Which led me to believe that I'd know if he loved me back.

"You don't have to exaggerate," I said, spinning my combination into the lock. "You've probably already had some."

He frowned. I knew it.

"Here," he said. "I got you something too. Well, I've had it."

He held out a braided leather bracelet, almost the same color as the cuff I wore with my pick. Not knowing what it was for or what to say, I took it.

"Birthday present," he said.

My birthday was in July, which meant he'd been holding onto this gift since before we'd fought.

Did this mean we were best friends again?

"Here," he said, reaching out to take it back. Okay, yeah, that made sense—but then he was putting it on me, right beside the cuff. I stared at him as he concentrated on the clasp. Was this the multiverse?

"Thanks," I said. "I love it." I really did.

"You do?"

I thought my admiration was pretty obvious. To reassure him further would just be excessive.

"Why's your mom going to the Records Building today?" I asked instead.

"I don't know."

"Probably the same reason they have us doing defense lessons."

Jonah leaned his head back against the locker, exposing his throat. I looked in at my shiny textbooks with their seldom-cracked spines.

He said, "Maybe we should just give them the ring so they can do the locating spell. Tell them what we did before—"

"That's the last thing we should do." I reached for the ring instinctively. "You read any of that book I gave you?"

"Yeah." He cleared his throat. "Some."

"Well, if you've ever wondered what would happen to us if the clan knew, there's your answer."

Jonah looked down at his feet. "This is bigger than us, Apollo."

Nothing is bigger than us. That's what I wanted to say.

He sighed. "We'll see what we can find out, if we can figure out how to do the Discernment."

"We could go tonight," I said.

"Are the clubs even open Monday night?"

"Believe it or not, not everyone plays video games with their little brothers and sisters and organizes their notes for a physics exam on a Monday night."

He looked away. "I already did that," he muttered. "You're not going to ditch me, right?"

"Scout's honor."

"Some kind of honor with another guy's ring around your neck," he said, glancing at Junior's ring—or Jade's ring, I supposed.

That wasn't flirting. Right?

He reached for his phone.

"What?" I finally managed. "Is it your Mom?"

"No. Courtney."

I tried not to read into the constipated look on his face.

We had Government together first period. We split up after class—me for Spanish, Jonah for French. For the record, I was a lot better at Spanish than he was at French.

We joined up in the halls before Physics and my stomach fluttered, the bracelet suddenly heavier on my wrist. I was all stomach and chest with Jonah. Every emotion was fed back to me, translated into nausea or butterflies or heart palpitations.

Taking the seat right behind Jonah, closer than we'd sat all semester, my magic filled me up completely. It shamelessly reached out to mingle with his. It tasted sweet. Like shooting hoops in my driveway as the sun went down. Like reading M&M a hilarious bedtime story together on Saturday night before making the biggest sandwiches known to man and passing out to horror movies. It tasted like skittles and Jack Daniel's on his tongue. It tasted like him kissing me back.

I winged the exam. I was tempted to write Jonah's name, get him to look at me so that he could mouth me an answer. He never would. I probably managed a C minus at best.

As Mr. Krasinski droned on and on, I guess I had written his name in my notebook anyway. When a magikalis writes a person's name, they can call that person from miles away, another city sometimes if the Call was powerful enough. He turned around, looking worried, like I'd had a good reason to do it other than my swan-diving GPA and pining for his attention.

"Jonah?" said Krasinksi.

Jonah snapped back around. "Mr. Krasinski."

"Do you want to explain the difference between static and electro-magnetic fields?"

Jonah made some vague answer. I added to it, watching his ears turn red with a heady mixture of affection and haughtiness.

I had to stop this.

Over the summer, I had asked Junior how to get over someone. I remembered it had been sticky hot, and I'd gotten even hotter with embarrassment when I'd let the words escape.

"Ahhh, young love." He had ruffled my hair then, and I would have given anything to feel him do it again. But I had hated it then. Like, I already had poofy hair. I didn't need any help with volume. So I had ducked away from him. Started for the door of whatever friend of a friend's place we'd been at—Junior was always moving.

"Sometimes they just don't love you back, *primo.* And it rips your soul out." He'd taken a drink from his beer bottle before jumping into someone else's conversation from across the room. I'd thought we were done talking until he said, "But you have to decide if you're going to walk away or be his friend. Either way, just gotta keep breathing. It'll get easier."

I thought that was the wisest Junior had ever sounded.

It still wasn't easier, I thought as we walked to PE, but it was slightly reassuring that someone else had lived through this feeling.

Jonah cleared his throat. "How do you think you did on Marner's quiz?"

Government. Ugh.

I shrugged, tearing at a piece of straw paper I found in my backpack. "Who knows? That old hag would probably mark me down even if I managed a B. She doesn't like me."

He stopped walking. I looked around confused.

"Someone doesn't like you? Hold on, the world's about to stop turning!"

I punched him in his arm. He laughed it off, because it probably felt like a butterfly kiss.

In the locker room, we changed for PE. Jonah moved into my line of sight, and I couldn't help it. Mostly because we were talking and it felt a little okay to look. He was shirtless, changing into his shorts. He would never do this on purpose to torture me. But he was dense enough that he wouldn't realize that seeing any of his skin, even the inside of his wrist or the back of his neck, tortured me. So basically, every filled out line I glimpsed—Jonah was equal parts baby fat and muscular bulk—made my heart nearly flat-line.

Before I pulled my stale gym shirt over my head, I caught a glimpse of myself in the full-length mirror at the end of the lockers. Long. Wiry. Jonah's opposite in every way. From far away, I dissociated a little, and I could see why people kept telling me I looked like shit. At least I accepted my legacy. Whatever.

Everyone ran today. I lagged after one lap, thinking Jonah would run ahead. Instead, he brought his steps closer, so that our arms touched for a moment and it instantly gave me more energy.

"Slumming it back here with the slackers, Clarke?" I said in faux shock. The effect was weakened by my panting.

"You need to quit smoking," he said.

"But then who will be your supplier?"

He smiled. "You need to throw."

"Does it get tiring?"

"What?"

"Sounding like Maddie?"

He looked forward, nostrils flaring. "I'm not going to stop until you stop trying to self-destruct."

Is that what I was doing?

Quinn migrated from her group of friends and seemed to suddenly notice Jonah's foreign presence. Our arms were in sync, breaths matching. Our hearts beat the same rhythm. Yeah, I know. It's corny. That's just how the whole Kindred thing works. It's not like I invented it.

Jonah said something to Quinn in French. She gave him a look that either meant she was laughing at him or he'd botched his pronunciation.

Then Danny appeared on our other side. Quinn rolled her eyes and ran ahead. Danny took off after her.

I heard them bickering as they got farther ahead, carried onward by their unresolved sexual tension no doubt. None of which was happening back here. Nope.

"What's that about?" asked Jonah.

"You guys didn't exactly include me in that conversation." The boost Jonah had given me was already waning. I'd noticed that, lately, the high from gathering receded quickly. "Also, they got their own . . . thing happening."

"She doesn't like me."

"Now you're the insecure one," I joked. "Everyone likes you, Jonah. You're the nice guy."

"I'm so tired of hearing that."

"Why do you care if Quinn likes you?"

"All *my* friends like *you*," he said like we were in grade school.

I didn't think that would be true if Courtney knew the dreams I'd been having about her boyfriend.

"Aren't we friends?" I asked.

Jonah's ears turned red, which was saying something since he was already flushed, but his expression was perfectly blank.

"Yeah, but it's different."

I didn't know what that meant. Even though it felt like we were closer than before—every one of my cards was out. Sorry, Mom—I still felt like he spoke a language I didn't get.

Like when we discovered we were Kindred, the moment we threw for the first time. I'm still not all that sure what got his shorts up in such a twist that night.

We'd talked our way into an upperclassmen party—I, *I* talked our way into an upperclassmen party—though we were only freshmen. Bored by the conversation and drama inside—and Jonah obviously feeling out of his depth—we found ourselves on a swing in the backyard, sharing a bottle. We'd always find ourselves going off alone if he felt uncomfortable or self-conscious.

I remembered the night exactly. It was almost winter. There had been a couple making out in the pool. I wondered what they were thinking. Then again, thinking probably was not at the top of their to-do list.

Jonah and I had been talking about the last lesson we'd had. We'd graduated to the Gathering classes that taught us how to control the amount of energy we gathered from our surroundings. As we spoke in low tones, we were both gathering.

He'd looked so relaxed.

"I know you're gathering right now," I'd said.

"I can feel you doing it too," he'd said, not opening his eyes.

I think, watching him right then, in the moving blue lights of the pool, that's when I knew it. Like, *knew* things were different between us. At least on my end.

"How does it feel for you?" he'd asked.

"Like . . . a sunrise, in my veins, or something. You?" I couldn't stop watching him. He opened his eyes.

"Like hitting a game-ending home run," he said, grinning uncontrollably.

We had noticed the sounds from the swimming pool and looked over at the couple.

I laughed. "Pretty sure they're past third base," I said, taking a drink.

Jonah's whole face got red.

"Are you blushing?" I had asked him. "That's adorable."

He looked down, taking the bottle from me and tossing back a drink.

"What's wrong? Have you never come across any sex in those books you're always reading?" I was messing with him, but apparently it had been the worst thing I could have said. Jonah threw the bottle down at my feet and left. Stunned, I watched it retch a few sloshes out of its open mouth onto the grass. I followed him out front to the street where my mom's Neon was parked, because I hadn't gotten the bug yet. (I would have totally waited until I was good to drive home. Cross my heart.)

The party house was on a cul de sac on a hill that overlooked the city. I walked up to Jonah, who was standing off the road in the weedy grass before the drop off.

The city lights were so bright at the bottom of the hill. But up here, it was dark except for the streetlights.

Standing at the ledge of the drop off, giddy with the alcohol, the magic, and the night, I laughed.

"Stop laughing at me."

I turned, surprised to find he was really upset.

"I'm not."

"You are. Because that was nothing to you. You've been with everything that has legs."

With great effort, I restrained a smirk. "Jonah."

He jerked his shoulder away from me.

The street lights went out. Jonah didn't notice.

"Just because I'm inexperienced—"

"I wasn't laughing at you." He looked so upset, I was about to just tell him. *Jonah, I like you.* Some people might have felt nervous about realizing such a thing and then just saying it. But it would have been weirder not to tell him. "I—"

"Enough!"

The wind picked up and came down the cul de sac, barreling into us, nearly knocking me to my death. I looked down at the bottom of the drop off, ragged branches coming out of the bluff.

"Jonah," I said sternly, feeling the magic. I grabbed him by the shoulders. As soon as I touched him, I knew. We were thrown back.

When he popped out of the grass, he'd looked like he'd stuck his finger in a light socket . . . again.

"Did that just happen?" he asked.

I had grinned back at him. "That just happened."

"Am I sitting with you?" I asked as I followed him to the cashier at lunch.

The only reason I was getting a chicken sandwich was because Jonah glared at me when I tried to walk away with only a Coke.

"Why wouldn't you?" He snagged a fistful of ketchup packets for his burger and fries on our way outside.

I watched his back for signs of a body snatcher. The last few months were a pretty cut and dry case for why I wouldn't, in fact, expect to sit with him.

I hitched my guitar and backpack straps higher on my shoulder. Teachers hated when I brought it, as though it was a huge inconvenience sitting over by the classroom door for the 53 minutes they had to endure my presence.

"Maybe Danny will even choose to grace the team with his presence once again."

I snorted. "Danny goes wherever the wind takes him."

"Did someone summon me?" Danny said, popping up between us like a Jack-in-the-box.

"That's funny. I'm sure the spell was for summoning demons," I said.

Danny threw his head back with a giant demonic laugh, and Jonah shot me a glare.

"What? He loves it."

Courtney was already at the table, posture perfect of course.

"Hey, Apollo."

"Hey," I said, slouching on the end of the bench, far away from JayCourt.

Jonah was dragged into a conversation about formal, which was swiftly approaching. Almost as soon as we sat down, he was acting weird. Quiet and tense.

I finished eating and turned around on the end of the bench, unzipping my guitar case. I didn't care about formal. I tried my damndest not to care about Courtney's hand on Jonah's thigh, or his hand always touching her hair.

"Oh. You play?"

It took me a second to realize Courtney was talking to me. I looked back at her while tuning.

"No. I just carry it around because it's pretty."

She looked confused as I strummed a chord.

"Ah. You're messing with me," she said with a strange edge to her voice.

Stupid question, stupid answer, I thought.

"You sound like you know what you're doing. Are you in band?"

"Nope."

Come to think of it, she was acting weird with Jonah too. Or maybe just generally weird because she kept talking to me. A sadistic thrill bloomed in the pit of my stomach that she might be questioning the nature of my relationship to Jonah.

Look, maybe I could have liked Courtney Christie if she hadn't come along and swept up Jonah's broken pieces before he had the chance to miss me.

16

Jonah

Maddie didn't look like she planned on coming out to Purple Haze with us later. Her hair was unwashed—"It's curly hair, Jonah. It gets dry!"—and she was in the yoga pants Grandma got her one year for Christmas that said PINK on the butt that she only ever wore when she needed to do laundry.

"I wanted to show you something," she said as we came into her room.

I sat on the edge of her bed then wished I would have let Apollo sit down instead. He stood by the door, hands in the pocket of my hoodie he still hadn't returned. Even though we spent most of the day together and he seemed like he liked the bracelet, I felt like I'd done something wrong at school to make him stand-offish.

Maddie turned her laptop to show us an article.

Lind Labs Welcomes Caterina Halsey, PhD, New Director of Research.

Below was an image of a blonde woman looking off camera, hands folded in front of her. Her hair and sharp-featured face made her look like a sixties Bond woman or something.

"Is that her?" Maddie asked Apollo. She dropped her voice. "The woman you saw out at Orville's?"

He swallowed and nodded. He looked like he was worried the woman in the picture would turn her head and see him.

She set down her laptop to crawl across her bed and close the door. When she came back, she read the article aloud. "'Dr. Halsey specializes in AI disorders and will advance its research at Lind Labs.'" When she finished, she looked at us like that was supposed to mean anything.

"Artificial intelligence?" I asked.

"Oh my *god,* Jonah. You seriously don't pay attention to anything ever unless it's the exact length of Apollo's eyelashes, I swear."

I opened my mouth to argue, face burning as I absolutely did not look at Apollo. Why didn't having a girlfriend exempt me from this?

"AI or immunotherapy is the cure *vampiria* have been researching against the blood song," Maddie said. "Remember? The effect of our blood on them."

"I remember that," I snapped.

Apollo stared at the screen over Maddie's shoulder. "How did you find her?"

"I honestly didn't even know where to start, but I was looking into the pro-cures in our clan. You know Talbot is one of them?"

Apollo shook his head. He looked a little sick.

"I was checking out their socials, and I found this link on one of their pages." She looked at the screen again, tilting it back. "She's pretty striking, right?"

"Their kind are meant to attract," said Apollo.

"So this woman was cleaning up after the blood crazy one you guys killed. And *she* is trying to find a cure for that state of mind. I can think of a few uncomfortable scenarios where these two things aren't a coincidence."

Apollo's eyes flickered over to me.

"Why don't you spell it out for me?" I said.

"Test subjects," she said, shoulders lifting helplessly.

Someone knocked on Maddie's door. She slammed her laptop closed. Mom looked surprised to see me in here and even more surprised to see Apollo.

"Hi, Apollo," she said.

"Hi, Isabel," he said, suddenly shy.

"What are you guys up to?"

"Homework," I said.

Maddie nodded.

"Dinner's going to be ready in about an hour."

"Can Apollo stay?" I asked.

"Of course," Mom said, because literally everyone loved Apollo.

When she left, I could feel him watching me.

"We're having chili," I said, a partial explanation for why I'd roped him into dinner with us. But mostly, we were all a little shook, and I just wanted him to stay until we could work out what all this meant.

He got this small smile that made my stomach flip. "That's my favorite."

"I know."

We filed into the kitchen. Mom told Apollo to help himself over Joss's excited shrieking. M&M were both restless in their seats. Dad made them stop with a look.

I gave Joss pieces of cornbread between Mom's bites of beans and watched Apollo get a bowl down—he knew exactly where everything was—filling it with much less chili than usual, and coming over to claim his place next to mine. I focused on Jocelyn's happy babbling as he squeezed in between Maddie and me.

I felt like I was seeing and hearing everything underwater.

Maybe it was what Maddie found.

Or maybe it was Apollo eating with us again for the first time in months, like nothing had happened. My parents noticed. He used to be just another one of the brood at the table, and now he was the guest.

"How's school, Apollo?" Dad asked.

"Okay," he said before launching into the explanation that parents always expected after that question. With parents, you can suddenly cite all the themes and connections your teachers had been trying to get you to see all year. He looked nervous though.

Dad had always liked Apollo. He thought Jackson, Apollo's dad, was a good addition to the clan too. He was always trying to be as inclusive as possible, so that none of us kids ever felt like it was okay to think we were better than sapiens. But I think Dad genuinely liked Jackson. I could tell he liked the simplicity of having a beer and talking about nothing but sports and politics. I think it let him believe for a moment that the fate of our entire clan wasn't, in part, resting on his shoulders. I could understand that desire to escape. I guess I kind of did that with everything. Baseball. Books. Courtney.

Apollo shifted, his leg touching mine. Neither of us moved away. I tried not to focus on it, but he was cold; I could tell even through his pants.

I shouldn't be thinking about anything through his pants.

Apollo laughed at the crazy stuff Miles and Macy were saying. It felt like I was seeing him as a guest right now, too. Or at least in an entirely new light. Maddie caught my eye and I looked away.

Joss started to get fussy, so I reached over and ran the tops of my fingers under her chin. She calmed down and tilted her head up so I would keep doing it. Then I fake sneezed to make her laugh.

I could feel Apollo watching.

"Are you coming to Jonah's game Saturday?" asked Mom.

I almost choked on cornbread.

It's not that I didn't want Apollo to come. I hadn't gotten around to asking. And now he would think I purposely didn't ask him. Maybe that was partially true, thinking of him and Courtney sitting together in the stands, chatting about guitar and colleges. And me. It nauseated me a little.

"Yeah, of course."

After dinner, when we got to my room, he said,

"I'll only come if you don't mind."

I pulled my shirt off. Joss had started slapping her tray—her new thing—flinging her dinner all over me.

"Of course I don't mind. I just forgot to mention it." I threw my shirt in the corner of the room, toward the mounting pile of laundry, wondering why I sounded angry.

When I turned to him, his eyes were burning into mine. "First game. Seems like a big thing to forget."

"Practice game," I said. "Seriously. Please don't make a big deal about it. We've kind of been going through a lot lately, so it isn't that crazy that I would forget." I turned to my dresser for another shirt.

I felt him step closer to my side, almost touching my bare skin, which lit on fire at the prospect. "Has your dad said anything, since we went out there with Maddie?" I could feel his breath on my shoulder. It sent a chill through me. I stood back, pulling my shirt on.

"No," I said, trying to place some distance between us. I felt possessed suddenly, like I had something inside of me, clawing to get out. I sat down on my bed.

"He was looking at you weird, during dinner."

"Yeah. I don't know." Truth was, I couldn't even fathom a scenario in which my dad knew everything we were doing. Panic spiked through me anytime I got close to thinking about it.

Apollo sat next to me, and that possessed feeling reared up again. Like my body wasn't my own. I swallowed, pressing my hands together.

I realized then that every time we had met up about everything going on, it had been here at my house. Which was weird because we used to spend a lot more time at his house.

But that was before.

"Maddie will be in here after she's done with the dishes," I said.

"Why?"

"Because now that she's had time to process that she found the lady you saw, she will have about four hundred questions about it."

"Are you going to formal?" he asked.

"Ugh!" I fell back on my bed.

"I take that as a yes," he said.

I couldn't tell if the gravel in his voice was derision or something else.

"I don't know."

He looked like he didn't believe me. "She'll have your balls if you don't. She's definitely expecting you to take her."

"It just seems stupid with all of this going on."

I watched him, still surprised by how different he was now. I assumed he looked tired for the same reason he had over the past few months. Even after using our magic out at Orville's with Maddie, holding onto his magic since then would have lasting effects. At least that's how they explained it in Sunday School a million years ago, when none of us ever thought we'd be prone to it, to how holding onto magic could mess you up.

Was this just a phase with him? Was there anything I could do to help?

"You and Danny have gotten pretty close," I said, thinking about them buddying up at lunch today.

He looked confused by the change of topic. "We just started talking after gym one day."

"Is he . . ." It felt like I was walking into a minefield. I didn't know how I could know someone as long as I had Danny and not just *know* like I did with Apollo.

"What?" he asked after a long silence.

"Like . . . have you . . . is he gay too?"

"Jayden just dumped him. You think he's just hanging out with me now because he might be gay?" His jaw muscles pulsed. "Being gay isn't a cult, Jonah. We don't induct people. You ought to know that."

It was the first time we'd acknowledged what happened the night before we stopped talking.

"I'm just trying to understand."

"Why are you suddenly interested in my love life?"

"Love life?" Something twisted in my stomach. "Do you like him?"

"*No*."

"Okay," I said, careful to keep my voice neutral. "I just figured I should probably know what's going on in your life."

"I don't ask about you and Courtney."

"You just asked if we were going to formal."

"Come *on*, Jonah."

"Sorry!" I pressed my palms to my eyes. Everything I said was wrong.

Maddie chose that perfect moment to walk in.

"Sorry," Maddie said, hugging her laptop to her chest. "Wouldn't take so long if you heathens would rinse your dishes."

"I rinsed mine," said Apollo.

She smiled at him. "I know."

She sat on the edge of my bed, a vaguely disgusted look on her face. I rolled my eyes, but Apollo distracted me by laying down beside me. I felt smothered between Maddie's heat and Apollo's whole . . . thing.

"Okay," said Maddie, opening a Word document, poised for note-taking. "What did you say Halsey was doing when you saw her?"

Apollo's eyebrows drew together. "I was driving, so I didn't see much. I just saw her, a couple of vans and people in Hazmat suits. She looked at me like she recognized me. It was creepy."

"You didn't say that before," I said.

"I guess I forgot."

"You forgot?" I stared at him. "That's kind of vital, Apollo. If she looked at you like that, then she must have seen us when that vampiris came after us."

"I don't know if she literally recognized me, but she did stare me down. Like . . . a challenge."

"Great. This is awesome," I said, standing up and pushing my dresser drawer closed.

"Jonah," Maddie said. "Mom and Dad?"

"Does it say where her lab is?" Apollo asked.

I turned around.

Maddie nodded, looking down at the article. "Apollo, I'm impressed."

Of course she was impressed. If *I* had suggested the same thing, Maddie would look at me cross-eyed. *Why would you assume the director of research would be in a lab?* I even mocked her voice in my head. It didn't make me feel any better.

"Huh," Maddie said.

"What? Where is it?"

"No. It's not that. This mentions she had a daughter."

"Had?" I asked, irritated by the topic derailment.

"Yeah. It doesn't give a lot of detail. But the author of the article is obviously biased, sees her as kind of a hero for her work. Which makes sense, because it looks like her daughter . . ." she trailed off.

"Maddie!" I said.

She looked up at us. "She lost her daughter to the blood song."

She had the audacity to look sad. I thought of that thing unhinging its jaw to swallow me whole.

"How would our blood *kill* one of them?" Apollo asked

It made me happy to hear I wasn't the only one affronted.

"Our blood doesn't kill them," Maddie said, looking back down at the article. "It makes them go crazy and then the Letum Antea comes and takes them away."

"What is the Letum Antea?"

"It's like their . . . Supreme Court. It translates from Latin as 'before death'. Looks like they took Halsey's daughter to reset her or whatever, and released her again. But she committed the same mistake, it says. They probably killed her," she said, her voice dropping.

"Damn, Maddie. You're a legit *vampiria* historian," Apollo said.

I lifted one of my hats for the strip of cloth. "Guess we'll know for sure if our guy could have been this lady's test subject."

Maddie took the cloth.

"Hazmat is for dealing with biological shit, right?" Apollo asked, scanning the article. "So maybe she was trying to clean up her own mess. Jonah, remember how his clothes looked all old and dirty?" His green eyes turned onto me, bright and worried. "That would make sense if he was her prisoner, or subject, I guess."

Maddie stared at Apollo a second longer than made me comfortable and handed the scrap back to me. "Strange that this Director, Halsey, would have missed that."

She pulled her phone out of her pocket. "Mom wants us to get ready for bed."

"She texted you?" Apollo asked.

Maddie shrugged. "She always does that. *Go to bed. Don't forget to turn off all the lights—"*

"Load the dishwasher," Maddie and I said at the same time. She grabbed her laptop from Apollo.

"I'll see you later, when you pick us up," she said. "What time?"

"Eleven thirty."

She closed the door behind her, and I felt like we were very alone suddenly. I fidgeted with the cloth.

"I'll get out of here," Apollo said, standing and stretching. I looked away.

I wanted to ask him to stay.

"Drive safe," I said instead.

17
Apollo

The sound of my car was too familiar to Tom and Isabel, so I texted them to meet me at the end of the block.

I was eager to get to Purple Haze. I needed a night feeling like I was doing *something*. Even if it was looking under rocks, trying to find someone who didn't seem to want to be found.

Safety. Family. Love. They felt like an illusion. Magic was all that was real, and I devoured it like a leviathan eats cities. It was the rope I held onto to keep my head above water. My parents were never really present. Whatever Jonah and I had before was a fragile thing now, and that was my fault. And now Junior . . . was that my fault too?

I'd told Maddie they should dress to fit in. I had specifically told her not to let Jonah wear his same boy-next-door blue jeans and plain T-shirt. I recognized the torn dark wash jeans as what he'd worn for at least three summers now—since he'd hit that last growth spurt—playing ball in the street and kneeling next to me as I worked on the bug. He didn't like wearing them to school because he thought they made him look poor. He was also wearing a black T-shirt. A T-shirt still, yes, but Jonah looked good in black. So good my bruised heart stuttered and almost checked out.

Maddie looked amazing too. She wore a draped purple top and black boots. If Jonah was He-Man, Maddie was a Willow-the-wisp. She just cleared his shoulders in those boots.

Jonah got the big, burly genes in the family. That aforementioned growth spurt had skyrocketed him to 6'1". It also exploded his chest. I remembered being envious that I hadn't grown the same way, that I didn't look manly.

I remembered being jealous of the girls that could touch him there.

"Dost thou approve?" Maddie asked.

I opened the door for her with a flourish and walked around to the driver's side.

"You didn't open my door," said Jonah.

I didn't know if he was joking or not. Usually when he tried to joke, that's how they fell: just short of being comprehensible and right on par with awkward.

He put his seatbelt on and leaned his elbow on the door, hand holding the roof. I stared at his bicep. He looked at me, and he looked like he knew what I was thinking, like he didn't mind. I lived for these moments when I could pretend that he felt this too. The hole in my chest got a little smaller.

But this was the guy who could eat within three seconds of opening his eyes from deep sleep. The guy who would correct the priest's grammar at a funeral. He had an 'or worse' fetish and a complete inability to see anything other than his own navel. I had to remind myself of these faults or I'd climb over the center console and into his lap. After reviewing the list, I kind of wanted to even more.

"Can we stop at the store?" asked Maddie.

"Sure," I said around a cigarette, shifting gears. I turned on the after-market CD player I'd rigged—you couldn't exactly Bluetooth into one of these bugs—and skipped to "Wake Me Up Before You Go Go."

"Wham," Maddie said, laughing. "It's all making sense."

"You shut your mouth, Madeline. George Michael is a god among men."

"You guys know what century it is, right?" Jonah grumbled to his window.

"And yet, you seem to know exactly who we speak of," I said, tugging at his hair.

He leaned away toward the window, muttering 'of whom'.

When we got to the store, Maddie hopped out like she wore those boots every day when I knew for a fact that she usually shuffled around in fleece-lined Wal-Mart moccasins.

The ground seemed a thousand feet down when Jonah suddenly moved into my space. Which was as good as his space, let's face it.

Ah. My cigarette.

I was surprised at his willingness to be close to me. Last night, he hadn't pulled away at dinner. But when I laid down next to him on his bed, he'd gotten away from me as quickly as possible. I was playing a dangerous game with our mutual love of that power surge when we touched, unconsciously trying to weave some primal love spell with scraping denim and brushing body hair.

He dragged my cigarette and leaned his head back. "God, that's good."

I glanced in at Maddie. "Get another. She's still shopping."

I was so pathetically eager to give him anything he wanted.

He took another drag.

Sopping up the burning magic, I dived through the cigarette, down his throat, and into his veins as they took the nicotine, as the blood pulsed with the chemicals. I came out on the smoke into the night. I floated on it up to the lights in front of the store. I sucked all the energy out, and the light popped.

Jonah looked up at it with no expression, then glanced at the store, reaching low to hold the cigarette to me.

"Jonah."

He looked at me, no longer lazy-moving-Jonah but alert-and-burning-gaze-Jonah.

"Don't."

I wasn't sure what he was talking about, but Maddie was opening the door.

I was going to tell him not to let me gather tonight. I was going to ask him to be my rock. What did he think I was going to say? Surely if he knew, he would have been all too accommodating. Let me help my poor, sick best friend who can't control what should be a very natural thing to control.

I pressed my fist to the bottom of the steering wheel. Those were the things I had to remember. Jonah, the good boy.

"What did you need to get so bad?" Jonah asked as I pulled onto the street.

"Never ask a lady about a sudden stop at the store, Jonah! Girls 101!"

"Yeah, Jonah. Don't you know anything about girls?" I asked.

He looked out the window, jaw tense.

We pulled up at Purple Haze, and I could feel Maddie's gathered energy. Her leg bounced up and down, shaking the car.

"Dealing with Wolves 101," I said. "Don't look at them with pity. Got it?"

"That's it?" Maddie asked. "They are orphaned people, and that's the only lesson you have regarding interactions with them?"

"Treat them like you would anyone else in the clan, and you'll be good," I said.

Jonah raised his eyebrows, and I could almost hear him wondering if that included the way Talbot had treated me. I still couldn't decide if he'd treated me badly or if that was just the sour feeling of rejection. *That* I was all too familiar with.

Inside, everything pulled me in, like it always did. I let Purple Haze soak through my sweatshirt, the T-shirt I had on under that, and the A-shirt I had on under that. I let it meld to my bones with its humid bodies and pumping music.

Maddie stopped walking, and we almost walked into her, along with about twenty other people whose flow she'd interrupted. "Okay. Plan?" she asked.

I shrugged. "Ask around. Don't be obvious."

"All right. Should we meet up in half an hour?"

"Sure," I said.

She was about to take off, but Jonah grabbed her arm. "Where are you going?"

"To engage," she said, gaze not breaking from the writhing room in front of us. "I suggest you try pulling your weight too."

He sputtered as she walked away.

"Should we just let her go off like that?"

"She's fine," I said. "I'm getting you a drink. You need to relax."

"No . . . I don't need—just stay close," he said. So I did.

We ended up lingering near the crowded bar as I waited for Junior's crew to arrive. As much as Jonah tried to look "casual", he looked like a hulking, sullen beast. I could just hear the thoughts firing in his brain: *Did that person think they were driving home? Do those two need to dance so close? Maybe Maddie shouldn't be talking to anyone alone.* His shoulders were up to his ears, as though he was walking through a storm rather than actively warding off clubbers.

I gripped his shoulder, trying to pull some of that tension out of the muscle there.

"Jonah."

He looked at me.

"Chill. Everything doesn't rest on you." I dropped my hand before he got the wrong idea. Which would definitely actually be the right idea.

"I know."

"Do you?" I asked, pressing my thumb to the crease between his eyebrows. He slowly pulled his head back to look at me. For something to do—aside from touching him everywhere—I grabbed a toothpick with a green olive on it from an empty glass on the bar and ate it.

"Gross," he said.

"Deal."

We watched everyone, and I swayed to the music with my hands shoved in my pockets. My hands were freezing.

Jonah's eyes followed Maddie around. She was laughing with a group who looked high on something that was definitely not magic.

"We're lucky she's helping us," I said.

"Yeah," said Jonah, but he looked mad.

Someone stopped in front of us, and suddenly, I understood why he looked pissed.

Talbot Erikson.

"Can we talk?" he asked.

I stood there for only a second before he grabbed my arm. I caught Jonah's irate look, nostrils flaring. His eyes were wide. *Don't*, they said.

We were here to get information though, and I was going to get my damn money's worth with this tool. Not that I'd paid for anything. That'd be weird.

As we moved away from Jonah, I felt his magic reaching out for me. Before I could process how funhouse-mirror this scenario was, Talbot released my arm and started moving. I didn't know that it could be called dancing.

I stepped closer but didn't dare touch him like that night.

"Heard anything about Junior?" he asked.

"No, but I'm sure the clan is 'doing everything they can'," I said.

He pushed his glasses up his sweating face. "It's not enough?" His blank expression made him look like a child.

"You have eyes, don't you?"

"What about on the streets?"

"Nothing," I said.

"And his girlfriend? Has she said anything?"

It hit me then. I was the only person who knew Junior had planned to come after me. "No."

Jonah popped up beside me before I could ask Talbot why he was suddenly concerned about Junior. Talbot hardly glanced at Jonah before sliding into the shadows.

"What did he say?"

I slipped my index through the ring, holding it up.

"Oh. Do you still like him? Talbot?"

I didn't want to look at Jonah and see everything I wished for—selfish, radioactive green jealousy—accompanying that question, but I had to look him in the eye when I said this.

"No, Jonah," I said. "I never even got the chance to like him."

To my disappointment, he looked very serious and composed. "You met him out at Orville's."

"You're awfully interested in who I like lately," I said.

His jaw clenched in a different way now. Determination. He stepped closer.

"I want you to show me," he said.

I almost swallowed my tongue. "What?"

"Show me what you feel," he said. My heart exploded into a million burning filaments. "When you gather it all and hold on."

Oh. "Jonah, I don't think that's—"

"I want to understand."

He saw Talbot talking to me and now he's trying to reconnect with me. He was jealous.

This was fine. I could do this.

I walked deeper into the club, making sure he followed me. I would join the baseball team and offer to help babysit M&M if it meant I got to be around him more. I loved him, but we were also best friends. We were Kindred. It made sense that he wanted to be around me.

As we started moving with each other, with everyone, the soda fizz at the bottom of my belly moved up. I leaned into him, suddenly bold with the chest-thumping bass and darkness. Jonah looked relaxed. Finally. Any reservations I had about letting him feel this high faded away.

I slipped my hand behind his back and under his jacket and shirt. Just as I thought, his skin was on fire.

We used to have this game where we would stick our cold hands or feet on the other. Jonah didn't try to inflict revenge. He didn't even flinch when my ice met his fire.

"Remember when we used to play that?" I asked.

"Yeah."

What was wrong with me? I'd kissed my best friend. I'd expected things to just be the way I wanted. I was no different than him, expecting everything could snap back to normal after.

All I wanted was the one person I couldn't have, the person I was closest to, the one person who I thought, for just a moment, might want me the same way. Now, we were in limbo, not moving forward or back, stuck under layers of scar tissue.

Some of the wolves who clearly followed Junior Doctrine were jumping up and down behind Jonah. Who knew what their flavor of the week was at the moment, but they all looked good and high. Someone was bound to give us what we needed for the Discernment.

Grateful for the distraction, I slithered between them with Jonah at my back, feeling their various highs. I never had to touch a single drug, because I could always lose myself in theirs.

I almost saw it unfold on Jonah's face, his whole body, when he felt it too. I wondered if he forgot he was with Courtney, because he was letting a girl back right into his loading dock. I kept an eye on him, on his hands, still and hanging like he had no idea what to do with them.

I moved into Lena's orbit; she was probably early twenties. She was a work of geometric truths: sharp cheekbones, heart-shaped face, Cupid's bow mouth. Her eyes, shrouded in dark makeup, lit up when I got closer. Sometimes we ended up dancing together.

I asked her about the spell. Had she ever done one? Or seen one? I told her that I was going to try to get someone to use a Discernment to find Junior. It was only a half lie. We were working on hunches here, but that's all we had.

She shook her head. "Discernments aren't pretty."

She put her arms over my shoulders. "They rip out whatever truth you're seeking through your blood and guts." She tugged my hair to emphasize her point. "You're left picking them up off the floor when it's done with you."

I'd always liked Lena. "Sounds painful."

"I've only seen it done once. It's hard to get the spell to go the way you want."

"Sounds like any magic," I said.

The girl Jonah was dancing with laughed at some undoubtedly straight-laced observation he'd made.

"Question is," she said. "What are you willing to pay for it? It better be worth the returns, because you'll have a hell of a hangover."

I'd pay anything to find him. He deserved someone in his corner, someone who wouldn't write him off as lost just because he was a wolf.

My answer must have been in my face, because it unlocked her. She told me how to perform the Discernment, and her words moved through me like a whisper over a grave.

I heard a scream over the sound of the music. It was a voice my ears were especially attuned to.

Maddie.

Jonah was already moving. I followed, eyes scanning until I finally found her purple top.

Talbot had her nearly backed to the wall. There was someone else by Talbot's side in a gas mask. My magic bled to the surface of my skin. Just like at the orchards.

I cursed myself for bringing them here.

The base of my skull throbbed in an effort not to give in to my fight or flight instinct. My eyes darted everywhere, looking for the source.

Jonah was already pushing them away from her. I stepped between Jonah and Talbot. Maddie or Jonah pulled at my sweatshirt but didn't say anything. Had they felt it too?

"He's just messing around," said Talbot.

He looked nervous, like the night he'd asked me to go to Orville's.

"What are you doing here with them?" he asked Maddie.

"What are you doing here with *him*?" Maddie demanded, her voice quivering.

He looked at her with the same cold look he had in his eyes at the orchards. *Let go of me.* "We can't understand what we don't know, Maddie."

Gas Mask grabbed Talbot's arm and stumbled away. I worried about Talbot despite myself, but Gas Mask dropped his arm on the way out and Talbot stayed by his side.

Behind me, I heard Jonah ask Maddie if they hurt her.

"No. *No*," she insisted, when he didn't let up. I watched them leave through the back exit.

"What happened?" he asked. "Why were you talking to him?"

"Bathroom," she said.

She looked like she was going to be sick. I felt like I was going to be. How could I lose track of Maddie? I shouldn't have let Jonah hold. I could only imagine what he was feeling.

We went into the men's bathroom because there was a line at the women's. There was one guy at the urinal. Maddie walked straight to a stall. We did our business, waiting for the guy to go. As we washed our hands, I could see Jonah was shaking. As soon as the door closed behind the guy, Maddie flew out of the stall and locked it.

"We need to do this now. If they're still out there—"

"They left," I said.

"They could come back with more," said Maddie.

"More?" asked Jonah.

"You felt it right, Apollo?"

"The vacuum feeling. Yeah."

"*Someone*," Jonah said. "Please explain what is happening."

"That was a vampiris. With Talbot," Maddie said, turning on the faucet. But then she stared at the water, like she didn't remember what she was doing.

I reached out and touched Jonah's shoulder, throwing some of what we'd gathered while dancing at the door, layering protection. Jonah realized what I was doing and joined in. It was less precise than the grid we'd hid Maddie with at the orchards, but it was something separating us and *that.*

"I thought it was weird when you'd told me he invited you to the borderlands. Alone. Clearly interested in doing *something* and then bailing," said Maddie. She looked at us through the mirror as she dried her hands. "So I picked his brain a little."

"Maddie," Jonah groaned.

"No one messes with Apollo like that," she said.

Tears of gratitude burned my eyes.

"We've been in the same study sessions with a couple other *magikalia*, and he's been going on about the AI movement lately, almost like he's recruiting. That person in the gas mask came out of nowhere. I knew it right away. What he was. But there was like, a protection spell around him—an Incognito or something."

"Just so I'm clear," Jonah said, holding up his hands, eyes closed. "That guy was a vampiris and someone was using magic to *protect him?*"

"You couldn't feel it when you got close?" Maddie's hands gripped the sink behind her, just as Jonah had done.

"I was a little preoccupied, Mad," said Jonah.

She blew a shaky breath at the strands of her hair that had come loose. "Talbot wasn't surprised to see him."

The night he'd approached me here, in this club, suddenly looked very different.

"Why the gas mask?" I asked.

"I'm not sure what that's about," she said, kicking the toe of her boot at the chipped tile. Maddie hated being unsure about anything.

"Talbot asked about Junior," I said, remembering earlier. "If anyone knew anything about where he was."

"I *seriously* hate that guy," said Jonah.

"Did you guys get enough to do the Discernment?" asked Maddie.

"Got something from one of the wolves, not much though."

"I think that's all you can ever get on this spell," said Maddie.

"I was with you the whole time," Jonah said, his brows furrowed in confusion.

"You were a little preoccupied," I said, repeating his excuse to Maddie.

He looked around. "We shouldn't stay here."

"I won't leave the wolves here like sitting ducks if they come back. With more." Nausea from our near-miss sloshed in my belly like a Mike's Hard Lemonade.

Jonah's eyes lit up. "We could do an Alert on the doors. Then we'd know if they come back."

"That's a good idea," said Maddie, looking relieved.

"Okay. We'll be back," Jonah said. "Stay," he told Maddie as we walked toward the door.

"I'm not a dog, Jonah."

"We already put a Protection on the bathroom.You'll be safe here," I told her.

She looked between us. Was she impressed? It was hard to tell; emotions were high.

When we got back, Maddie snapped into action and dropped to her knees.

She had pulled her purse into her lap and was digging through it. "You have the scrap, Jonah?"

Jonah dug in his pocket for it.

"We need things," I realized. "Dirt, twigs, outside things. Maybe we should—"

"We're getting this over with," Maddie said. "Now."

She dumped her purse out, hands flying over the contents with tremors. She picked out dental floss, a canister of Morton's salt, and a pack of wooden matches and tossed them at my feet. There were other things too, random things like the balled up plastic bag from the store, a twisty metal spiral thing, bobby pins.

I settled on the floor. We would be improvising with some things like the matchsticks for twigs, but that had to be half of what all magic was—bullshitting until something sparked.

"How did you know what I'd need, before we even knew how to do the spell?" I picked up the salt, turning it in my hands. The picture of the girl on it had always seemed sad to me.

"Research," she said like it was a dumb question.

It was true that a lot of spells were written down, but going by the book was never as effective as hearing the spell from a magikalis's mouth.

I lifted the metal tab on the salt container. I felt dizzy, like the spell had already shoved a brain scrambler up my nose and ripped it back out. Jonah knelt down beside me, which steadied me.

I poured the salt on the floor, smoothing it into a flat sheet with my palm. Maddie leaned forward, fingers digging into her knees. I took two matches out, drew a circle into the salt with one and laid a match on either side of the circle.

"Give me it," I told Jonah. He handed over our clue and I pulled out my pocket knife

"Hey," he began. I opened it and pressed it to my skin on my inner arm. "Apollo!"

Maddie put her hand on his arm. She understood enough to know that this was part of it. To discern, you had to give yourself over to the spell. To become part of it.

The blade was too dull to cut a tomato, so it took some digging, and I focused on the pain like that's all there was. Blood welled slowly. But it was a thick, deep red, and it would be just enough. I picked up each match and painted them with my blood. I laid them back down in their places.

Jonah picked up a headband from the pile Maddie had made and wrapped it around my arm. I didn't think it was necessary, but I wasn't complaining as each brush of his fingers on my skin gave me a little more strength, a little *more*.

I put my hands down on the ground, the salt cutting into my palms.

I had nothing to give this spell. I hoped it worked. I let that hope percolate into the words I whispered.

I unwound a piece of floss. I kept whispering. I wrapped the two matches with the cloth from the vampiris's shirt. My whisper turned into a prayer. I folded it all into a tight bundle and the words came out of my throat louder than a whisper, more forceful than a prayer. It was a desperate plea for something that would help me find Junior, or at least rule *this* possibility out. I bargained for something that would tell us whether we were in danger. Because now I felt responsible for not only Junior, but for my best friends.

I picked up the matchbox, took a breath, and struck the matches on the side. The combined flame from the two matches flared, and then settled down. I touched it to the greasy material, and the flame flared again, before turning black. I blew it out.

The smoke climbed up through my nostrils and jerked in my gut, like I was being flipped inside out. Static filled my ears so loud, I couldn't hear anything else.

The bathroom's pinkish fluorescent glow was replaced by black hole darkness. But it wasn't just the sound and light that was gone, it was an all over feeling of being stretched to impossible limits.

And I was thirsty.

There was a frenzy inside my body. Still the pain, and just, this wild feeling of not being in control but of being restrained all at once.

Someone thrust something into my face, and it was like a dial was turned up on everything. I rubbed my face into it. I wanted to consume it. In a very far away part of me that was capable of thought, I remembered that vampiris in the orchard, throwing itself around, forgetting it was bound by the restraints of society, of humanity.

The bathroom lights flickered and went out. Someone was screaming, but I couldn't tell if it was the spell or I was actually hearing it. I felt the despair, an animal in pain.

The spell was supposed to give you a clear insight not confuse us more. I wondered if it wasn't working right because I had so little to give it. What did the blood I'd poured out for the Discernment mean in the grand scheme of the cosmos and all its knowledge? Nothing.

Someone took my hand, lacing their fingers in the negative spaces, anchoring me *here*.

Jonah.

I gripped his hand and held on until the darkness and shaking stopped. The pain and screaming. The thirst.

But then the emptiness came. The spell stopped where we'd taken its life.

I opened my eyes to blood on my arm. To our clasped hands on my thigh, knuckles white as bone. I didn't let go.

Maddie stared at our hands too.

"What did you see?" she asked.

I opened my mouth to speak and croaked instead. Maddie handed me a water bottle.

I broke my frozen hand from Jonah's and took a drink, which turned into half the bottle. I handed it to Jonah, still clenching the blood-matchstick-shirt combo—saying it like that, it sounds juvenile, but it was the most powerful magic Jonah or I had ever done.

Instead of taking the water bottle, he reached over and freed the bundle from my fingers. As soon as he did, I felt a little lighter, but sucked dry. So empty.

Maddie took the bottle from me. I wanted to rip the plumbing from the walls and drink and drink and drink—

"There was someone screaming," Jonah said.

I should have known he'd see everything I did when our magic was practically interchangeable. It didn't matter that I did the spell. He's here. He's part of me. Whether he's touching me or not. And whether he wants me to be or not, I'm a part of him.

"And it was dark, with this . . . sound, repeating, blocking out everything else. And then," he stopped here and looked at me. "Insanity. Just chaos."

"Thirst," I nodded. I swept the salt away with trembling hands.

Pounding on the door made us all jump. We helped Maddie jam everything back into her impossibly deep purse.

When I stood up, my vision blanked out. Jonah grabbed my arm, giving me enough of a pick-me-up to be able to move my legs.

Jonah jerked the door open and a sapien walked past us. "Someone get her period in here?"

Jonah turned around like he might deck the guy.

Maddie pushed him out.

Outside, the cold was a shock.

"Do you want me to drive?" Jonah asked once we were in the car.

"What?" Maddie laughed, high-pitched and strung out sounding. "You can suddenly drive a stick?"

"Apollo taught me," he said.

I dropped my forehead to the wheel. "I don't know what the fuck is happening."

"We should talk about it. But not now," Maddie said.

I wanted to talk about it now. I wanted to talk about what it meant that Talbot was with a vampiris. I wanted to talk about whose screams those were. I wanted to talk about how thirsty I was. Would I ever stop being thirsty?

"He needs to rest," said Jonah.

Their careful tones pissed me off. I wasn't the one who'd disappeared off the face of the planet. I wasn't the one who consorted with *vampiria.*

We were at a dead end, and I was nowhere nearer to bringing Junior home.

I clenched my teeth and started the bug.

I parked down the block again. When they got out, I followed, ignoring the tremor in my legs.

The crunch of my shoes on the asphalt was sharp in the heavy night. The smell of sprinkler water on grass was thick.

Maddie hugged me. "We'll figure this out. We'll figure something out. For tonight, eat, hydrate, sleep."

"What are you? My personal trainer?" I asked, but it didn't sound funny.

She kept hold of my arm after breaking the hug. "What you did tonight was amazing. Both of you," she said, glancing at Jonah, who was a steel barrier at her side, eyes darting up and down the street. Sometimes he forgot he was the little brother.

She took off toward the house.

I leaned against Jonah's door, taking out a cigarette. Everything from the spell, from seeing the undiluted terror on his face when the vampiris had reached for Maddie ran through my head like a skipping CD.

"Is this why you stayed?" I asked, holding out my cigarette, the end an orange warning.

Jonah took it and flicked it to the ground. He held my arm, the one I'd cut. Then he held my neck. He leaned his forehead to mine. He was a breath away. I felt like I was going to shatter.

"I need you to be okay."

"It's not about you," I managed.

I wanted to tell him that this was not how straight guys were with their best friends. But I couldn't. Because I started crying, and if I opened my mouth again, things would get ugly.

And it wasn't just about Junior, or about Jonah and me. It was also about this thing inside of me, and I felt like if I could just find Junior, if I could just get over Jonah, then maybe I could also control this.

"You should stay." His voice cracked.

I was hurting him.

I shook my head. I was categorically unfit to handle being in the same bed, the same zip code as sleepy, hot-blooded Jonah who holds his platonic best friend this close.

So he hugged me and pulled away too soon. "Text me when you get home," he said before heading down the street to his house.

I picked up the cigarette he'd thrown, the ember burned out to grey ash, before driving home on autopilot.

Thank god I was too exhausted to dream.

18
Apollo

I was still very much out of it after the Discernment. Nothing Lena said could have prepared me for this emptiness. So in English, I studied the quad outside the window more than the motifs in Robert Frost's poetry.

"Mr. Tormey?" Mrs. Del Toro always used last names, as though we were already the doctors, lawyers, and professionals we were destined to be. "Can you talk a little bit about the poem?"

I focused on the white board, scanning over "Stopping by Woods" to refresh my memory. I'd read it (and SparksNotes) before going to Jonah's yesterday.

"He—the speaker," I corrected, knowing Del Toro would get on me if I didn't use proper terminology, "is considering suicide."

Someone clicked their pen in the sudden silence.

"Can you explain how you came to that conclusion?"

"Um." I scanned the page. "The speaker is between places throughout the poem, like, he's in limbo. In one part, he's standing between the woods and the 'frozen' lake. Life and death. I think when he says that 'the woods are lovely, dark and deep,'"—my voice cut out here, thinking of the darkness when I'd done the Discernment. I thought of Junior and couldn't breathe for a moment—"he's tempted to give it all up, and go in, but he has some shit—*things*, to take care of."

Mrs. Del Toro stared me down for a long moment. "That is a powerful interpretation. Thank you, Apollo."

I went back to staring out the window, wondering how Jonah was doing in Holcomb's class with that novel he hated.

After class, I hitched my backpack and guitar on my shoulder and started for the door.

"Mr. Tormey," Mrs. Del Toro said. "Will you please stay for a moment?"

I set my guitar down and watched everyone leave.

"Please have a seat," she said, gesturing to the desk in front of hers. "Do you have anything you'd like to talk about, Apollo?"

"No," I said, confused. And a little concerned that she was suddenly using my first name.

"Are you certain? I'm a good listener." She waited for an uncomfortably long time, until I was forced to repeat myself.

'Everything is fine' couldn't have been farther from the truth.

"I can't help but suspect there's more to your behavior than you're letting on."

I shifted in the chair. Why did I choose to sit so close to her desk? "What behavior?"

"When you bother to make it to class, you're often removed from what's going on, among other things. Your thoughts on the poem today, along with everything else, the skipping, the lack of engagement, are concerning to me. I believe it's time we speak with your mother. Maybe involve Mr. Hasson and Principal Carver."

Mr. Hasson was a bearded "cool" counselor with whom I have never exchanged a 'hello'. Principal Carver was actually cool, but he had a deep bass voice, which had been terrifying the fine young people of tomorrow since first setting Conversed-feet on this campus. I did not want that voice directed at me with disappointment. Likewise with my mom. I didn't want any of this to come down on her. My leg was shaking at the thought.

"I'm in trouble for how I think?" I asked.

"No, Mr. Tormey. You're not in trouble." The gentle way she said it was the worst. "However, I think it could really help for you to speak with someone, and since you won't talk to me, I wouldn't be doing my job if I didn't send you to someone who can help."

"I don't need any help."

I should just tell her: *I've been in love with my best friend for four years and things are a little fragile between us. The only person who kept me afloat over the summer is missing. Also, magic is the only thing keeping me going alive, but I'm pretty sure it's driving me insane.*

"That's the thing about help," Mrs. Del Toro said. "Most of the time, we get it when we don't want it."

Our dining room always felt so cold to me, with the glass table top and blue placemats to match the rest of the kitchen. It was practically Antarctica in here. I pulled Jonah's hoodie sleeves down to cover my hands before resting my arms on the icy table.

Mom had brought me home after meeting with the principal and counselor about my concerning behavior. The whole affair came off like an anti-drug after-school special. I probably would have enjoyed myself a little more, center of attention and all, if I hadn't been so out of it from the spell.

She set a cup of jasmine green tea with honey in front of me. It was my favorite.

She took a breath. "Apollo, you've got to exhale, baby." She always said that. Holding magic is like drawing and holding a breath. Releasing is when you finally exhale.

The cup warmed my hands through the sleeves. Mom pulled her knee up to her chest, heel on the chair. I'd noticed I got the habit of sitting like that from her.

"I know you're not doing drugs, but this holding is worse than smoking weed."

"Doesn't your generation refer to it as dope?"

Her mouth pulled into a grim line.

I couldn't lie to her, so I was left with silence.

"Tell me how I can help you," she said.

"You can't." I wished I could tell her what would help, but I didn't even know.

She watched me drink my tea. It felt good going down. Tea helped. Maybe not in the grand scheme of things, but right now, it was warm and solid. Liquid. Whatever.

"Maybe you should start seeing Dax."

The clan psychologist. Yeah, that's a whole bunch of nope.

"I'll work it out." I could barely look at her.

"Okay. I will give you this chance to get it under control. But if you keep crossing the line and skipping school, then I have to make that choice for you. Do you understand?"

I nodded down at my tea.

"It's just like anything. Too much of a good thing isn't good. And I remember how hard it is to find that balance. But you have to put space between you and the magic until you're able to throw it."

Problem was, the outlet was already open, and I was still fucking up.

I nodded, hoping that was it.

"I don't want you staying out all hours of the night anymore either. Not with what happened to that wolf."

"Junior."

"What?"

"His name is Junior," I said, a little louder.

"Okay."

I couldn't read her tone, but I was too fragile to linger on that part of the conversation right now anyway.

I cleared my throat. "To be clear, you don't mean I can't go to Jonah's, right?"

She looked like she knew I needed this concession.

"You can go to Jonah's. I just feel like you need to keep closer to home right now. Are we clear?"

"We're clear." I'd never bothered to keep my nightly outings quiet, because I didn't even realize she'd noticed me gone.

"You know you can talk to me anytime. Anytime you're having trouble. I follow an excellent vinyasa channel that could help take your mind off gathering." Uh oh. First the tea, then the yoga and meditation. There would probably even be a stack of books on my dresser in the morning. *Achieve Your Goals with Deep Breathing, Finding Your Inner You,* and the like.

Later, as I was re-stringing my guitar in the living room, Dad came in.

Look at me! Not on drugs!

Really, I was just killing time until the Clarke household was ready to receive me for dinner.

Dad sat on the edge of the couch.

"I heard about the meeting with the counselor."

I hated the idea of them talking about me in private, talking about how to fix me.

"Yeah," I said, as I threaded the fourth string through the peg. I was tired of talking. Not figuratively. My vocal chords were exhausted. "Kinda want my money back."

I could feel the pity emanating from his face so I kept my head down.

"I know you're not on drugs, Son."

Everyone was so sure I wasn't on drugs, but I totally tried a hit off something Junior had rolled once.

"I don't get exactly what you're going through. Just what your Mom tells me, but I get feeling like life is hard sometimes and wanting to distract yourself from that."

I ripped the fifth string through the bridge. I wasn't mad that he was lecturing me or that he assumed our experiences were at all similar. This achy, wistful feeling was the opposite of anger. I just didn't know what to do with it.

Dad stood from the couch, lingering like he wasn't sure he wanted to say what he was thinking.

"You know my door is always open, Apollo. Anytime you need me." He squeezed my shoulder and mussed my hair on his way past to his office and closed the door.

I pressed my fingers into the ends of the strings until it hurt.

19

Jonah

I couldn't stop watching Apollo as we cleaned the kitchen together after dinner.

Maddie and I watched how his eyes rolled to the back of his head at Purple Haze, how he'd thrashed around like his own body was a prison. Only he and I had heard the terrible scream that had pried his own out of him.

I'd been all for him resting after the Discernment, but I'd never seen him so unlike himself.

Selfishly, I missed the old Apollo, before he was obsessed with finding Junior. But that was only because I didn't like change.

Seeing him so focused on Junior, I wanted to know this new him too though. It was like unlocking a bonus level.

"Where did you go after class today?" I sounded about as casual as Dad trying to ask if I had "adequate protection, just in case" while giving me The Talk.

He scrubbed at the spaghetti pot with a focus he rarely got with anything but guitar. "English teacher sent me to the office to powwow with Hasson and Carver."

"Ugh, Mr. Hasson is so weird. Like . . . too eager or something."

He laughed, which is exactly what I was going for. But then I processed what he'd said.

I dropped the bottle I'd rinsed into the strainer. "Why did you have to see Principal Carver and the counselor?"

"They think I'm on drugs. They even called my mom, but—well, let's just say she threatened me with yoga to manage my holding."

Cold sweat broke out along my back. My heart felt like it was going to bust out of my chest. *He's admitting it.*

"Your mom's right though. I hate seeing what it does to you."

He rolled his eyes. "I throw, Jonah. But when I don't, holding makes me feel good." He tried to push off the counter away from me, but I pulled him back.

"Well, aren't there other things? Things you enjoy that you could . . . I don't know, substitute it with?"

"Oh, sure. Like binge-eating, anonymous sexual encounters, maybe some acid trips."

I only realized I grimaced when he covered his mouth to hide his smile.

"Please," I said. "Don't do any of that. I was thinking more along the lines of guitar. Haven't seen you play in a while before today at school. That was cool. Or exercise?"

"Exercise? What is this strange ritual of which you speak?"

I laughed, stopping as he patted my cheek.

"Only you would recommend working out, Golden Boy," he said.

I grabbed his wrist and pulled his arm behind him, leading him to my room. When we got there, we were both out of breath and laughing. Maddie raised her eyebrows, like *what happens in here stays in here.*

Whatever. We weren't doing anything.

I let go of Apollo's arm, but he bumped right back into me, like we were opposing magnets. We both went still as we realized Maddie was arranging pillows and, weirdly, a bowl of popcorn on the floor of my room.

"What are you doing?" I asked, a little afraid.

"*We* are watching a movie," she said, throwing a thick comforter down and messing it up a little.

"Maddie," I said, like I was talking to a crazy person. "We need to figure out our next step."

What I really wanted was to be done with all of this, but if Apollo wasn't, then I couldn't be.

She stepped back to survey the blanket. When she toed a fold, it didn't look any different after she pulled her foot back, seemingly satisfied.

"Jonah," she said, mocking me. "I'm just setting the backdrop. Mom and Dad are going to wonder why we're all scampering around together. This way, we can talk without seeming sus."

"Who actually says 'scampering'," asked Apollo, turning to me.

I held out my hands, introducing my sister who sunk down onto the comforter in a cross legged pose. She was looking up at Apollo.

"What movie are we watching?" he asked, sinking next to her and grabbing a handful of popcorn.

"Apollo—" I was going to tell him we don't have to do this if you're not ready to talk about it.

Maddie shrugged. "Nothing special."

"Madeline Ruth!" Apollo said.

"What, what is it?" I said.

"Only Apollo's favorite movie," said Maddie, grinning as she opened her laptop.

"What? Hocus Pocus?" I asked.

"No. That was years ago. And besides, Max isn't his type anymore."

I looked at Apollo, settled back against the pillows, knees drawn up. I could swear he was blushing. Had I ever seen him blush?

"I thought it would help to have something comforting on while we talk about this," she said, pressing her laptop's space bar. I looked away before I could see what movie it was. I didn't want to know what perfect male specimen was his type now.

"I think we should tell someone about Talbot with the vampiris," I said.

"Admit we were at Purple Haze?" asked Maddie.

"Anonymously," I said. I couldn't see anything wrong with the idea. I'd thought of it from so many angles, it made me dizzy.

"Okay," said Maddie, nodding. Apollo watched her like she would make the final decision. "That's something to consider. Let's go over what we know." She turned toward Apollo. "This might be hard for you to revisit, but we can stop anytime."

He shook his head.

"Why would you have heard screaming?" she asked.

"The thirst," he said, voice cracking. "That had to be the vampiris, since we did the Discernment on his clothing. Since I was, like, in his head."

He pulled his pick in and out of his cuff, thumb swiping over the bracelet I'd given him. I shivered and lowered myself to sit down next to him.

"It was all distorted," he said. "Because the vampiris was seeing everything through the blood song."

You can't see and feel these things, and be okay after. I wished I could do something—anything to make him feel better. I gently squeezed the back of his neck and dropped my hand to his back, rubbing it. I could feel our magic intertwining at the touch, which seemed somehow too intimate right now with Maddie here. I dropped my hand.

"So, somehow, he was being exposed to our kind's blood," Maddie concluded.

"What if he had a good reason?" asked Apollo. "Talbot, I mean. We have our reason for keeping all of this under wraps."

I tried not to read it as concern for Talbot. I seriously wanted to pummel that dude.

"What good reason could he have for hanging out with the kind that wants to literally drain us?" I asked.

"So, I have a theory," said Maddie. "You're not going to like it. After you guys killed the one that went crazy on you, the new head of AI research at Lind is out there cleaning up the aftermath?"

"There was no aftermath," I said.

"Maybe Lind Lab is near the orchards. And Talbot had asked you to meet him there, Apollo, thinking you were a wolf. It's a little strange, all of it together, isn't it?"

"There's nothing out there, though," said Apollo, staring at the computer screen as impossibly beautiful actors threw witty quips at each other.

"What does Talbot have to do with Halsey?" I asked.

"There's a lot of *magikalia* in San Alvarez who are pro-cure. But it's not something you go waving around unless you're serious. A lot of the clans won't even entertain it. No one can ignore the necessity of experimentation on both our species to get a working, field-tested formula. You can't exactly test this stuff on rats."

"Do you believe in it?" Apollo asked.

"No," Maddie said. "I don't believe a symbiotic relationship with a creature who goes crazy at the scent of our blood is the answer to anything. But we learned Talbot *is* pro-cure."

I remembered Cody Iver trying to talk to Maddie and I a couple weeks ago, and Talbot acting like the group's ringleader. But then—

"Wait," I said. "He was . . . trying to get Apollo for the *vampiria's* experiments?"

"Maybe Talbot is working for her," Maddie said, with a concerned glance at Apollo. "That would explain his *friend* at the club. He jumped in when Talbot got too excited. Think about it. He believes in finding a cure and she's researching immunotherapy. Talbot led Apollo to the *exact* spot where a crazed vampiris was roaming. Almost like it was set up. Tell me I'm not crazy," she said.

My brain refused to process anything beyond how close Apollo had been to danger, if not death, how close I had been to losing him when we hadn't even been talking. My last words to him would have been mean and untrue.

"There's something else," Apollo said, quiet and resigned. "What aren't you saying?"

"You should be asking what this has to do with Junior." Her voice was unbearably gentle as she stared at him, head tilted. "What it *could* have to do with him, if Talbot had been looking for a wolf that night," she amended. "Wolves would be an easy resource in testing a cure, don't you think? Alone with no protection from the clan," she said.

"He wasn't alone," Apollo said, an edge to his voice.

"And he would have had clan protection if they'd known," said Maddie. "But if he presented them with ample opportunity . . . " She trailed off.

Apollo didn't look at either of us, eyes still locked on the computer screen.

"It wouldn't go over well with the treaty for her to be using our kind toward this end. There's probably some sort of stipulation that she use synthetic blood. But from what I've read, she's pretty prolific for shirking the rules. She wrote her PhD thesis on—"

"Maddie," I said. "Pretend like we're not as smart as you. Shouldn't be hard, I know. Why target Apollo if he was only supposed to be targeting wolves?"

"Well, that's why he left, is my guess," she said.

Apollo drew his knees closer to his chest, wrapping his arms around them.

"That's why Talbot wanted to meet with you alone. I mean, you run with them," she explained, voice gentle.

"So," I said. "What do we do with all of this, frankly, terrifying information?"

"I think we should leave it up to Apollo. It's his friend," Maddie said.

"He's part of our clan," Apollo growled. "I just want someone to realize that Junior isn't this lone ranger!"

"We do realize that, Apollo," Maddie said, her fingers tugging on his sleeve.

He didn't look at either of us. His clenched jaw seemed to relax when Maddie leaned her head against his shoulder.

20

Jonah

I opened my eyes, focusing on the small glow from my night light. I'd dreamed about Apollo. Anytime I'd dreamed about getting farther with Courtney, the details were all blurry. This was not. So much so that my face could have cooked an egg.

I got up and took a shower as cold as I could stand it.

When I got out, I texted Courtney: *What do you want me to wear to the dance?*

I was dreading the dance. I didn't mind people watching me play, but I didn't like people watching me in intimate moments. I didn't even like it when people looked at me in the library (reading is a very intimate activity).

The morning light danced on my ceiling. I stretched to unplug my night light, dropping it to the floor.

Courtney: *Can I come over with my dress tonight? You'll need to get something in the same shade.*

She already had a dress? I hadn't even answered her about whether I would go or not until just now. Had she planned to go without me anyway?

Me: *Sure. I'll see you then.*

Courtney: *Miss you.*

I pretended I didn't see it until after I got dressed.

Me: *I miss you too, Court.*

And I did. I missed her hair. I missed her laugh and her rapt attention when I answered a question in English. She never said, 'It's good to see you with a book, Jonah.' She expected more than baseball of me. She didn't know enough to expect anything other than normal from me which felt easy.

At Sunday School, I hovered over Apollo, making sure he ate.

"That spell probably wouldn't have taken such a toll if you were taking better care of yourself," I said.

I was too nervous to eat. Nervous about seeing Apollo after that dream I'd had. About Talbot and the vampiris he'd been with. About anonymously tipping off the clan.

"It wasn't just that," he said.

I didn't miss his non-denial. He looked closer to falling apart every day.

Maddie stepped up on my other side, looking over her shoulder. "You haven't seen Talbot, have you?"

Apollo shook his head. "What do you think they did about him?"

"I don't know," Maddie said, again in that sad, sensitive voice that she conjured just for Apollo it seemed.

At the sight of Graham, the entire room fell silent.

"Another wolf is missing," he said.

The club. Talbot and the vampiris. That could have been one of us. It could have been Maddie. I closed my eyes, forcing myself to breathe.

"Lena Tamayo," Graham said.

Though I didn't know her, it still felt like a wound had been ripped open. Another one of our clansmen, gone, just like that.

Apollo looked grey.

"The Bureau provided intelligence of a vampiris sighting just before Tamayo was reported missing," Graham went on. "A vampiris had lost control of its faculties near the boundary and was detained by the Letum Antea. We are recommending a curfew. At this time, it might be prudent to withdraw younglings from school.

At least until we have more information. Or until our missing return home."

All at once, a hundred voices echoed against the high ceilings.

"Please," said Graham, looking distraught by the disorder. "It is best, as always, in these situations that we remain calm, and proceed as we always have. In vigilance and solidarity."

His words were about as useful as lighting a single match to keep us all warm.

After the meeting, Apollo came up to me while Zarine talked with some of the elders. Mom and Dad weren't far off, herding Joss, Miles, and Macy to the door.

"Let me know what happens," Apollo said.

After the meeting, Mom and Dad forbade us from leaving the house. I threw a bouncy ball against the wall, annoyed and relieved at the same time. I needed to tell Courtney I wouldn't be able to go to formal. That fact didn't bother me as much as it should have.

My door opened. I spun around in my desk chair, ready to snap at Maddie for not knocking. The sight of Apollo instead, hair long enough to hang over his forehead now, punched me in the gut.

"Who always lets you in? Macy should know better." I meant it as a joke, but I couldn't conjure a light tone. I didn't want him here. Not *here* where I'd had that damn dream. I clenched the bouncy ball in my fist.

"Your dad let me in, actually."

"Thought everyone would be locked out like we're locked in."

He kicked his foot back onto my exposed bed frame. "I always have a free pass to your house," he said with a wry smile, running his fingers along my headboard. His musician's hands were always touching things.

His mom obviously wasn't putting the shackles on him. If anyone should have a leash, it was him. At least I could keep an eye on him if he's here instead of out partying.

"Besides, it isn't those of us who have families to keep them safe that need the concern. It's the wolves."

The circles under his eyes definitely looked deeper since the meeting earlier. His tone was so conversational, I wouldn't have known he was mad if I couldn't feel his magic snapping.

"They have a sanctuary for the wolves at the records building," I said.

His arms were crossed tight over his chest, his stare challenging. "Wouldn't you feel like a stray dog being given a cardboard box to sleep in for the night?"

"I hope they will. For their own sakes." I started throwing the ball again. I kind of couldn't handle looking at him right now.

He exploded from the edge of my bed where he'd been sitting and caught my ball out of the air. "I *just* talked to Lena!" His voice was shaking. "We saw that vampiris with Talbot!"

"Right, and we let someone know." I kept my voice even and low. "They're handling it."

"How are they handling it? What is the clan doing?"

"There's nothing else *we* can do, Apollo." I snatched my ball back. "I've already lied to everyone. My *dad*."

"I know, Jonah. It's a huge inconvenience being bound to me." He sounded close to tears.

I felt helpless. When he did that, it was a fight neither of us could win. When he seemed light enough to blow away, fragile enough to break.

"That's not true," I said. "That's not what I'm saying."

He swallowed, nodding. When he ran his fingers along my bookshelf, it felt like he was touching me. "I'm not giving up. But don't worry. I have an insurance policy." His quiet voice was a ruse; he was too keyed up to sit down. "I took your book."

I looked at the place where I kept my well-loved copy of *Aristotle and Dante Discover the Secrets of the Universe.* He'd taken it for a Locator or Discernment. Apollo knew most of my dark secrets; one of them was my obsession with Sáenz's novel.

He took off his cuff bracelet that held his first pick and set it in the empty space of my bookshelf, the bracelet I'd given him for his birthday still circling his wrist.

I cleared my throat. "When did you take *Aristotle and Dante*?"

"Jonah, you don't even notice me half the time," he said, tilting his head.

I stood up. "You think I don't notice you?"

He scoffed.

My fingertips found his jaw, sliding back to tilt his head up. He had to know. "You know you're not one of them, right?"

"May as well be." He licked his lips. His gaze flicked down to my mouth and back up to my eyes.

I wanted him to forget about Junior, and Talbot, and ignoring me for half a year when we could have been—"No. You're not one of them. You're mine."

Then my lips were pressing against his. I meant more than just having a solid place in the clan and by my side, but being so much a part of me that he couldn't be a wolf.

I pulled back, breathing hard. With my hand on his neck, I rubbed my thumb over his Adam's apple. I felt his breath on my lips.

"Don't mess with me," he said, eyes closed. But it was so weak.

"I'm not. I swear to god, I'm not." I didn't bother hiding how wrecked I was.

He moved in slow, hands light as feathers against my jaw, like he thought I'd back away.

He opened his mouth slowly against mine. A stampede of wild horses filled my chest. It felt so unbelievably good, I shivered and didn't stop, almost like I couldn't get warm but I was hot all over.

I pulled him to me again. Harder. Flash of the dream. I kissed him until my mouth hurt. We slowed down, experimentally navigating each other.

"I've missed that," he murmured against my neck.

"What?" I whispered. I didn't really understand how he could form sentences right now.

"That feeling of our magic being together."

My breathing sounded embarrassingly loud. He definitely felt my heart under his hand.

"I could feel it when we were far away from each other," he said. "And at school and stuff, but it's better like this."

This was what we were protecting, why we couldn't expose ourselves. *This.*

I kissed him again. And again. And again.

His fingers dug into my sides, like I was a life raft. I was fine with that.

I needed him too.

He sat back on the bed, and I climbed over him. I couldn't stop smiling as I leaned down to kiss him again.

My phone went off in my pocket. I jerked back. Apollo caught the pad of my thumb between his teeth and lips. I dived down again and he moved his hands up my sides, over my shoulders. I dropped a little of my weight down against him and he gasped.

"Is this okay?" I asked, breathless.

"Yes," he said, hands moving down to hold my hips, not letting me shift my weight off of him.

My phone went off again. Everything got really clear, like the feel of him, hard underneath me, our ragged breathing, how much time had passed since the first time my phone went off.

"Why?" I said, sitting up on my knees. I dug through my pocket, but my jeans were too tight now and my fingers were useless.

Finally, I got it out and read the messages.

Courtney: *I'm on my way now. Okay?*

I jumped up.

"Fuck. Courtney's on her way. With her dress." I sounded ridiculous, but there wasn't a lot of blood left in my brain for thinking just then.

He laid back on my bed, folding his hands on his chest. He closed his eyes and would have looked like he was sleeping except for the current situation in his pants.

"What am I going to do?" I clenched my phone like it might give me a Magic 8 ball answer. Really, all it would likely tell me was 'vintage rose'.

Apollo stood up.

"You could always tell the truth," he said, crossing his arms.

His jaw was clamped, opposite of his open mouth a few seconds ago. I could still feel his pulse under my thumb, racing. God, I did *not* want him to leave.

"I can't even think about it right now." I wasn't sure if I meant telling the truth or what just happened.

"Why don't I go, so you'll have plenty of time to think before Court gets here."

His words echoed in my brain as he left my room.

"Apollo." I followed him, but he was already halfway across the empty living room.

He opened the door and went out, shutting it quietly behind him. Apollo never slammed doors or cupboards, never left them open. He always meticulously cleaned up after himself. It made me unbearably sad.

"Do you love him?"

I spun around.

Maddie was on the couch, her hands over her closed laptop.

Oh god. My door was open and she was out here the whole time. What was I thinking?

Well, the answer to that would be I wasn't. Not at all.

"I don't know, Maddie! I just . . . we . . ."

"What?" she asked.

I dropped my head back, staring at the popcorn ceiling. I felt like I was under a very strong microscope. "I was trying to help him."

"By making out with him?" she hissed. "'Cause that's what it sounded like."

I ran my hands through my hair, pulling it.

"Just because he's gay, doesn't mean that he likes every guy he's friends with. It doesn't mean you can make him feel better by doing things like that."

I looked at her. That's where she was going with this? She let the question of my sexuality go, just like that?

"That's not what I thought," I said, realizing how wrong it all was.

"Fine. You're so comfortable with him, it might be difficult to know where the line is between being in love and loving your best friend. Regardless, you liked him enough to lead him on. If you plan on pretending like something didn't happen between you two *again* and staying with your girlfriend, you will destroy him. *Go* talk to him."

Her words punched through me, and I had to drop to the couch. It devastated me to even entertain the possibility that I was the reason he was going through this. If I believed that was true, I would have gone after him right then and told him to stop being stupid. But that's how Apollo was. He didn't see himself as good enough. But he was. More than.

I could feel all the music he'd ever played in his mouth when he kissed me back. I could feel all the times he touched my chest when he thought I was asleep to calm me down after a night terror.

There was a knock on the door, but Maddie wasn't done.

"You could have talked to me anytime about what you're going through, Jonah. I'm sorry if I didn't make you feel as though I was a safe space. But if you don't care about him like that, if you're just experimenting or whatever, it's downright cruel."

She gathered her laptop and power cord up. When she walked by me on her way to her room, she looked like she was about to cry.

I didn't want to be cruel or lead anyone on. I didn't know how to fix this. All I wanted was Apollo.

I wiped my face and opened the door.

"Hi," Courtney said.

"Hey," I said, hoping I looked normal.

She faltered. "Can I come in?"

"Oh. Yeah."

She looked around. "Where's everyone at?"

"Bed, I guess." I shut the door and almost locked it. I didn't. Whether because I thought this would be quick or I thought he might come back, I don't know.

"I'm sorry it's so late. I couldn't get out of there. Mom wanted to 'bond' with us after dinner by watching this horrible movie—are you okay?"

"Yeah."

She started walking to my room.

"No!" I said. She looked at me, startled. "Let's sit in here."

She smiled. "Okay." She came to the couch, and I noticed the dress bag in her arms. She laid it on her lap and patted the cushion next to her. I sat down.

"So, my dress." She unzipped the bag. "I was thinking you could do a matching tie or bow tie, whatever you want. But please don't do a bow tie," she said, laughing.

She pulled the dress all the way out, and I didn't see why she felt the need to do that.

"Do you like?" she said, twisting a little, so the bottom swished around. Just like a Disney princess. In vintage rose.

But I wasn't listening. I thought about how I couldn't even go.

I thought about how Apollo's kiss six months ago had been a question. My first answer pissed him off. But tonight . . . that was my real answer.

I could still feel him under my hips, the pulse of his throat against my thumb, his stuttering breaths between each kiss; every time he gasped, I tried proving to him that he shouldn't be waiting for it to end.

I thought about how it had never felt that *right* kissing Courtney. No, I couldn't take that answer back.

Maddie's voice came into my head: *You'll destroy him.* She was right. Only now, I knew, I'd be destroying myself too if I didn't make good on my answer.

I'd already hurt Apollo, and Maddie, Mom, and Dad. Now I had to hurt Courtney, but at least neither of us would be living a lie. I was going to have to confront every lie I'd been telling myself.

I guess you were wrong, Mom. I am not such a good boy, after all.

I pressed my finger against my sore mouth as a kind of self-punishment and took a breath.

"Courtney. I can't go to formal."

21
Apollo

I tried telling myself before I didn't care if he went to a stupid school dance with his girlfriend. She was his girlfriend. I had pretty much told him to go. And before tonight, I was finally learning how to be around him again.

I *hated* him. I hated that he chose Courtney. I hated myself for hating him for choosing Courtney. Mostly, I hated that he kissed me back *again* and let me feel like he chose me.

I drove. I didn't care where I was going. Eventually I ended up sitting at the end of the pier. Déjà vu. I closed my eyes and reached out. I couldn't feel any *magikalia* nearby. The crowds had been driven away by the overcast sky and icy wind turning the waves into silver blades. I could have been the only person left in the world.

I couldn't move. I didn't want to move. I'd already tried to tell him with everything in me, in my body—god, to finally know what it felt like to be wanted back—that this would work if he'd just give it a chance.

I wanted Jonah to lose control. And I had thought he was. I could feel it in the way he'd arched his body against mine, mouth searching for the deepest part of me. I had badly wanted it to be real not just some experiment, but it was May all over again. My hope was blown to shrapnel.

I only had myself to blame for falling in love with my Kindred. He was practically my brother.

A notification broke through the sound of the ocean roaring. I got my phone out so fast I almost dropped it into the water.

Mom: *Are you still at Jonah's?*

Everything inside me deflated.

After what just happened in his room, he knew all the parts I usually kept from him. Then he pulled away, taking all the oxygen out of my lungs, my brain, my blood with him.

Mom: *It's probably time for you to start heading home.*

I was tired of being told what to do when it didn't matter. Junior and Lena were gone. Talbot was gone. All of them had talked to me before disappearing.

Gone.

Mom: *Please answer so I know you're safe.*

I walked back to my car at the far end of the parking lot, the last one left.

It looked like a storm was coming. I sat on the hood and watched the sun set. The wind picked up, rocking along the sides of the bug.

I really needed a hobby. Maybe Jonah was right about that at least.

I started laughing. Then I couldn't stop.

When I got to Quinn's, I was hysterical. I thought I'd lay in her hammock until she found me. When I came around the side of the house though, scrubbing my wet face with the heels of my hands, I heard talking.

The hammock was already occupied. Quinn and someone else, rocking slightly. One of them was tracing the other's palm in the air. I recognized the voice. Danny.

After eighteen years of practice, I was pretty good at leaving without making a sound.

I needed to find Lind Lab.

The trees got thicker as I took the 110 out of San Alvarez to Orville's. The houses were next to go. Leaving the city behind for the orchards shook something loose inside of me again, and I was clenching the steering wheel and chain-smoking.

I didn't bother cutting the engine before I got to the clearing. Nothing had happened the last time we'd been out here. Not a fucking rat scurrying through the grass.

I walked across the road, my steps echoing without any noise from the city or sea to muffle them. The night seemed devoid of even the natural night sounds, like nocturnal birds, insects, or even the wind that had been at the beach. I looked up for the clouds, but the moon's glow was either too weak to illuminate anything or there was no moon tonight. I probably should have looked up the moon's current phase beforehand.

The silence pressed closer, almost suffocating. It was a bit like walking through an alternate dimension. I thought of astronauts out there in space, taking steps on distant, dusty moons or just floating outside their ship in nothingness. I felt that emptiness.

Closer to the old Miller house, I couldn't see any lights like I had the night I'd been out here with Talbot.

Kkkshhhh—

Every hair on the back of my neck rose. Was it an animal?

I started walking again.

I remembered Jonah's half-asleep face waking up when I pointed out here. I remembered watching the vampiris, not thinking of it as a sentient creature. And maybe they aren't, really, when they get to that point. But before that point, what kind of life had it lived? Did it believe in a god? Have a job or go to school? Did it love anyone? He. Did he love anyone?

I reached into my pocket for the piece of shirt, only to remember that Jonah had taken it from me.

Deliberately placing each step on the soft ground, I walked to the nearest tree.

I was gathering and it made my head airy with magic. My heart beat loudly in the silence. I strained to see through the blanket of darkness. Were there things out here that would hear my heart? I shivered and couldn't stop.

I took my phone out.

Jonah: *We need to talk.*

It must have come while I was driving. Something inside me walked to the edge of the world, and then walked off.

I wanted to see him. I wanted to talk to him. I didn't want him to know I wanted these things.

I answered and put my phone to vibrate. I backed up so that I was touching the tree. The clearing by the sagging farmhouse looked dead as ever. I was just going to have to go over there. I pulled magic from the roots digging through cold earth, from the salt lacing the mist in the air, from the moon, wherever it was. I thought about Junior's philosophy.

We could hold the stars.

I pushed off the tree.

Something moved in the clearing. More than one something.

I opened my eyes wider, trying to see how a cat sees at night. The way *they* do—Halsey's kind.

I stayed very still. Shapes glided between the trees around me. The clearing was so dark. I itched to muffle my pounding heart with my hand. But I couldn't move, because I knew I wasn't alone anymore.

Something slammed into the back of my head. The ground crashed against my forehead. I thought maybe I should check for blood.

"Hm."

That was definitely a person. I tried to look at the source of the voice, but the movement detonated pain through my head. I closed my eyes, listening, staying very still until I didn't even have to try anymore.

22

Jonah

After Courtney left, I put his cuff on and texted him.

Me: *We need to talk.*

I felt horrible for breaking things off with Courtney, but I couldn't wait to see Apollo again. I was free to be with him. If that's what he wanted. If he could ever forgive me.

I scrolled as my room got darker, waiting for the response bubble.

I woke up without the aftershock of a nightmare coating my skin for once. I'd had that same dream with Apollo, but it wasn't just a fantasy anymore. It had happened. I had instigated it.

I turned my hot face into my sheets, smelling his eucalyptus and aloe soap and the faint scent of Camels.

I thought of Apollo watching me feed Joss, talking to M&M about their science projects, him taking Joss onto his lap after dinner and letting her mush his face. When he bumped his leg against mine, smiling, when we beat the Knicks on NBA2K. When Apollo really smiled, it was like the sun.

I was so obsessed with normalcy, I'd never tried applying a label to myself. Would I have ever even questioned what I was if Apollo hadn't kissed me? If he hadn't fallen for me? Heat moved through my whole body.

I thought about him laying back on my bed when I told him my girlfriend was on her way, how crushed he'd looked. I needed to fix things with us.

The sound of a text notification had me tearing my covers apart for my phone, eyes still blurred from sleep. I fumbled it in my hands before reading the message.

Apollo: *Looking for Lind Lab at the orchards. Come help or don't.*

I saw the time. It was almost eleven. This? This was his answer to me wanting to talk.

But then it sank in. A second wolf was missing. He was pissed about the clan's lack of action. He was pissed at me. And he'd gone out there again.

I tore out of my room into the empty living room. A dim light was on in Mom and Dad's room. Maddie's too. I burst in, closing the door as quietly as possible.

Maddie was laying back on her bed, laptop propped on her chest. She sat up when I came in.

"Jonah! What the hell?"

"Read!" I said, thrusting my phone at her.

She read it. Her face went white.

"He's out there with *nothing*," I said. "No protection whatsoever."

"Tell him to leave," she said like it was obvious.

I laughed humorlessly.

"Do you know Apollo? He wouldn't listen if I did. He went out there on his own, *knowing*. The first time he'd seen the crazy vampiris, he came to get me. Because he knew he had nothing without me."

She pulled my phone out of my hand and started typing.

"What are you doing?" I asked, fingers caught in my hair as I tried to pull it out.

"I'm telling him he needs to get out of there."

"What if he doesn't?" I get being mad, but did it justify doing something this reckless? *Please, Apollo. Please don't,* I thought. I don't even know what I was praying he wouldn't do.

"Let's just see if he answers. Maybe he will."

"Maybe he won't."

"Jonah, you need to calm down."

"Has that . . . ever worked," I began. "In the history of anyone telling a person to calm down?"

"You're panicking."

"He's—" I fought for the right words. "He's been really down on himself. And holding magic," I said. "It's like he's on this path to self-destruction. How do I stop him?"

"Go. Get dressed. Wear black, and bring a weapon," she said, echoing my own words.

I put on jeans and a hoodie. My phone remained stubbornly quiet. I grabbed my pocket knife and bat before leaving my room.

"He hasn't answered," I said as I came out, meeting her at the door. She looked over her shoulder down the hallway.

"Let's go."

I tried the door, but the knob didn't budge. But I could feel the buzz enter my hands. On instinct, I started gathering it. "What? What's—"

"I was afraid of this. I think Mom and Dad put a Protection on the house. I heard them talking earlier." She looked up at me, trying to catch my gaze. "You didn't feel it?"

"They locked us in?" I wasn't used to our parents not trusting us. Not that it wasn't deserved, but why did it have to be right this very second? "What are we going to do?" I hated how helpless I sounded.

She touched her hand to the door. "You've done this spell before. Where's the Discernment?"

"The . . ."

"The shirt, wrapped around the matchsticks," she said.

I ran back to my room, knocking things over on my dresser and catching them before they could make a clatter.

I brought it to the living room.

"Apollo's blood," she said.

I instantly knew where she was going with this. God, I loved my sister.

"Maybe I can break the barrier," I agreed.

"You're going to have to be fast, Jonah. They'll probably feel it."

I took it to the door and closed my eyes. I saw the bathroom at Purple Haze. Apollo cutting himself and dipping these matchsticks into his blood. Yes, I could feel it. My magic started to pulse to life.

I focused on the Barrier. My magic recognized Mom's and Dad's. The raw force of their love and protection brought tears to my eyes. I hated to think about what they would go through when they noticed their Barrier had been broken. They would know one of us is Kindred to be able to throw the magic required break theirs.

They would know right away it was me. Sometimes, I wondered how other people didn't see me glowing when Apollo was around.

"Is it working?" asked Maddie.

It was hard just having a bit of Apollo's blood to power me rather than him standing with me, touching me. I used that, I pulled magic from my own desperation and wrapped the grid of the Barrier around my fingers. And broke it.

I swayed a little, dizzy from the release. When I pulled the door handle, it gave.

"Go, go," said Maddie.

She manually unlocked the Tahoe so she didn't have to deactivate the alarm, which would be a dead giveaway. We were basically banking on them being asleep right now.

I opened the door, a little dumbstruck. I'd never done magic like that before without Apollo. It felt surreal. I didn't like it. I wanted him back.

After closing the door behind us, as quietly as possible—had to account not only for increased parent hearing but increased magikalis hearing—I stepped off the porch and almost stumbled. Maddie grabbed my arm and led me to the car. I couldn't have been more grateful that she'd butted her way into this whole thing.

"Do you have enough left to do Incognito?"

"I need to have something left to help him."

"Yeah, but we won't even get there unless we get out of here without drawing Mom and Dad's attention. Here," she said, tossing a plastic bag in my lap.

"Trail mix?"

My head was pounding. It seemed that doing magic without Apollo was not in my best interest.

I've missed that, he'd said. *That feeling when our magic stirs awake.*

"Every bit counts. Drink some water too," she said, lifting a bottle from the center console. I ate and drank and concentrated on Incognito.

I finished off the trail mix as she drove us to the orchards.

"This is the dumbest thing we've ever done," Maddie said.

I didn't feel myself gaining more strength, but I sensed we were getting closer to Apollo. My magic could sense him.

I stuffed the empty baggie into the door handle and sat up. I rolled down the windows, trying to echo-locate him or something.

"He's probably just walking around out here, smoking his death sticks."

"No," I said. "He knows they'll smell them." I scanned the trees. We were outside of town now. We were close.

"Try that little road up here that we went on last time," I said.

She slowed down until we saw it and pulled in. We drove in a few yards and saw the bug. I fell in relief against the seat. Sweat rolled between my shoulder blades.

"You know, he probably wouldn't have done this if you hadn't misled—"

"I know," I snapped. I started taking off my sweater, but then, I couldn't see him in the car. I couldn't see him anywhere.

"Fuck. Maddie. He's not here." I opened the car door before she'd even stopped.

"Jonah!" I heard her say as I got out and walked over to his car. I jerked the door open. Empty. He was *gone.*

Maybe I'd imagined feeling him. But then, he *had* been here. His car was right here.

"He gave me his pick last night," I said when Maddie caught up, holding up my wrist. "So we'd each have something for a Discernment for this exact reason. And I freaked out on him. I'm an idiot."

"Here," she said, shoving my bat in my hand.

"What did you bring?" I asked, scanning our surroundings. I could hardly see a thing, it was so dark. My chest felt tight around my lungs. I remembered hiding in that basement in Mississippi, wondering if I'd die down there.

"Mace, taser, one of Mom's good knives."

"The ones grandma got for her?"

"Yep. Hope I don't have to use it," she said.

I stopped walking. "I'm so sorry." I was sorry for involving Maddie. Sorry for mine and Apollo's actions that night, the first domino in a long, twisting snake.

"If things go to shit, I want you to drive straight home. Don't stay."

"Looks like they're already kind of going that way," she said, her voice shivering.

"What? Why?" I asked, dread uncurling in my stomach as I looked for whatever she'd seen.

"Mom's blowing up my phone. They know we're gone."

Which meant they knew. They knew what I was. I started shivering.

"We don't have a lot of time, then," I said. We'd gone a ways from the car and still hadn't seen or heard anything.

"Fuck! He's not here."

"Jonah."

I leaned my forehead against a tree. When I opened my eyes, I could just make out a corner of the Miller place through the trees.

I held out my hand. "Give me Mom's knife."

When she did, I started carving his name.

"You're Calling him." Her voice was full of awe.

I remembered when Apollo had Called me in class. I had felt all warm with the guarantee that he was at my back and that line of communication had opened between us.

I held onto the tree when I finished, waiting, breathing as quietly as I could.

And then it hit me. Him. I could feel him. My heart started racing and anxiety squeezed my chest like a vice tightening.

"He heard it." I dropped my head against the tree. Apollo was scared.

"How do you know?"

"I can feel him," I said, but it was barely a whisper, because I already knew. I got up from the tree. The bark left an imprint on my palm.

Maddie returned the knife to the sheath.

When we started walking to the road, I felt like he was closer, like playing hotter-colder. I was getting hotter. I started running. Something jerked my arm right before I got to the asphalt.

"Jonah. No! You're going to get us killed."

"He's out there!"

"Are you sure?"

"Yes!" I said, a sob choking me. "I'm fucking sure."

"Okay. Okay." She crossed her arms, tight, and stomped her feet on the ground a little. She looked up. "If you can still feel him . . ."

She didn't say it. It was too heavy. *If you can still feel him, he's alive.*

"What do you want to do?" she asked. She was crying.

Dad told me he knew how helpless I probably felt. Now it felt impossibly, horrifically real. Apollo could die because we had thought we were invincible. We hadn't even had a chance to be together without walls. Without secrets.

He couldn't die.

I thought of the woman in that picture in the article. What she'd done to her own kind to try and find this cure for the effect our blood had on them. It was that powerful. It was a weakness she'd stop at nothing to overcome.

I needed my mom and dad.

"Where the hell were you?" Dad asked as soon as we opened the door.

Maybe he'd kill me before I could save Apollo.

"There's only one way you could break that Barrier," said Mom, her voice no less terrifying. "So start talking."

Seeing them made tears run down my face. My feet were lead on the threshold. Maddie squeezed my hand as she passed.

Dad's face flickered to concern. "What's wrong?"

"The *vampiria* have Apollo." I almost couldn't get the words out. I was trying not to break down.

Dad laid his warm hands on my shoulders. "How do you know this?"

My face crumpled. Hot tears cut through the ice of my face. I explained everything almost in one breath. I told them we were Kindred and everything we'd done.

Mom led me to the couch and pushed me down. I stood back up, but my knees buckled. I could feel everything the spells had drained out of me.

"How do we get him back?" I asked.

Dad placed his hand on my chest. "You have to breathe, Jonah."

"What if something happens to him? They could be using him for their experiments. We have to . . ." I was breathing weird and fast again.

"Please . . ." I managed.

"Maddie, get a bag," Mom said, her voice calm. Calmer than it should have been.

Why weren't they doing anything? At least yelling at me for keeping this massive secret about myself and Apollo.

I stared at the digital clock on our cable box, glaring green. I heard crinkling and felt the bag scratch my cheek.

We were running out of time.

The time glared brighter until all I could see was green.

"Here. Breathe," said Mom.

But I didn't know how to do that without him.

23

Apollo

I heard voices as though from the bottom of a hole in the ground.

"We've never had one this young."

"They're pretty much useless at this age. But Dr. Halsey is obsessed, says all data is valuable."

I had the disorienting sensation of moving through space.

I barely had to squint my eyes open before white light pierced them into submission. I could see that we were moving down a wide hallway. The lights reflected off floor-to-ceiling glass walls standing between me and people in all white working at tables and along the back walls.

I felt sick and exhausted.

Alarms rang through me as hands touched me. Something pinched my arms, my inner thighs, my neck, and other places that I couldn't pinpoint. I tightened every muscle, trying to suppress the shuddering. If I moved, they would know I was awake and administer something to put me out. I was terrified frozen.

I peered through the slit in my eyelids. Gas masks, just like the one with Talbot at Purple Haze.

They said nothing. I felt a pinch and a pulling as the masks hovered over me. I glanced out of the corner of my eye to see a bunch of vials. Most of them empty. Some full of . . .

Blood.

I didn't need to hold my muscles from shuddering anymore. They all went slack.

I couldn't move. It was just like out in the clearing, after I'd been hit. My whole body limp, bones like bendy straws, but I was awake.

What had they done to me?

All I could hear was static.

I forced my eyes open. Didn't make a difference. I was in complete darkness.

I reached out with my fingertips. They were the only part of me that didn't hurt to move. I was on a cold, hard floor. With . . . a rough texture. Cement?

Where were the sterile halls and rooms? The gas masks and white coats? *Dr. Halsey is obsessed,* someone had said. Where was that vial of my blood, currently?

No. Don't freak out. Don't overanalyze it.

Go back, before that.

Dark figures in the clearing. Being hit in the head. That voice. *Hmm.* As though someone had just stumbled upon me. I guess I kind of was just standing there like an idiot.

Where had they come from? The only structure for miles is that farmhouse. Either way, it seemed I had found Lind Lab.

How long ago had I texted Jonah? Would he come? Fuck.

How could I help him from in here when I could barely walk? Would he feel me? To think of Jonah having to deal with this cold darkness nearly unraveled me.

Breathe.

Focus.

If Jonah was here, somewhere, maybe I could signal him somehow. I looked around for any type of window, but looking didn't make a difference in pure darkness. And moving my head made bile climb up my throat.

I reached out with my magic. I reached for him. I couldn't sense anything. I felt useless. Deaf, dumb, and blind, exhausted and hungry. Starving. I still hadn't been able to shake the thirst since the Discernment. Fat lot of good that had done us.

I reached into my pocket for my lighter to find everything had been taken. I only had my clothes. Thankfully, I'd worn lots of layers. But my shoes were gone. Who takes shoes? The blood thiefs?

Thieves, Jonah would correct.

I almost laughed to think of them trying to manufacture any kind of cure from my sick blood. Would that just keep them from going crazy at the scent of an addict's blood?

I tried to stay calm, but my chest felt like it was caving in. I couldn't even tell how long I'd been out. It felt like a week since I'd stood in the clearing. Is this what it felt like when Jonah had his panic attack at school? Would I ever go to school again? Would I ever hear him correct me again?

It was so dark it was hard to tell if I was dead or alive. That scared me more than anything. I guess my only real indication that I was alive was that my heart was pumping so hard, I could feel my entire chest jerking.

A blanket of warmth suddenly fell down around me, and I heard Jonah's voice. *Please.*

Instead of asking questions, or wondering how I was so lucky to feel him, his magic like the warmth of a fire on a cold night calling to me, I pulled it over my head to keep the monsters out.

I woke up with a start. I had to get up and do something; I was so cold. I rolled onto my hands and knees and cried out, when I put weight on my wrist. I vaguely remembered falling on it weird out in the clearing.

I tried again, gasping with the effort. My entire body was a rusty bike frame.

I needed a point of reference, a wall. I felt with my hand before I took each crawling step. My head pounded, but I had to find a way out. I stopped, dizzy, then inched my way down the wall.

As I shuffled along, it was stupid, but I thought about Jonah. Did that text mean he was going to keep being the same stupid Jonah? Or did he realize what he did to me with that kiss last night? Just before he had dived back down to me, I recognized the hunger in his eyes. It's what I'd felt for years. That's why I thought he'd lost control. Joke's on me, I guess. Again.

I tried to listen around the constant sound of static. I couldn't be sure if it was generated somehow or if my ears were making sense of the silence. I breathed, focusing on what I could smell. Cold concrete. Wet, dark earth—was I underground? That would explain the silence, the complete darkness. Then . . . chemicals? Something salty—bleach! Okay. And behind that, something earthy and damp. *Wet grass.* I realized my heightened sense of smell was for this exact prey versus predator scenario. Thanks, biology.

I imagined digging up through the ceiling of my prison to the surface. What was up there? What would I smell?

Trees.

It hit me so suddenly, I could almost hear the branches creaking in the wind. And—gasoline fumes! God, these assholes better not have touched my car.

And fainter than it all, but more than I could stand, surely more than was safe, the smell of Jonah's cologne and his heat burning like the brightest star. I inhaled until it was gone, hoping to god he wasn't stupid enough to get caught.

I couldn't even tell how much of this room I'd covered. Taking off one of my shirts to mark my progress, I hugged myself, trying to keep some of the warmth I'd generated.

Throughout my 'self-destruction' as Jonah had deemed it, I had never experienced such a complete betrayal of my body. I'd felt tired, sure, exhausted to the point of hardly being able to stand, but I could always gather and force it forward.

I touched the wall, pressed my palm flat. I reached inside with my magic, my fingers dug at the concrete wall, nails bending back with my effort.

I thought about all the bodies, like worker bees where they'd wheeled me around on a cart. Surely I should be able to pull something from them.

I waited. I pulled until I felt like I was turning inside out. And then I felt something. Not organic life, moist and salty, but a flicker, deep inside the wall. I called with everything inside of me to the electricity, to the spark and acrid smoke. I knew it was there, and that was half the battle. But it was either too far or the walls were too thick or I was too weak.

I gave up everything—Mom squeezing my foot through the blanket and hot cups of tea, Dad and I jamming together, Quinn and Danny in the hammock, reading bedtime stories to M&M, Joss's delirious giggle, Maddie calling us idiots, Junior's heavy arm slung over my shoulders, solid and warm, Jonah riding passenger in my car—*god,* his smile, and magic, always magic around me. When that was all gone, and I was just an empty shell, that's when I felt it.

Once, I'd gone camping with Jonah, Miles, and Tom. Tom had tried to show us how to start a fire with just sticks. It seemed like it took hours of twisting those sticks onto one another. But when we saw the smallest puff of smoke go up, it was a huge victory. That's how much power travelled to me from its source, down the structure and through this wall. A tiny puff of smoke. But I caught it, and I held it close to me to keep it from going out.

I kept moving, letting the electricity drive my legs and breathe for me. It felt like I'd been walking for hours.

Just when I thought I was close to my shirt on the ground, shuffling my feet all along the way so that I wouldn't miss it, the wall changed. I stopped, feeling. It wasn't concrete anymore. It was smooth, cold to the touch. Glass.

Relief flooded through me, but then I realized glass meant see-through. Glass meant that maybe someone was on the other side . . . watching me.

In this dark, in this silence, the thought terrified me. I dropped into a heap below it. Broke out in a sweat, pressing my hands to my head. Everything in me absolutely did not want to be watched by whatever was behind that glass.

I'd been walking so long too, so for me not to have noticed this when I'd started my trek around the room, for me to not have gotten back to my shirt—they'd seen me this whole time. This room must have been massive. Or maybe I was going in circles. Maybe I was just losing it.

I reached up and felt the seam between the glass and the concrete, trying to feel some kind opening, something coming through. But there was nothing.

I stood, facing that glass wall with my blind eyes. I stepped forward, everything in my body screaming not to touch it, to duck back down and hide. I put both hands on it anyway.

If Jonah was anywhere nearby, I might be able to throw the small amount I'd gathered from the electricity and break it. I tried pulling more, but it was as though a graveyard was on the other side of the glass.

It felt like the floor dropped from under me. If there was a vampiris on the other side of this glass, there *was* no life on the other side of that glass. I stopped gathering; magic excited them.

I hit the glass instead.

"Doesn't matter any way!" I screamed, beating so hard my teeth jarred in their sockets.

The glass didn't reverberate at all. It was as though I was a moth flying against it. A moth with no light. Sounded about right.

24

Jonah

I woke up, face wet and a hard lump in my throat. I'd been crying in my sleep.

I couldn't remember how I'd gotten to my bed. Then I noticed it was morning. *No.*

I flew out of my room, vision going dark for a second from standing too soon, to find Mom, Dad, and Apollo's parents at the table. Jackson's face was a mask of dark circles and pale five o'clock shadow. Zarine's eyes were completely bloodshot. Maddie was sitting on the floor at the kitchen door, knees drawn up to her chest.

"Why did you let me fall asleep? We have to go!"

"We have to take care of some things first," Dad said in that voice that told me to shut up and sit down.

"Dad—"

"Jonah. We have to take certain steps to do this right. We've got a meeting in an hour, but you need to talk to the Tormeys before we do."

Zarine studied me like she would crack the code as to where Apollo was. It felt like cold water had been dumped down my back.

They knew we were Kindred.

That everyone was out here talking about what we were to each other without Apollo here beside me, it felt completely wrong.

Zarine's face rippled and broke out in a new bout of tears. "Please, Jonah. What happened?"

"We'd already decided—" I began and stopped, putting my head in my hands. "Well, I was trying to talk him into stepping back." God, and here I was blaming it all on him.

Dad leaned against the counter, arms crossed, like he was trying to hold himself back. His urge to protect even extended to my best friend, his sixth child basically.

"To let the elders take care of finding Junior. And Lena," I added. I could hear Apollo chiding me for forgetting either of them. "He was supposed to . . . he wasn't supposed to do it alone."

Zarine dropped her head. She noticed Apollo's cuff, which I was still wearing and compulsively turning. All my feelings for him felt very visible under her gaze, which made everything I'd done so much worse.

Apollo looked so much like her.

"I don't understand," said Jackson. "How did you guys get caught up in all this?"

Apollo looked like his dad too—the jaw, the curl in his hair.

Then I remembered. "Talbot. You need to find Talbot Erikson," I said, looking at Dad who frowned. "He's pro . . . pro-cure. He might have been the reason Junior was taken. He thought Apollo was a wolf too. He asked him out to the clan boundaries."

"I already told them," Maddie said, leaning her head back against the wall. "He's gone."

"What do you mean? He's been helping them. You need to find him and question him. He may know—"

"We have reason to believe whomever he was helping realized he was a risk," said Mom. She had stopped twisting her coffee mug in front of her.

"What? What do you mean?" I stared at them.

"Talbot Erikson is dead," Dad said. "We went to speak with him and found him . . . "

He didn't even have to finish. I cut my eyes to Maddie and she closed hers.

My head pounded. If the *vampiria* killed him and he'd been *helping* them . . . I clenched the edges of my chair, trying to keep myself together.

Zarine took my hands, and I immediately wanted to pull away. I felt too bad. "Why would Apollo do this? Why would he try to take this on by himself?"

"We got into a fight yesterday. But before that, he's been—"

"Holding," she said, understanding everything. "But if you two are Kindred"—I tried not to flinch at it being said aloud—"then he would know, certainly, that he had no power without you."

I looked down, because I couldn't stand it anymore. I was sorry that I couldn't explain why he'd be so careless. I was sorry I couldn't explain why I'd been so careless with him last night. I was sorry that we'd kept our secret for nothing.

"So, what?" asked Jackson, tearing his eyes away from Zarine, his voice breaking. "We petition the Bureau for reinforcements?"

In all the times he'd hung out with us and Dad, I'd never heard Jackson Tormey discuss what we were or anything about our species, actually. Before now.

Dad let out a shaky breath. "We gather our own reinforcements."

They'd made a plan while I'd been asleep.

"But the Bureau, Tom," said Zarine.

"Let me worry about the Bureau. That route takes time we don't have."

I didn't understand everything, but I did understand that going without the Bureau's knowledge could be bad.

"I know how long these things can take," said Dad. "With one of our own dead and three missing, I won't waste any more time with the politics."

Dad dropped his arms and pressed his palms against the counter behind him. I don't think I'd ever seen him look uncomfortable once in my life.

"We do need Graham on our side," he said. Jackson nodded. Zarine chewed her thumbnail, looking at nothing. "He'll have to gather a group of those willing to fight with us. For now, we'll be petitioning the Letum Antea."

The *vampiria's* version of our Bureau.

"You've got to be kidding me." I sat back in my seat, ripping my hand through my hair.

"Jonah, I thought it would be best to keep you in the loop. Do not make me regret that decision."

I took a breath. He was right. I had to be on their side.

Jackson asked the question I was thinking. "I'm confused as to why we would involve the group that we believe is behind this."

"With the information Maddie provided—" Dad pointed a look at her. "I still would like to know how you came about that information, young lady. We think that this new research director might be employing her grim methods without the Letum Antea's knowledge. Erikson's death is further evidence that the Letum Antea has no hand in this."

"Why would they be above killing one of our kind to send us a message?" I asked, straining to keep my voice calm.

"And if we warn them, they'll just get their people lined up and ready to fight," said Jackson.

"We have no proof that the Letum Antea isn't aware of what she's doing and condoning it," Mom said.

So her and dad had already talked about this. They were relying on the fact that the Letum Antea would stand by the treaty.

I banked on my Dad having all the answers—we all did—but how could he justify this? We'd be working against ourselves, giving our position away before we made a move.

"This risk would be too great," he said. "The treaty would be null if they're allowing this to happen. If they find any truth in our claims, they could make her stand trial."

I felt like everything, every logical thought, was coming to me slowly and through layers and layers of padding.

"So, what now?" I asked, ready to actually do something.

Dad tapped his finger on the table. "We get Graham and make contact with the *vampiria*."

I felt helpless, knowing that we had to jump through all these hoops before we could *move*.

I got up from the table.

"There's something else, Jonah," said Mom.

My stomach felt like a rag that had been rung out. I turned to face them all.

"You will have to tell the clan you two are Kindred for this to work," said Mom, her arms crossed tightly over her chest.

They had to know why I'd never said anything. It wasn't that I didn't trust them, but that was *our* secret. It was the only way we could protect ourselves from separation.

This was exactly what made us break the rules over and over, and now we'd have to face it anyway. That didn't matter right now though. I'd take any risk to get Apollo back. To bring him home.

"The clan will need to understand how you know he's in danger," she said, putting a hand on my cheek before following Dad and the others.

I didn't see how the clan could choose not to help. How would any of them turn a blind eye to this with their own kind on the line? I could almost hear Apollo saying in my ear, *because one or two . . . or three of us don't matter in the big scheme of things. Especially those with no families to look out for them.*

25

Apollo

The only thing I had to tell that time was passing was by how frozen I was from sitting on the floor.

I tried to remember anything about those people in that lab that might be useful. Maybe next time they came in, I could talk to one of them. If they ever came back for me.

I stayed underneath the glass wall so they wouldn't see me and tapped the glass with a numb finger. I considered digging through the concrete.

The constant deafening static stopped. Then a cracking, hissing sound, like when the aide talked over the intercom at school.

"You'll never break it."

It was a woman's voice. I wondered if it was the one I'd heard in the clearing.

I still couldn't be sure that I hadn't fallen asleep and this was some sort of delirium. I pinched my arm with my nails. Felt that. But I could feel in dreams, too. I'd felt my heart soaring and then crashing. I'd felt desire—*god*, had I felt desire. I'd felt pain. I'd felt fear, too, in dreams, but not quite like this.

I tried to speak and failed, throat raw. I tried again. "Did you forget to pay your electric bill?"

"I've stripped your senses to weaken you."

I snorted. "I was doing that just fine on my own."

No answer, but the static didn't return. Like the line was still open.

I couldn't handle the silence again.

"My clan knows where I am." In this pitch black, I still couldn't be sure that I wasn't talking to a voice in my head.

"They haven't come yet," she said, almost like she believed me and wondered what was taking so long.

"Pretty thoughtless of you to let your experiments out to play. We made quick work of him, though, the one you were looking for." If it was Caterina Halsey, maybe I could piss her off, so she'd come talk to me in person. Maybe she'd turn a fucking light on and I'd have some modicum of a chance for escape. Or at least a fight.

I did not want to die like this.

I didn't want to die.

There was silence. Then light seared my eyes.

Well, that was easy.

I squinted, my vision blurred and not as responsive as I would have liked in a lion's den. The room was exactly what I had thought. A massive, concrete square. Except for the window behind me.

"Stand up." It sounded like a very calm, logical order. "Talk to me face to face."

I thought about telling her it would be a little difficult given that she'd had me in here like an animal without food or water, and so I was a little off my game. But it probably wasn't in my best interest to show all my cards.

I pushed myself up, willing everything in me to look composed. She was probably going to be the last person I saw before I died. I turned to face the glass.

It was her. The blonde woman Maddie had showed us on her laptop. The woman I'd seen on the road.

She didn't look like a teacher or a 60's pin-up anymore. Maybe it was the man's button up shirt, or her hair, which was no longer flawless. She looked like a slightly frazzled mom who just got the kids to bed and was about to settle in for a glass of wine.

Except for the part where she didn't look like a mom at all.

She tilted her head the slightest bit, like a bird of prey regarding its dinner. Not sapien. Not even *alive.* I fought to hold back a shudder. My instinct was to gather from the light so that I had some power at my disposal, but I also knew, instinctually, that she would sense it.

"That Judas of yours told me about you. I've had your number for a long time, Apollo."

Was she trying to intimidate me? I had other ideas at my disposal though. "We know what you're doing."

"You do?" A small smile played at her lips. It made her beautiful.

"We know about your daughter." Maybe I should have saved it. Maybe it was going to get me killed right now by the look on her face.

Her mouth twitched. What little conversational manner she had disappeared. I was right, nothing but death in that room.

"No one could possibly think it was my fault. I loved my daughter beyond everything," she said, like she was quietly defending herself to some unseen jury. Or I was the jury. She cared that I knew she hadn't hurt her daughter.

But just as she had flown off on that strange tangent, she was back to removed prison guard.

"You have interfered with my purpose here, Apollo Reid Tormey."

Ah, my wallet. I hated that she knew my name. I hated hearing her say it.

"I've been watching you since you drove by. That was foolish." She paused. "I know you killed my subject."

Was that a vampiris trait? The negative of a poker face. Why would anyone who had evolved to drink the blood of other creatures ever have to lie? Top of the food chain, right? You didn't see lions or sharks going around being accommodating with their prey.

We were predator and prey with only a glass wall separating us.

I had been hugging myself to stay warm. Now, I dropped my arms to make myself appear bigger.

"Don't flatter yourself. I cannot stand that," she said with none of the usual conversation markers, no movement of hands or mouth. Just flat speech from a featureless mannequin. "You are not here for killing my subject. They all die at some point or another. Since you fell into my lap, however, I will put you to good use. You will serve a greater purpose."

"Let me guess," I said. "A cure for our blood."

"You just know it all, don't you? I see youth has not changed much over the years, between species."

She leaned forward on her arms. She was so close to the glass. I wanted to be brave enough to walk right up to it, close enough to see the color of her eyes. Then I'd spend the rest of my life trying to forget. If I ever got out of here.

"It is an unfortunate turn of evolution that we've come to covet your blood so absolutely that it drives us mad. It was, unfortunately, the crux of El—my daughter's undoing," she said, stumbling on her daughter's name—Elizabeth? Eleanor? I couldn't see her using a trendy name.

"But then," said my captor. "That's where the problem began."

She pushed herself up. Her bare arms made me envy her inability to feel cold. You couldn't feel cold if you were dead, right?

"In my experience, it is those single-mindedly intent on helping you who hurt you."

I cleared my throat. "How do you figure?" Though I thought she might be onto something with that. Teachers. Parents. The clan. Jonah.

"Do you ever question your leaders, Apollo? Their ability to manage you, your loved ones, themselves?" Her voice sounded musing, but I was kind of flattered to be asked.

She wasn't looking at me, and that made me feel safe to answer. "Doesn't everyone? It's human nature to doubt and question."

She looked at me then, making my stomach clench.

"You would not gladly give your life to a cause?" she asked.

I didn't want to give anything away that could be used against me.

"You kind of flushed my free choice down the toilet already."

"You're very different from your companions."

"Companions," I repeated, feeling faint.

Plural. We were right.

She turned away, arms crossed. "Mr. Erikson came to me so dewy and idealistic."

"Yeah? And he's still a tool." I was too afraid to ask if Junior was still alive.

"I really have nothing against your kind. Well, now, I am not being entirely truthful. It hardly seems fair that one species should exist solely to be the scourge of another, does it not?"

Fear locked up my jaw.

"Nevertheless, my true fight is with my own kind."

"I don't understand." My throat was a desert.

"No, nor could you ever. But you don't have to. Once I develop a cure so that our kind are not reduced to slathering fools in your presence, I will hold a key."

"A key?"

"I hope to help people like my daughter. I will change how things work."

This is when it hit me. She actually believed what she was doing was good. And she needed my blood for it.

Exhaustion, hunger, fear, and adrenaline all won out against what I had hoped would be intimidating posture.

"It will be your time soon, Apollo Reid Tormey. Until then," she said, and the lights went off.

The static began again. I clawed at my ears to try to get it out.

I wasn't even hungry anymore. Just tired. And freezing. I didn't know if I felt weaker from that or having my main fuel source of magic suddenly taken away. How does someone in my position get comfortable enough to fall asleep in a lion's den? The answer is you don't.

I actually wanted to see her again. Maybe it was Stockholm syndrome. Or I just missed the light.

In here, darkness and light were completely literal. Before this, I was so poetic, so deep, and darkness was everything that wasn't Jonah. I couldn't think about him anymore though. It was like, you begged the universe for something to happen. You want it so bad, you need it, you'll die if this thing doesn't happen, but when the universe spits on your favorite Pumas and then pushes you on your ass, you just can't put your eggs in that basket anymore.

I tried to count seconds to mark the minutes, curling down a finger for each one, so I would have something that was real to hold onto in here, but I stopped. Because it didn't matter. Time didn't exist without anything to mark it by.

You'd think it would be easier to think in pure darkness. Instead, you can't separate thoughts from delusion. So when Philip Riley, a friend from kindergarten, showed up next to me, digging a stick into the concrete, asking if I wanted to come over for his birthday party, I said yes. When Gertie showed up, telling me that he who lies to himself will lose what he loves most, I just went with it.

I didn't know who 'he' was that lied to himself. Funny that I hadn't forgotten a single word of the fortunes she gave me. They'd felt like these heavy burdens I hadn't stopped carrying.

In darkness, he finds death.

If you took the two fortunes together, they fit like puzzle pieces. Jonah was the one who lied to himself and lost me. Though it wasn't his fault he was losing me. It was my own stupid fault. And now I would die here.

In darkness.

It was airtight, that prediction. Mostly, it was freeing. I was basically just waiting for someone to pull the plug.

At least I knew what this placed looked like now. There was some comfort in knowing it was empty, aside from me.

No. No monsters here. They're on the other side of this wall behind me.

The light came on, waking me out of an in-between sleep, the kind when your biology teacher is droning on about the anatomy of a cell, and you can still hear the lecture, but your chin slips off your palm, and you jerk back awake.

I massaged my neck as I scrambled up the wall and walked to the middle of the room—chamber? Cell?—to face her.

I turned to the window, like a dog rolling over to be warmed by the sun. But no warmth came from the light. Just Caterina. She looked like a Siberian queen, crossing snow drifts to get to her daughter. To save her. From what exactly? The blood song and her own broken mind? Or maybe her government, the Letum Antea. *Before death,* Maddie had said. And they had come for Caterina's daughter.

"I've deprived you of everything. What are you without your senses, Apollo Tormey?"

Ha. She was waiting for me to lose my mind.

"I was wondering the same thing." Maybe if she thought I'd given up, she'd lose interest in me.

"You have maintained yourself though. Why? What could someone as young as yourself have fueling such strength and fight?"

I wasn't even sure anymore.

But that was a lie.

Jonah, laughing, his light brown hair looking golden in the sun.

Dad nodding along as we jammed to Stairway to Heaven.

Mom running her fingers through my hair, telling me my magic tasted like stargazer lilies.

Caterina never looked away as she talked. Maybe all *vampiria* did this. Maddie would probably know. But usually, when you talk to someone, there's a lot of glancing around, looking down or to the side. Caterina's eyes never left my face.

"And yet," she said. "I keep coming back here."

"I would ask you to pull up a chair, have something to drink—" *Oof.* Wrong thing to say to this one.

She smirked though. I'm gonna count that as a win.

"You talk more than the others. You sound like Elise."

Elise.

The others.

"She was full of life, of wonder. And so, I am curious. What would draw her to you?"

Me? I wondered.

"Where does your magic come from?"

Ah, here it was. The elephant in the room.

"What does it smell like? Taste like?"

Huckleberry honey, I heard my mom's voice say.

"How strong could your pull be? You're, what, maybe seventeen years old?"

Excuse you. I'm going to be nineteen in nine and a half months.

For some reason, I didn't want her to know that I was underage, that I technically couldn't use magic. Though the point was moot.

"I can hardly believe I left cheese for the mice, and what do you know? It worked. It's quite humorous really, how easy it was."

"What cheese?" I asked. I hardly recognized the low, tortured baritone of my voice.

"Just the smallest scrap of nothing, and you two still found it. You truly are extraordinary."

Of course she would have been careful enough to thoroughly clean up after herself. The shirt from her escaped patient had been nothing but bait. How dumb could we be?

"Not so very loquacious now," she said.

"Maybe if you turned on the heat." My teeth were chattering and not just from the cold.

If Jonah—if no one had come for me yet in the days it had felt like I'd been here, then nobody was going to come. It would hurt less if I accepted that.

Halsey turned off the light, an abrupt end to our conversation. I stood there, heart pounding in the darkness, waiting for her to come back. But I felt too much like a dog pathetically waiting for his master to return.

I turned around and slid down the wall.

Something was different.

"I want to feel your blood song," she said, but it didn't come through the intercom. It sounded closer but muffled somehow. "I want to know what that madness feels like."

"I think you're already there," I said, voice cracking.

She was in here with me, in the dark.

Game over.

"I need to understand what Elise felt before the end. I would like to feel it with you, Apollo." She said it as simply as if she were asking me to help her pick out a new color for the walls of my cell.

She was going to kill me. I had no power to stop her.

It was good I got used to the idea of being alone before Halsey abducted my sorry ass. Why was I even fighting anymore? Maybe I wanted to feel it too. Let Halsey carry me to the end. What would it be like? To just let someone else lead, even if it was to death.

Then the light came on. When I saw her, my flight instinct kicked back in. Yeah, I wasn't inviting her to dinner anytime soon.

I didn't dare look around for the way that she must have come in. I couldn't take my eyes off her. She had on a gas mask, like the ones I'd seen before, working above me. She hadn't worn one behind the glass.

I watched, paralyzed, as she took it off and dropped it to the floor. She didn't do anything for a moment. She was as still as death.

Then her chest expanded. She was smelling the air.

The mask protected them from our scent, I realized. That was why the one at the club had worn one. And the ones who had been taking my blood.

"Yes, I can smell it. It's beautiful," she said, her eyes like a cobra's eyes now, ready to wring the life out of the mouse. She took a step closer.

I stepped back.

"Oh no. Please don't. We haven't even reached the capper." She definitely looked like she was losing control.

All my gross motor skills were useless. Breathing had already kind of started to fail me.

"You were wondering about your friend, weren't you? The one you were looking for." She stopped, looking like she was having difficulty speaking or swallowing.

How did she know that? Talbot? The traitorous bastard.

"Someone you love," she said.

I stopped. My head pounded like a tribal drum.

"Gilberto Sanchez?"

No.

I jumped when the sound of screaming came through the intercom. The same scream I heard during the Discernment. Mystery solved.

"They say it tastes better with fear," she said with a furrowed brow, almost apologetic. She nodded her head, glancing behind me.

I turned as a massive form hit the glass.

Junior.

He mouthed my name. He was almost unrecognizable. All sharp cheekbones and sunken eyes. She had been starving him, just like she was starving me. But he'd been gone so much longer and it showed.

I thought about how I had felt here and how I was someone who was used to being lonely. Junior was different. He was special and so loved.

"His appearance startles you. Yes. I was curious to see if you would still have power without any food. Turns out, *magikalia* have an unending supply of magic."

"It isn't unending," I said, my voice cracking, unable to take my eyes off him. I walked up to the glass.

'Te amo,' he mouthed.

I cracked. My eyes flooded so that I couldn't see his face for a moment.

"It isn't?" she asked, her voice returning to the cool, detached scientist she was when the glass separated us.

"It fades if we don't gather enough. It kills us if we hold on too long. We're made to only hold it for a finite amount of time. It's like radiation, when you hold onto it for too long."

He must have noticed Halsey behind me, because he threw his whole body at the glass again, beating it. He was crying.

Por dios. On my way.

He'd come for me, because he cared about me. All because I'd fallen into Talbot's trap set for a lonely loser just like me.

I reached up for his ring. I wanted him to see it, to know Jade had looked for him, his mom, me. That it had led me to him. But it was gone, taken from me with everything else.

"He was cut from a sturdy lot, that one," she said. "Over the course of his time here, I've taken four pints. And look at him. Still so robust."

He didn't look robust to me at all. I hated what she'd taken from him. Drained his blood and magic and stripped him of everything and he. Still. Fought.

She shouldn't have given me that idea.

An older vampiris came into the room with Junior. I only caught a glimpse of his face—ice white skin, deep circles under his eyes, black stubble—before he stepped behind Junior.

I beat my fists on the glass.

"Junior!"

The vampiris barred an arm over his chest, pulling his head back to an ugly angle, before latching onto his neck. I reeled back like I'd been hit.

Halsey's voice rose over my cries. "The cure comes first, so I have had to keep a controlled mind. But I've been missing the key component in my study of your kind: I should know why my daughter died."

I wanted to destroy her for throwing Junior's life away, for taking away mine. I had to fight otherwise everything Junior went through to get to me was pointless.

Maybe if I could get her under the power of the blood song, she'd be vulnerable enough to miss a step.

I turned to face her and opened my arms.

She came at me fast. I felt every pierce and rip of her biting into my neck with her face buried, smelling, sucking.

Vampiria could drink from anywhere probably, but the neck, that was prime territory right there. How easily the skin tore open for her. Digging down past my muscle and tendons must have been more complicated, because it was excruciating. All of my muscles twitched helplessly. My knees gave. She held me up.

She'd lost all her scientific cool. Only instinct left. Talbot's cause was pointless. We couldn't ever let them have a cure, because they'd still be animals.

The cold encroached, taking every limb, every finger and every toe with it. It was a horrifying feeling, having everything in your body sucked out so quickly through such a small crack.

I didn't want to be alone. What I wanted didn't matter, because the darkness came from every direction, just like the cold.

26

Jonah

We fanned out, approaching the clearing I had led them to. I could feel Apollo getting closer.

We were here, finally.

Graham Jones had stood in our living room hours before, after I'd had to give up my secret.

"Why didn't you come to any of us?" he'd asked. "We could have helped you."

Would they have helped without the threat of Apollo's death? Or would we have been separated?

My eyes snagged on the farm house now, golden and sagging in the late afternoon light, like a dream. The sun would go down in a couple of hours.

"He's in there," I said.

As we got closer, keeping my shit together was a struggle. But I had to. Dad had made it clear that if I wasn't required on this mission to save Apollo's life, being his Kindred, I'd be at the back of the charge if I'd even be here at all.

Someone threw up a Barrier as we all moved toward the house. Everyone pooled their magic.

Dad to my left, Mom to my right, walking a little in front of me so that I almost kept stepping on the back of her boots.

She refused to stay behind, though Dad had asked more than once. She finally gave him a look that was usually reserved for us kids. She didn't even say anything, and he had grabbed her hand and said, "Okay. Okay, you're right. We're stronger together."

"So we're just going to knock on the front door like we're borrowing a cup of sugar?" I had to clench my jaw to keep my teeth from chattering with every word.

Dad scanned the clearing, his eyes seeing far more than any sapien's could see in the fading daylight. He finally looked at me.

"It's politics, Son. Not an action movie."

I knew just how much politics, because Dad and Apollo's parents had to convince Graham to do this without Bureau approval.

"It's Apollo's life!" I argued.

It had taken everything in me not to lose it while we wasted all that time. In response to my outburst, Dad put his hand on my shoulder and pulled me back.

Mom paid us a sidelong glance walking ahead with the others. I jerked to follow her, but Dad held me back.

"I know you're dealing with a lot at this moment, but I need you to focus. You're letting your emotions take control right now, and fear excites them."

He was right. I needed to keep a clear head. I had to be able to go beyond myself to experience whatever Apollo was feeling.

Our defense instructor, Steve, was ex-military, which I could see was really paying off right now as he directed some people to move around the house in groups.

We approached the door with three others. I was in awe of how many had come together to help Apollo. Quinn Young's parents were here. Danish and his crew. Zarine's friend, an older woman with silver blonde dreadlocks whose magic snapped at the air like a whip.

The others pressed up against the walls surrounding the door. They'd heard us anyway. The beating hearts were a dead giveaway.

I could hear, feel, and taste Apollo's magic stronger now.

Dad put his hand against my chest. It steadied something inside of me. He banged on the door with his other hand.

The smell of old, damp paper filled my nostrils. And . . . oil? And something else. Something deeper and colder. Something ancient.

The door opened a crack to reveal the face of a middle-aged man. He had kind of a hooked nose and heavy eyelids. Everything in me reared back. This was a vampiris. There was no doubting that. His flashing glance took us all in. He opened the door a little wider, glanced down at Dad's gun. He laughed.

"Now there's a sight." He sounded like William Shatner as Don Carter in The Twilight Zone. "I could snap your neck before you even pulled the trigger."

"And I can turn your body inside out with nothing but a thought," Dad said in a dry tone, but his hand against my chest was tense as stone.

"At the expense of every vampiris here bearing down on you. Ah," he said with a slow, rolling laugh. "And a man of my age knows a fine vintage when it comes his way."

This was so far from the monster that came after Apollo and me in the orchards.

I realized he sounded like a man in a show from the 60s, because that was probably his heyday. His age was probably the only reason we weren't being charged right now.

"Hence, the gun," Dad said. "We're here for our people. Turn them over and this will be simple."

"We don't make a habit of playing with the local indigenous," the man said, sneering at the others behind Dad. His eyes fell on me, and Dad's hand pushed harder against my chest.

"Says the cannibal," said Dad.

"I'll speak with my superior," the man said and shut the door.

Dad kicked it.

Though he had spoken so calmly to Dad, the vampiris turned around with unreal speed, his face almost feral.

Dad had told me before we came he wanted me to stay back and let the elders take point. I wasn't trained. I wasn't old enough or experienced enough. As he was saying all of this to me, I knew there was no way in hell that I wouldn't fight. But now that I was faced with the reality of a fight with our undead predators, my nerves faltered.

The rest of our clan poured into the space around us and the walls of the strangely quiet place came alive.

Facts came to me in flashes. Four vampiris in this room. More came in through a room at the far end, and from the balcony around the top, running and jumping off. Everything had been stripped from the house. I could see ghosts on the walls where all of the shelving and pictures once stood. Doors were gone. Windows covered. Though it was still light outside, we could just barely see with the flashlights we carried and the bit coming in through the half-open front door.

The sounds of physical exertion, of our people fighting, their heavy breathing and grunts of pain, echoed off the empty walls.

Our movements were uneven, clumsy, while the *vampiria* had speed and strength on their side. Despite our enhanced senses and the magic pounding through our veins, we were still heavy, *living* bodies. And aside from Steve Murphy, no one here was military trained.

Then, gun shots, impossibly loud.

I saw an opening and ran to the door at the far end, praying I wouldn't get shot. Flashlights strobed against the walls, making the floor seem uneven. Mom screamed for me.

As I got closer to the door, Apollo started fading. I took a few steps back, trying to feel him again.

Something grabbed me, then I was flying into one of the living room walls. Pain stabbed up and down my entire side. White lights and black stars filled my eyes. My hands fumbled for the safety on the gun Dad had given me. Though he and Mom had taught us how to use guns safely, I'd prayed I wouldn't have to.

A vampiris dressed in all black knelt in front of me. She was younger than me—physically, anyway. She looked like Black Widow. She lurched into me, and the pain in my ribs knocked the wind out of me. She ripped out my hair as she was pulled away.

I looked up to see Zarine's friend, the woman with dreads. I'd never noticed her before tonight. Sweat poured down her face. Her eyes were bright and alive. She plunged a knife into the girl's eye socket and set her on fire. I had no idea where she'd pulled the magic from for that. There were no lights, no electricity it seemed.

Something hummed below my feet though.

"Come on," she said, helping me up. "We gotchya, kid."

"Thank you, Gertie," said Mom, appearing with Dad and Steve, out of breath. They'd somehow cleared the room.

As I stood, Apollo faded again.

"He's down. He's—" I wasn't breathing right again. Not now. "He's underground or something."

"We'll find a way down," said Dad. "Should be a cellar door somewhere."

The rest of the clan moved toward the hallway.

"I know it's hard," said Mom. "But concentrate. Where is he, babe?"

I stopped and took a breath, ignoring the stabbing sensation in my side. I could feel him, like a beacon of cool blue light. I threw some of my magic, gathering again the moment it left me, waiting for it to echo back.

There.

"Over here!"

I ran to an open doorway in the kitchen.

"Wait, Jonah!"

I don't know who yelled it.

A man grabbed me by the neck but let go in almost the same instant, hands going up to his head. I could feel the magic in the air so I knew it was beyond his control. I could still feel his bruising grip squeezing my throat. Someone set him on fire, and with my ears ringing, I realized the smell of the burning girl was still in my nostrils.

I pulled energy from the burning *vampiria* and the presence of the clan. I was shaking everywhere. Whatever I had expected, it wasn't this. I only hoped none of our side had fallen.

Dad and Steve led the way down the cellar stairs. I kept checking behind to make sure everyone was accounted for. Mom, Gertie, and more people with Graham behind us.

As we reached the bottom of the stairs, we could hear the others were fighting for their lives. For Apollo's.

I felt him expand inside my chest as we took the last couple steps, closer to him.

I've almost got you, I thought.

I clutched the rickety banister and threw up over the side. My eyes were burning. The burning bodies maybe. The restless, all-consuming magic in fire filled the air with its cloying heat. Maybe the whole building was going up. I pulled from it.

When we opened the metal door at the far end of the basement, we were blinded, darkness chased away by sterile fluorescent lighting.

It was a lab bigger than the house above. There were four vampiris behind glass walls who looked up from what they were doing as though they hadn't heard anything outside the doors. They put down their implements and emerged from their glass rooms. One of them came at us, his lab coat flying at his sides. He jumped off the wall and kicked Gertie down.

I was starting to see that these things who looked mostly sapien were more like insects or weightless animals.

I jumped on him from behind as he stood over her. He swung around, flinging me off. I was seriously tired of flying into shit.

I stood up and all the magic I'd gathered blew out of me, knocking them all to the ground. One turned to dust, scaring the hell out of me. It was like I'd incinerated her from the inside out.

Apollo's magic pulsed, faintly, but I'd know it anywhere. We were getting closer.

I found a small room that kind of looked like a sound studio. There was a table with a broken window above it. Then I saw him, on the other side of it, laying in a cement room. I climbed onto the table, ready to leap into the room, but something pulled me down. I fell to the floor, hitting the back of my head on the hard ground.

I was face to face with a woman under the table. It was her. Face covered in blood, Caterina Halsey looked high.

"Elise, I hear you!" She was looking right through me.

I noticed someone else underneath her, facedown in a hospital gown. He was big with shaggy black hair. Not Apollo.

Caterina's face twisted. "You smell like him," she said. She lunged at me, but Dad tackled her.

I clambered on the table again. My ribs felt like they were stabbing me from the inside.

The temperature changed drastically when I got through the window. I thought I'd be able to see my breath if there was more light.

I gathered Apollo into my lap. He was all bloody and so cold, I wouldn't have known if we were too late if I hadn't felt my magic reaching out for his.

"Be careful," Mom said. "If he has a neck injury . . ."

"Mom." Tears filled my eyes. "He's not . . . he's . . ."

"Jonah?" His voice, usually warm and a little raspy, sounded like dried leaves crunching underfoot.

"We're here. We're going to get you home."

His neck had an open wound. I took off my sweater and wrapped it over the wound, tying the sleeves under his arm. Hopefully the pressure would stop some of the bleeding.

"You're here," he said.

I pushed his matted hair from his forehead. Being able to touch him again felt like touching starlight. I nearly shattered with relief.

"With the whole Calvary," I said.

"I'm tired, Jonah."

"It's okay. You can sleep now."

All the weakness I'd felt up to now was burned away with him against me. I stood up with him in my arms.

Through the cutout into this concrete room, I could see Dad blasting Halsey with magic. He drew and drew, dimming the lights, making their machines cut off and on, causing the whole place to shake, and she kept running into it, the flesh on her face starting to flake away like burnt paper.

"Junior's dead," Apollo said, just above a whisper.

Was that Junior I'd left beneath Halsey?

Dad limped to the window to help me get Apollo through.

I needed to get Apollo away from the body of his friend. I wanted to see him in his bed at home with his parents who were going crazy without him. I wanted to warm his freezing skin, to hear him tease me, to see his eyes, green like sea glass, looking at me.

Dad gripped my arm to help me over while holding Apollo.

Mom leaned against one of the table legs. Slowly, my brain processed what my eyes were seeing: Halsey, hair black with char, holding her there. My vision tunneled.

She had my mom, and I was going to tear her apart.

"You've destroyed my work," said Halsey.

She shouldn't have even been able to talk.

"Now you know what your daughter felt," Apollo said against my chest.

"I could have saved you all," said Halsey, either ignoring Apollo or not hearing him.

Mom's eyes locked on Dad, like she was trying to tell him something.

"Like this? By imprisoning our people . . . doing tests on their blood?" Dad was barely holding himself together.

"Ending world hunger by causing a blight is no cure," Mom said, and it sounded just like Maddie.

"It appears as though our new director had plans of her own."

We looked up to find a short man had come into the lab. His olive skin and grey-green eyes the color of moss on ruins made me feel a bizarre tug of attraction that sickened me. I knew what he was, because I could feel the suck, all my magic and life being slowly drained and something cold snaked through the air.

Halsey tensed in fear, but the man kept his distance.

"Lael," Dad said. His voice was as taut as a guitar string. I remembered Apollo changing his strings, twisting the pegs tighter and tighter, until sometimes one snapped.

The stranger nodded, acknowledging Dad in return.

Lael turned to where Halsey was gripping Mom. "Caterina Roselyn Halsey, Née Conti," he said. His voice was smooth and controlled. "Turned in 1923 by Armelio Davide Pesco." I heard the words, but they were like a foreign language. He sighed. "I had higher hopes for you, Dr. Halsey."

Halsey didn't seem to hear him. She kept staring down at Mom. At her neck, but some invisible leash held her back. Dad knelt down. He was freaking out. I knew the exact feeling.

"Let her go," I said, the threat shaking my voice.

"Jonah, no," said Mom, glancing at Lael.

"Ah. Now I see," Halsey said. "You and that one are bound . . . by your . . . magic? How quaint." And she smiled like it actually was. The dried blood on her chin, or maybe it was her fried skin, cracked.

"Let her go," said Lael. "Come to me, Caterina. No more blood will be spilled."

"I will not come to heel like a dog," she spat, but she didn't move. It was like she was stuck between wanting to attack my mother and being unable to. We'd learned about bloodfathers and bloodmothers of *vampiria* covens, and how they could access the thoughts of their children. Maybe they could exert some sort of physical control over them too.

I closed my eyes and took in a burning breath. It didn't choke me this time. My magic called to Apollo's, and I threw Caterina off my mom.

She flew back underneath the table, a green fire surrounding her like a corona. Pale green, like Caribbean water, like Apollo's eyes. Mom ran to Dad. He wrapped his arms around her, heedless, for a moment, of everything around us.

"You need to leave," said Lael. "Now."

I didn't understand why he was letting us leave, but I wasn't about to question it. Not when his presence weighed so heavily. We made our way to the door as he strode to Halsey.

Before we left, I turned to see him drinking from her. It reminded me of the one Apollo and I had seen above in the orchards. The whole body sucking.

We emerged from underground into a smoke screen. I pulled my sweater up with my teeth to cover Apollo's face.

"Look for gas masks!" I said, remembering the one at the club.

The living room was completely engulfed on one side. It was taking much longer to burn than I would have guessed.

Fireproofing. Of course they would fireproof a building. Their bodies were like kindling.

I looked around, eyes burning and watery.

I ran as hard as I could for the door with the smoke saturating everything.

I had a sinking feeling as I emerged into the sweet, clear cold air.

"Zarine," I yelled. I don't know if I was calling out to her or calling out to someone to find them. It was chaos, everyone coming out of the house from different exit points.

Dad and Mom came up right behind me.

"I'll grab a mask and find them," Dad said, squeezing my shoulder.

The dew on the ground seeped into the knees of my jeans. I still held him. I couldn't let him go, though my arms screamed too for oxygen.

"Apollo," I said to let him know I was here, but I was watching our people gathering. Were we really going to make it out of here?

Then I saw Zarine and Jackson. She had blood all over her. She searched the crowd and when she saw me and Apollo on the ground, her face broke open. She started sobbing, coming toward us. I couldn't see where the blood was coming from, but she seemed to be moving okay.

She stared down at him, her hands shaking as she pulled my sweater away from his mouth, revealing clean honey skin below the mask of soot. He stayed motionless, leaning against me.

"He's okay," I told her. I was trying to assure myself too. "I thought you knew I was leading us to him."

His eyes were deep in shadow, his face concerned even while unconscious. If I hadn't been able to feel his heartbeat in my entire body, I would have probably been freaking out.

"I wasn't thinking, Jonah."

"Are you hurt?" I asked.

I couldn't stop staring at all that red smeared on her shirt.

"Oh." Her face fell. "Gertie. She was . . . "

The woman who saved me. "Is she okay?"

"No, Honey. I was with her when . . . "

I couldn't speak.

Jackson appeared and stared down at Apollo like he was in a trance.

I leaned over Apollo and whispered that he was going home and that I would see him soon.

Zarine looked at me with teary eyes.

"I see how important you are to each other."

"Wait," I said and unclasped Apollo's cuff, putting it back on him. I wanted him to know I'd found him.

She nodded at Jackson. He leaned forward to take Apollo from my arms. But Lael watched from a few yards away, the building going up behind him. I pulled Apollo closer, getting to my feet.

"That was quite a display of willpower," he said. "I am impressed."

He looked between us like we were rats in a maze. Others stood in a wide semicircle behind him, a couple wearing gas masks, some not. I could instantly see that they weren't ours. They were too still. Too at ease with the smell of bodies burning and the cracking of the wood beams giving way. Too aware of the blood we all wore.

"We warned the Letum Antea we would be getting our people back," said Dad. He and Mom looked prepared to fight again.

"So you did. I was informed a little late. I regret that you had to be victims of that radical, Halsey. But I'm here now in good will."

"We've already lost people." Was Dad threatening this asshole?

"I see that. Casualties are too frequent in battles that aren't theirs to fight." I couldn't tell if he was patronizing us. "What of our death tally? And our research," Lael said, looking at the building. The flames licked at the air. The sun still hadn't set, and the sky all pink and orange. Purple like the shadows under Apollo's eyes.

Lael pulled his attention from the facility, his eyes as hungry as the flames. They landed on Dad. He was waiting for an answer.

A group emerged from the back of the house. Two of our clan with a girl between them, each of her arms draped around a shoulder. Lena.

"I hope you're not implying you knew what was going on here," said Graham. I was surprised. He'd seemed so resistant to doing anything without the Bureau's blessing, and now he was like a freaking outlaw.

"Why is that?" asked Lael.

"The treaty," said Dad. "It's pointless if one of the parties violates the territory lines, let alone abducts the other's people."

"As I said, I am here in good will. I was not aware of the late Ms. Halsey's gross violations." He didn't look very sorry though.

Another small group from the clan came around the side of the building, carrying someone—a body. I saw the dreads, bright and grey. Gertie.

Lael's eyes came alive on them.

"She's elderly. She has no family left—I can smell that." He turned back to Dad and Graham. "Let us harvest her blood. We could call this even."

"No," I said. She saved my life and died for Apollo. There was no way in hell I was leaving without her.

"She's coming home with us," Zarine said, her voice even and clear. "She's blood, and that is family."

Lael shifted at the word 'blood.' "I see. You desire to bury her and mark the resting place."

None of us said a word.

"Or, I can heal her," he said, eyes devouring the scene. "Make amends for the trouble our wayward director has caused."

"She's dead," I said.

Lael looked at me. I felt cold down to the hollow of my bones.

"No matter." He stepped forward.

"Get back!" I gathered so much so fast that I could see it hit everyone like a shockwave.

"You're not going to want to do that," he said.

His face abruptly changed. Like the one who had been at the door, how he had changed into an animal.

Lael looked at Dad. "Shouldn't you be teaching him that?"

One of the others standing behind Lael, who had been still as a statue up to this point, shifted.

"Hold your ground," Lael ordered, barely raising his voice. All of them appeared to be held by the same invisible control Lael exerted over them. "The Bureau will be hearing from me."

Dad didn't acknowledge the threat.

"Leave now before you can't," Lael said.

Zarine and Dad closed ranks on either side of me. I knew Jackson and Mom were close. I could feel them. I could feel everyone's magic. I was terrified *they* would feel it too as we walked back to our cars on the road.

27

Jonah

I hated giving speeches in class. I'd feel sick to my stomach the entire week leading up to it. I always anticipated the worst. That I'd be called out for knowing nothing, for being an idiot, for being a liar.

So as Dad drove me to the trial, I obsessively went over it all in my head. Since Zarine would stand trial for Apollo, she and I had sat with a counselor and went over it all. Convincing the Bureau that we had to break the laws we did still felt like it was mostly my responsibility. Since I'd actually been there.

Dad put his hand on my knee, which was bouncing up and down. "You're shaking the car," he said.

God, I missed Apollo. It had been two days since I'd put him in the back of his parents' Blazer.

Mom and Dad weren't letting me talk to him. They'd taken my phone away and put me on house arrest almost immediately after we'd gotten home from Orville's. And that was fine. I'd basically just laid in bed imagining all the worst-case scenarios. But this was the worst case. It was exactly what we'd been afraid of and it was tearing me apart that I couldn't be there for him.

I'd had a lot of coffee. So much that my mom cut me off and then Macy hid my water tumbler full of contraband because I was being 'rather irritable'. Which was fair; my blood type was pretty much blonde roast at this point. It didn't help with the ball of anxiety in my chest when Dad woke me up to leave for the trial.

But I had a plan. Last night, I knocked on Maddie's door. When she let me in, I had laid on her bed like old times as she looked down at me, biting the skin around her thumb nail.

"What am I going to do?"

She had closed the door, leaning against it. "There is a way you guys can be together."

I sat up.

"I don't even know if they do it anymore," she warned. "You can ask for a Leveling Sentence. If you both chose it, I don't think they would need to separate you."

But our magic was literally bound together. I didn't understand how not separating was going to be an option if we could still throw before coming of age.

"How is that possible?"

She took a deep breath. "It was in that book Apollo gave you. Didn't you read it?"

"The Kindred book? I didn't finish it."

"Right. So, the Leveling sentence would bind your magic for a specified amount of time."

The bed felt like it swayed underneath me. "I didn't even know that was possible." I vaguely remembered that but I assumed it had been embellished.

She gave me a look like 'of course you didn't.'

"How much time?"

"Are you serious about this, Jonah?"

"How much time?"

"I don't know. It varies case by case, depending on the severity, I guess."

Why did it feel like I was trying to sculpt stone to get her to say something?

I didn't want to know this answer. Not really. "What's the longest you found?"

"Ten years."

"Holy . . ." My legs went wobbly and I slid off the edge of the bed onto the floor.

We'd live like sapiens for an entire decade. But we'd get to stay together.

"Well, fifty years in one case, but that was an extreme case. And over a century ago."

"Stop. Just stop," I said, grabbing her trashcan to hold between my legs. I felt like I was going to be sick.

"You guys kind of put the entire treaty in jeopardy, so one way or another, they have to make an example of you."

"Okay, I get it. I'm pretty much doomed either way."

She took the trashcan and put it back. I dropped my head between my knees. The bed frame dug into my back.

She put her hands over my elbows. "It'll be a huge sacrifice. But you just have to ask yourself, is he worth it?"

What if Apollo didn't choose the same? Or worse, what if we weren't given a choice at all?

"What would it feel like, do you think? What if we were to run into a situation like the one at Orville's again? What if we run into *Lael* again?" I'd told her everything that night when we got home, and I'd finally convinced her to stop hugging me. I ran a shaking hand down my face. This was far too much to process on a handful of hours of sleep.

"You'll just have to keep your heads down and not be the cavalier little desperados you've been for the past couple months, won't you?"

"Giving this up to stay together . . . it's the mature choice, right?" I didn't know why I was even asking, but I wanted to know what she thought before I went and asked to be cut off from my magic to stay with Apollo.

I'd be asking for this in front of Dad. I remembered Deschamps and Perron. Kindreds were often in love. Shame and guilt tore at me. Shame for my dad thinking I might be gay and guilt that I would even care about that right now. I was going to have to face that shame down if I wanted to be with Apollo. I couldn't hide anymore.

"Does it seem like it's going to suck?" Maddie had asked.

"Well, yeah."

"Then it's the mature choice. I've seen you get through harder things, Jonah." Awkwardly, she rubbed my back. "You're stronger than you think."

In the passenger seat of the Tahoe, I felt very small as we drove farther from San Alvarez. I took out the penny Miles had given me before we left.

"This is my lucky penny. I found it at school. It kept me from getting beat up by Caison Moore. Keep it in your pocket."

"Thanks, M."

Miles and Macy had never been bothered by being lumped together with their joint nickname. They were never bothered by constantly being in one another's presence. Apollo and I had always been that way, since day one. I would have gladly spent every day and night at his house or with him at mine. There was something new between us now that needed to be acknowledged. I was too afraid to let myself fantasize about it. But first, I needed to protect it to find out if it could work. If *we* could work.

"Dad?"

"Hm?" He looked over his shoulder to change lanes.

I'd been thinking of my dad as this barrier when he could have helped us all this time. He wanted to help me, which was . . . well, it should have been obvious—he's my dad. But I'd been too afraid because our Kindredship had been so bound up in this secret of killing the vampiris and all of our own shame about the situation—anyway, it was complicated.

But now it was all out there.

Mostly out there.

"I want to be with Apollo." I thought it would be so hard to say the words, but it was the easiest thing in the world.

By the way he looked over at me, not like I was some kid that didn't know anything, but like he was proud of who I was becoming, he knew exactly what I meant.

"I know, Son."

Relief rushed through me, knocking the wind out of me. I laid my head back and closed my eyes, rubbing the penny between my fingers.

When he pointed out the building, it reminded me of the old records building. My legs felt detached from my body as we walked up. Dad pulled open one of the big carved doors, and when I stepped inside, I felt like an inverted image of Tom Clarke, walking down these halls. The law breaker. The vampiris-killer. The aberrant son.

The off-white hallway and harder-than-stone benches had to be the most depressing thing I'd ever seen.

"Do you want anything?" Dad asked. "Restroom? Some water?"

My dad's solution to every possible ailment, even, apparently, a trial for my freedom, was water. I shook my head, not trusting myself to speak.

"All you have to do is tell the truth, Jonah. It will be tough. They're going to hold you to a list of charges, but just keep your cool."

With the speeches, I had to walk straight to the front of the class before my thoughts won and I ran for the door. I opened the door before I could run away.

My first impression was that the whole thing looked exactly like the courthouses on those mid-morning judge shows. Familiar faces stared at me from the audience. People who came to help us save Apollo and the wolves. *Lena and Junior,* I reminded myself. Graham next to Zarine in the front. I'd never seen that expression on her face. She looked so rigid. Mad, I realized. Which was worrying.

Hector Garcia, the Bureau President sat at the podium up front with six others. Maybe it was the essence of what the Bureau was, a body who managed our species (or maybe that Apollo and I had essentially been breaking the law since we were fifteen), but I'd always been a little wary of President Garcia. Or at least my idea of him. Now that he stood as the gatekeeper to my freedom, to being with Apollo, I desperately tried to see something I could like. He looked nice, actually. He had glasses on his round face, something you don't usually see among *magikalia,* because our eyes didn't age as fast as sapiens' did. I wondered how old he was.

Behind his glasses, his large brown eyes passed over us.

"Good morning, Brother Clarke."

"Good morning, President Garcia."

His gaze rested heavy on me.

"I know it was a long drive, so we'll try to be expedient."

That couldn't be good, right? Dad's face betrayed nothing.

"We have some difficult business to sort through today. Clan Leader Jones provided sparse detail regarding the evening in Orville Orchards. And so here we are, at the trial for Jonah Clarke. As a youngling, Jonah Clarke is joined by his father Thomas Clarke who will stand trial with Graham Jones at a future date. Is that understood?"

Dad nudged me.

"Yes," I said.

"You have committed more than one criminal act according to our laws, laws put in place to protect the integrity and safety of our species."

I nodded, then realized I should answer aloud (for the record?). "Yes."

"The charges are withholding a Kindred bond, which encompasses illegal use of underage magic, and crossing the boundaries of our territory. Were there any witnesses to the event in question, in which you used magic?"

"No," I said. "Well, a vampiris. We used magic when he attacked us." *But he's dead.* I was already royally screwing this up.

"Attacked?" said Garcia, as though this was news. "Tell me exactly what transpired."

I felt like I told it all out of order, like the pieces weren't fitting together right. The pressure to explain, to prove, without a shadow of a doubt, that we had been following a trail was agonizing.

"That is . . . quite honestly, incredible," said Garcia. He stared at me for a moment longer than was comfortable before looking down at my file or whatever.

"Let us move to the genesis of the hunches that the Letum Antea had taken members of your clan in custody."

Dad explained that things I assumed Maddie had told him. That we thought Caterina had to have been working as a rogue agent. Garcia's face changed minutely. Maybe the Bureau had been keeping tabs on her too, I thought, hopeful.

"If you will recall, President Garcia, I spoke with the Bureau a week ago about what was happening in our territory. The Bureau chose to let it play out. The Bureau's inaction should be also be taken into account before meting out punishment to my son and his Kindred."

Garcia nodded, and surprisingly did not look mad. "Unfortunately, prior to the dire circumstances, Mr. Clarke still broke the law."

I clenched my fists at my sides. I couldn't believe he was still so focused on our bond.

"And you knew of this bond, Brother Clarke, and chose not to bring it forward to the Bureau with which you have been employed almost a decade?"

"He didn't know," I said.

Dad lifted his hand for me to wait.

"I didn't know," he said. "Not for sure. I think if you review my records, you will come to see how that hunch might have been possible."

I looked up at him. What did he have in his records?

He looked down at me. "I had hoped he would come to me on his own. However, he and his Kindred were afraid of separation, as any Kindreds at their age and with their intimacy would be."

Garcia nodded. "Yes, we've reviewed your file and see you are already familiar with such a dynamic."

Dad knew someone else who was Kindred?

"Putting aside the question of Brother Clarke's innocence, everyone needs to understand the purpose of those laws. Do you see how this coincidence of Kindredship results in arrogant, impetuous decisions?"

I thought of the broken glass and Halsey on top of the wreckage. I remembered the spine-chilling sight of Apollo alone on the concrete floor of that room.

"Without our Kindredship," I said, my voice surprisingly even. "Halsey would have killed Apollo. Once I was near enough, he was capable of protecting himself. She would have gotten away with everything she was doing and likely would have kept abducting our clansmen. We helped expose her to the Letum Antea, who made sure we got out of there alive."

Garcia stared at me. I took his silence as an opening.

"With all due respect, Sir, if Kindredship hadn't been so stigmatized, if there was more support in place for people who are Kindreds, we wouldn't have been so afraid to come forward." I looked at each face behind the podium. Maybe I felt like they should take a little more responsibility for their unrealistic laws.

Dad put his hand on my shoulder and squeezed once.

"Rather than be separated from my Kindred," I said. "I want the Leveling Sentence."

"Jonah," said Dad, appalled.

My stomach turned, and I worried that Maddie might have been wrong. Maybe this meant something else.

The room broke out in discussion. Garcia turned to the other Bureau members at his sides.

Dad pinched the bridge of his nose. "Maddie," he said under his breath.

"That is an archaic practice that we have not used since before the turn of the century," said Garcia. "Before separating Kindreds became standard." He looked at me like he didn't know how I would have heard about it, like he had underestimated me.

I waited, pulse fluttering like a hummingbird in my throat.

"Given the severity of such a punishment and further, the impossibility of committing the same crimes, I believe implementing a Bind until you are of age will suit."

They were going to do it. They were going to take my magic away. My knees turned to jelly. I had to hold onto the podium. Two and a half years. It wasn't as bad as the worst case Maddie had brought up, but it was still unfathomable. And why did 'Bind' sound so much worse than a 'Leveling Sentence?'

Dad turned to me. "Think about this, Jonah. It is not a decision to take lightly."

"I have. I accept the punishment," I said.

"That's a brave decision, Mr. Clarke. You must be a very good friend," said President Garcia. Strangely enough, that didn't make me feel any better. "We'll break for the time being while my cabinet and I deliberate."

My heart was pounding. Before I could even process what was happening, everyone was standing.

In the hallway, I leaned back against the cool wall, pulling up my sleeves, forgetting that they were buttoned. Mom made me dress nice for this. Garcia didn't care that I got straight A's, so why would he care if I was wearing a band T-shirt?

"Jonah," said Dad. I could tell he wanted to talk me out of it. I tried to look confident and assured, but I was tired. It was like everything that had been pushing on me was finally releasing its pressure.

"I know how much you love him—"

"I won't leave him." I said, ignoring the heat in my face. I gestured toward the door, feeling nauseated. "Besides I already asked for it."

I just wanted it to be over with.

"I stand by your decision, Son, however miserable it will be for you. And it will be miserable, Jonah. Magic is what you are."

"I'm also Apollo's Kindred. Being without him would be worse."

I expect Dad to fight more on this, honestly. But he agreed.

We filed back in to wait for the ruling. President Garcia took his time straightening the papers on his podium.

I wanted to scream.

"In the matter of Jonah Clarke, we deem he used his magic out of necessity."

I sagged in relief.

"In the matter of the Kindred bond that was deliberately hidden, we find Jonah Clarke guilty. Let the record show Mr. Clarke has asked for the Leveling Sentence until coming of age. This will be enacted directly after the hearing."

A flash of heat went up to my face at the immediate reality of this. I had no idea what binding my magic would entail, but I didn't think I would like it.

"In the case of Bureau member, Brother Clarke, we understand your intimacy with the situation, and your service to your clan and the Bureau have been taken into consideration. You are hereby placed on probation until your own trial."

"I understand," said Dad.

As we stood in the depressing hallway, watching everyone come out, I tried to savor the feeling of my magic. Even without Apollo and being unable to tap into it, it was always there. An effervescence deep inside and behind every movement. I had no idea what it would feel like without it.

Someone from the clan pat me on the back as they walked by. Someone else tried to comfort me.

We found Zarine after the crowd thinned. I'd seen Apollo with that same cross-armed posture before, like a string about to snap. I was far enough away, that I didn't hear what she told Dad, but she gestured at the door and looked pissed again. She shut it down when I reached them.

"You did wonderfully," she told me.

I didn't feel like I'd done anything wonderfully. I wanted to ask about Apollo. I missed him desperately, and I just wished someone would tell me how my Kindred was. I get that with everything else it was low on the totem pole, but it would have been a nice insurance policy against completely freaking out.

Unexpectedly, she hugged me. "You're strong. You'll be okay. You'll both be okay." Belatedly, I realized the hug was probably to hide the fact that she was crying.

We were directed to a private room in what looked like a medical wing. I was wondering how I would fit on the small hospital bed, hoping I wouldn't have to actually lay on it.

"So you're on probation?" I asked Dad, trying to distract myself.

He nodded.

I felt awful that he had to worry about his job, about taking care of us all along with all of this.

"I'm so sorry, Dad."

He pressed his lips together. "Just learn from it, Jonah."

"Yeah," I said with a weak laugh, "Looks like I'll have years for that." I didn't want to think about what was coming, so I kept talking. "You said you suspected, but you didn't know for sure."

"I've always known."

This was news. "How?"

"I could sense the restlessness of your magic. Your agitation around him."

I fidgeted with my sleeve.

"I don't think many would have known," he said, "but I know how it feels when one of our kind gets around his Kindred."

"But how could you know—"

"I'm a Kindred too."

"What? Mom?"

His smile was soft. "I didn't know for certain, though. It's just like I told them, I wanted to see if you would come to me with the truth."

I nodded. "Why didn't you say anything about you and Mom?"

"It feels very personal, sharing something that deep with another person, don't you think?" he asked with a small smile and knowing glance.

I swallowed. "Yeah," I said.

"Your mother and I didn't meet until after we were both twenty-one. We had more training and control. It's less of a risk for Kindred of that age to be together. We're required to report our Kindredship, but we never had to worry about separation. We were also never confronted with the life-threatening situation you were. If we had been underage and run into something like that, then we likely would have made similar decisions, broke the same laws.

"Ultimately, it made us stronger. Your mom and I didn't need help navigating our Kindredship. So I figured you two would be okay. I figured you wouldn't do anything stupid."

"I swear, I never did. Not until that night.'"

"I know, Son."

"So you guys never told anyone about you?"

The door opened to admit one of the cabinet members and a guy in scrubs.

"They'll be in shortly after you're under," said the cabinet member. He'd been the youngest of all of them, just a little younger than my dad.

"I have to be under anesthesia?" I asked.

The Bureau member looked surprised by the question. "Yes."

The nurse gestured to the bed. "Here, why don't you lay on the bed so we can get you hooked up?"

As he put the IV in, I looked at my Dad. "You'll stay, right?"

"Of course." He had that serious furrow between his brows, but having him here made me feel braver for what I was about to undergo.

"What do they do during the ritual?" I asked the nurse.

"Whole bunch of chanting and repetitive hand movements," he said.

I wanted to laugh, but his face already started to blur.

28

Jonah

"I have to see Apollo."

Dad looked up from his phone. I could already see the 'no' forming.

It had been four days since the trial and I was going mental. Dad had watched me on the drive back and over the next couple days. I told him I was fine, because I didn't want him to know that I felt scrubbed raw inside with my hands tied too tight behind my back. I didn't want him to know I wondered if I'd made the right decision—no. This was the price to stay with Apollo.

I hated to think of him going through this too after everything else. If he'd made the same choice.

"I've done everything I was supposed to do. But if you think I'm gonna sit here for another minute without knowing how he's doing, I'm going to go insane," I said to the black TV I'd been staring at all morning. I resisted punching the wall for emphasis.

I saw him set his phone down out of the corner of my eye. He leaned forward, elbows on his knees. "The Tormeys probably want to spend this time with their son."

"What do you mean 'this time'? Is he okay?" I looked at Mom, who had been talking with Zarine every day. "Did she tell you something?"

Mom was sitting on the floor in the middle of the living room, open photo boxes all around her. "He's okay," she said in that placating Mom tone. She set down the stack of photos she was sorting. "He's recovering. He just went through something very traumatic. Not even taking into consideration that he'll be undergoing his binding in a few days too."

So he'd chosen it too. She knew she'd dropped me the information I'd been desperate for and smiled.

I took a deep breath to get control of myself. "Exactly. And I'm his Kindred. He needs me."

She cut a look to Dad. That meant I had a chance.

She exchanged a look with Dad and sighed. "Call Zarine. Check with her first."

I found Zarine's number with shaking fingers as I walked to my room. I was afraid she'd say no. Afraid she'd say yes. Afraid to hear that he wasn't doing well. Afraid to hear he didn't want me. It felt a little like a Jane Austen novel—*May I call on you?*

If Jane Austen novels had cell phones. And guys who liked other guys.

Zarine wanted to talk before I went up to see him. My stomach twisted. He had worse internal injuries? He didn't want to see me anymore?

I followed her into the living room, bright with all the blinds open. For some reason I'd imagined pulled curtains and incense, like some sort of purification rite. This might have been more to do with how little I knew about Apollo's current state than my vague understanding of Zarine's spiritual beliefs.

She stood in the middle of the entry area, rubbing her arms through her cardigan.

"After his sentencing, he's going to be . . . recovering. Not just from the events of what happened to him but not being able to turn to magic like he did before."

I swallowed and nodded. He was going to be forced into being sober. I hadn't thought about it until just now. Having our magic bound was going to be so much worse for Apollo than me.

"I don't necessarily believe in prophecies, but Gertie gave me one before she passed. She said . . . " She took a breath and crossed her arms. "She said that if he loses you, he will lose himself." She shook her head, then looked up, searching my face as though to make sure I was worthy of him. "He looks at you like you're the air for him, Jonah."

"He's never going to lose me." If only she knew what my heart was doing right now.

"Good. I need you to be careful with him."

"I won't ever let anything happen to him."

She nodded.

"We were idiots. I'm sorry." Then I felt bad for saying that about him when he was sick. Was he sick? Had that been a bite on his neck?

"Everyone makes mistakes. Just don't make one like that ever again."

God, which one was she even talking about? About hurting him the night I'd kissed him? Had he told her? Or was it going along with him to Orville's? Letting him talk me into using our forbidden magic to play detective?

"Go on up."

That was all I needed. I walked up the stairs, stumbling once. Face burning, I didn't look back to see if she'd seen.

His room was dark and stifling. His bed was so loaded with blankets, I couldn't see him, but I could hear his breathing. Strong and even.

I felt a thousand times better being in here with him. And the Bureau must have overlooked how my pretty much nonexistent magic would still wake up around him. I'd been trying to get used to not feeling it since the binding, but here it was, reminding me it was still there.

I walked over to the window, wondering if I should wake him up. I picked up his cigarettes from the dresser. It was a new pack, two missing. Sometimes Apollo smoked in the house with the window open, though his mom forbade it. I turned a cigarette over and put it back in the pack. Luckies. I don't know where I'd even seen that.

I was so nervous, I was sweating. The window slipped up smoothly and silently, unlike the two basement windows in my room which had to be rocked in their frames. Overuse, Dad had said; I thought of Apollo folding himself through them and smiled.

"When'd you get here?"

I jumped and hit my elbow on the window. I looked over at him to see the blankets had been thrown back and he was sitting up on one arm, looking thinner than ever. I shut the window. I was an idiot for opening it.

"'Bout five minutes ago," I said.

My heart beat hard in my throat. I thought I might throw up. I started crying instead. Nice.

"Damn," I said. "I thought I'd be able to keep it together." I looked away to wipe my face.

He watched me without saying anything, like he wasn't sure I was in the right place.

"It's just really good to see you. To see you up. Okay," I babbled. I meant not lying nearly unconscious in my arms.

He looked down at his hands on the blanket.

"It's good to see you too."

Shoving my hands in my pockets, I walked toward his bed. "Can I sit?"

"Yeah."

I sat carefully. "How are you doing?"

"Alright, considering."

He didn't look alright. He had a bandage around his neck, and his usually amber skin was drained of color. He still had the dark circles under his eyes, but I don't know how much of that was from the way he deprived himself, from holding.

I was burning to ask what Halsey had done to him, to know how much he suffered so that I could share it with him, but I couldn't make my mouth work. When I did, it said the wrong thing.

"Can I stay the night?"

He looked at me strange. "Yeah."

It was rare to have no idea what he was thinking.

I stood. "I'll get a blanket from Zarine."

"Take one of mine."

"No. You get cold easily. Sorry about the window. That was stupid."

"You're all sweaty," he said with a small smile.

"Yeah," I said. Did he know I was nervous?

He rubbed the edge of his comforter between his fingers. "I was wondering if you'd turn up."

"I texted you after the trial."

He looked up at me. "Mom said you were the one who carried me out."

"I couldn't let you go."

We stared at eachother. We'd both chosen to stay together. He had chosen me even after the way we'd left things.

"You still have yours?" I asked.

"For now. And you . . ."

"Castrated? Pretty much."

"Jonah," he said, voice soft.

"It's okay. I'll be okay." I'd given up a part of me to be with him, a part of me I didn't know I could live without. I would have to learn. And if I had to do it over again, I'd make the same choice. "Guess they didn't bank on anyone being as codependent as we are."

He just stared up at me.

Maybe Mom was right. I should have given them more time. I felt better than I had in the last two days, but this wasn't just about me. I should have realized that a long time ago.

"Thank you," he said. "For saving me."

"I didn't . . . I mean, of course, I came for you. But it wasn't just me."

"I know. Mom told me. She told me about Gertie. Funeral for her and Junior's tomorrow. I can't really talk about that right now." He swallowed. "Lena's okay though . . ."

"I'm so sorry, Apollo."

"It's not your fault." He shut his eyes for longer than a blink. "Here," he said and pushed a blanket toward me. "I'm going to take a shower. Been laying in this bed all day."

I stood there stupidly until he started to get up. I jumped to his side.

"I got it," he said.

After he'd got some clothes and went into the bathroom, I laid the blanket on the floor. Whenever I stayed over, I usually took the couch. I didn't want to be that far from him. I hoped he didn't ask why I was choosing the floor.

I laid there, listening to the shower running, unable to imagine what he went through. I knew what I went through while he was gone. And I didn't ever want to feel it again.

The shower turned off. The light from the bathroom grew brighter as the door opened. He was wearing his sweater again and Adidas joggers. Hiding whatever happened to him at Lind Lab.

"You have some clothes here, from a while ago," he said, looking at the couch. "If you want to be more comfortable. If you're staying."

I closed my eyes. "Do you not want me here?"

"Of course I want you here."

I got up and walked over to the couch. "Have you eaten anything?"

"God, yes. You sound like my mother."

I stared at a pair of my basketball shorts and a long-sleeved T-shirt. No wonder I left it here. I never needed the long sleeves. I took off my pants and put on the shorts. I took off my shirt, but when I picked up the shirt, I could smell something familiar. The room was filled with the steam from his shower and that scent. Apollo's soap.

"Did you wear this?"

"I got cold." Absently rubbing his bicep, he looked cold now, even with the sweater.

Pulse thrumming in my neck, I went to him. We just looked at each other like we were memorizing each other's faces.

"I have to see," I said, clenching my fists at my sides. This entire day was a study in self-control. "Or I'll keep having nightmares about it."

When he struggled to pull off his sweater, I helped him stretch it over his head.

"This is it," he said, voice rough. He wouldn't look down as I took it all in. The bandages. The bruises.

"Does it hurt?"

He nodded.

My throat painfully tightened. "Can I touch you?"

Apollo shut his eyes and nodded again.

I rubbed my thumb just on the edge of his bandage, right over his Adam's apple. My fingers shook but my touch on the bandage was lighter than air. I could feel him swallow.

"She bit you," I said.

He nodded. "But she didn't give me any of her blood, so the doctor assures me we're all good. Guess she wasn't looking to adopt."

I trailed my fingers down and gently laid my whole palm against the bruises on his side that looked like they were made by fingers. To think of her holding him tight enough to bruise . . .

"Did they take your blood?"

"Yeah."

"Where?"

He held out his arms where it was clear some kind of needle had been plunged in. Something that took his blood from him. His life. His magic.

"There was a less appropriate area below the belt too—"

"Jesus. Apollo."

"Yeah. That's it." He dropped his arms. "Well, fucked up my head too." He laughed humorlessly.

"I'm sorry."

"I didn't invite you over to make you grovel." He swayed a little.

"Bed. Now."

"Yes, sir," he said but followed.

I pulled the blankets over him. When I turned to go to the floor, he touched my arm.

"Will you . . . get in with me?"

Like there was any way I'd say no.

I lifted the blankets and scooted in beside him so that we were facing each other. I reached out to run my fingers along his arm under the blanket.

"Is this okay?"

"Yes."

I laid there, memorizing every detail of his face.

"Mom doesn't want to talk about it," he said, his voice hoarse. "It's all I can think about, though. She told me I was down there for about twenty-four hours. It felt like longer. A lot longer. I think because it was all . . . dark most of the time—remember the Discernment? It felt like . . . days, or something. I couldn't tell if I was alive or dead."

I didn't know what I could say to make any of this better, to take any of his pain away. "Your mom thought she lost you, and it nearly destroyed her."

"I thought I'd never see them again."

He had tears running over the bridge of his nose. I rubbed the pad of my thumb across to catch them. "Your parents love you. They fought for you every second you were gone."

"I was going to let her have me," he said. "Halsey. Let her keep drinking until there was nothing left and I was as dead as Junior."

I took in a breath.

"But then I felt you, Jonah. I was able to throw her off of me. She already had me. I was going to die, but then I had the power to keep her back. Because of you. I thought I'd never see *you* again."

He was grabbing my shirt in his fist.

"There's no reality in which I'll be apart from you."

" 'In which'," he repeated with a teary laugh.

When my fingers found his cracked lips, he opened his mouth, breathing hot pants against my skin. I slid my hand very carefully around the back of his neck and pulled his mouth to mine.

I remembered our first kiss. The second he grabbed my hand, I'd felt something charging up. Not just our magic. It was something I had never taken the time to realize I was feeling. Before that moment, I'd been ignorant.

It seemed stupid to be thinking about that right now, but when Maddie and I found his empty car, that was my first regret, how I acted the night he showed me how he felt.

I grew up watching my parents be in love. I'd wanted that before I even started liking girls at school. Before I even knew what a relationship was. I'd read a lot of books, and romance fascinated me. And with Apollo, that night in May, the idea of being with him like that had knocked the wind out of me.

I used to think there was only one path to love.

Nudging his mouth open with my lips, I tasted his toothpaste and what I could only describe as *Apollo*.

The smell of him was all around me in his bed. That was my favorite scent in the world.

This kiss was so much quieter than when I'd kissed him in my room the other night.

He pulled back, and embarrassingly, I chased him.

He butted his chin against mine. "What are we doing, Jonah?" He sounded tense. Edgy.

"I lied."

"You lied."

"When I said I didn't feel anything." I watched his face, but it was as blank as when I arrived. I would probably cry again if he didn't feel this. I felt *hectic*. "Back in May."

It just seemed so pathetic a consolation prize after what he went through. *Turns out, I was lying to myself all this time because I'm a coward, but, bro, I love you.* If he even felt the same still.

He pushed at my chest. "You're with Courtney." His voice nearly broke my heart.

"I'm not." I slid my hand up his arm.

"What happened?"

"I don't want to talk about it. I just want . . ." I didn't know what, I realized as I stared at his lips. Not just to kiss him again.

"It can't be the way it used to be, Jonah. You know I want more. And you—"

I kissed him again, cutting him off just like I did that night at my house. Only gentler. "I want more, too."

His mouth twisted up in that arrogant way I'd seen him do so many times. Even though I knew I'd probably roll my eyes at whatever he was about to say, it was a comfort to see it now.

"You didn't say you didn't feel anything when I kissed you the first time. You said 'I'm not gay.'"

"Well, whatever. I lied. I'm a liar," I said, flustered.

He touched my neck, moved his fingers into my hair. I closed my eyes, my stomach tugging at the possibilities. Of him returning what I felt. Of this between us.

"Or maybe I'm not gay, and I just love you." I opened my eyes. I couldn't believe I'd said that. My words stumbled forward. "Or worse. Maybe—"

He put his fingers over my mouth. "No 'or worse.' Say it again."

"I lied."

"Not that."

When he tried to pull away, I pulled him back to me.

"I love you." I swallowed. "Apollo, I want to be with you."

It felt so good to say it. To know I wasn't forcing myself to believe something I didn't feel anymore. But at the same time, something unlocked inside of me.

"You love me?" he asked with a shy, sweet smile.

"Yeah. That's what it's looking like." I sighed in a very put-upon way.

He pulled me into a big tight hug, and I rolled back a little to bring him half on top of me.

When our lips were sore and other things were begging not to be noticed, we laid back. I couldn't stop pushing my fingers through his hair.

"You were always touching Courtney's hair," he said, and his voice almost sounded like his old self. "I thought it was just her."

"I thought so, too. I think it's just hair," I said, marveling at how good it felt to run *his* through my fingers.

"Good to hear."

"But I've always been obsessed with yours."

"Nice save. I think you may have a fetish, Jay."

"You're not allowed to call me that."

"Because Courtney called you that?"

"No. Because you called me 'Jay' when you were mad at me."

"Maybe it's starting to grow on me."

"Yeah, right," I said, the edge of my smile pushing against the pillow.

When he spoke, his voice sounded wobbly. "I didn't know it was possible for you to choose something like this. Just to be with me." I savored that dip in his voice that was just for me, that had always been just for me. "Jesus Christ, Jonah. What are we going to do?"

"Be together, I guess."

He leaned his forehead against mine.

I threaded my fingers through his over and over. How could something so simple feel so amazing?

Apollo had always made me feel a little less cool. Less easy going than I thought myself to be—he always riled me up. Now, it was pretty clear why. I had to face everything I'd been denying about myself, afraid of the way others would see me, afraid of the way I'd see myself. I had to face all of that to give us the chance we deserved, to show him how much he meant to me.

"So," he said, and his voice suddenly struck me as sexy. "Are you bisexual? Or . . ."

I'd been afraid of this question honestly.

"I don't know. I mean, I guess. I liked Courtney and girls in general, but you . . . everything is louder with you."

"Louder?"

"That's the perfect word. Don't question it." I took a breath. I guess we were doing this. "After we stopped talking and Courtney took an interest in me, I panicked. I felt like everyone would wonder why I wouldn't want to be with someone like her."

"As opposed to someone like me."

I scoffed. "More like, you'd never be with someone like me."

"Right."

I had to remind myself that for Apollo to kiss me, he'd have had to be dealing with these feelings before then, unsure of where to put them as we rode to school, and went to the beach, and played video games, knees and elbows brushing, and laid together on our beds on lazy days, reading or listening to music or just talking about anything that came into our heads.

"So, are we, then?" I asked.

"'Are we'?" he repeated, trailing his fingers down my palm. An almost unbearable spark of pleasure clenched at the base of my spine.

"Together?" I asked.

He took a shuddering breath and moved on top of me, his thigh going between my legs.

"Oh," I said, but it was all breath.

He put his hand on my chest while we kissed, and I thought, *this is what skin is for.* That and his weight on top of me felt amazing. I felt guilty for my body's instant response when, really, it was a foregone conclusion.

His hand moved down to my stomach, fingers tracing the skin above my waistband.

This. This is what skin is for. I couldn't stop thinking it, rapid fire as his fingers dipped under my boxers.

I gasped. Grabbed his wrist. "Don't." I was afraid of how good it would feel. Afraid of Zarine coming in, though his parents had zero history of being as intrusive as my family. Afraid I would do something wrong.

Apollo grabbed my hip. His grin was somehow tempting and innocent. Hysterically, I thought of boyband idols on posters. That and his rough touch made me want to pull him all the way on top of me, have him straddle me the way Courtney had.

"Why are you so shy all of a sudden?" he asked.

"I'm not," I said, releasing his wrist.

He looked different. Better. Healthy. Perfect. Could being around his Kindred really bring that much color back to him? Or maybe being around his hopefully-soon-to-be-boyfriend-without-his-head-stuck-up-his-ass did that.

"You are. It's adorable."

We kissed again, and he moved his hand lower.

"Apollo," I said through my teeth, but I couldn't stop him this time because that clenching pleasure was running all the way up my spine and down my body.

"Yes, Jonah?"

"We shouldn't." It was unclear how I was forming speech; I was such a mess.

"Why not?"

"I don't want to . . . exert you."

"Ooh, fancy word."

His hand slid lower and found skin. I gasped, gripping his hips, trying not to move.

"You know how many times I thought about us like this? It never felt right with anyone else because I always just wanted you. Sweet, thick-headed, book nerd, human garbage disposal Jonah."

I couldn't believe I was laying in Apollo's bed. That he was saying these things. And it wasn't just the touching, which was incredible. It was him. The way he was watching me, the way he wanted me and made me feel so good about wanting him too. It felt exactly right.

I found my way to him too, and he let his breath out in a puff against my neck.

I surged up to kiss him, bumping my teeth painfully against my lips. "I'm sorry. I'm sorry it took so long," I said in a rush, sounding totally uncool. I kissed his chest, warm from being under the blankets, from . . . *this.*

I pulled him tighter against me. It felt so good to have his skin on mine.

"You feel *amazing,* Jonah."

"Apollo," I said, gripping his bicep, which didn't help matters. Like at all. "Slow down. You're going to make me . . ."

"That's the idea," he said, voice so rough I thought maybe he was close too.

And well, that was the end of the story. All those books I'd read neglected to mention the awkwardness of clean up.

"You should have just touched me like that to show me how much I'd be into it," I whispered after catching my breath.

"What?" he asked, voice gravelly in my ear. "And lose the chase?" He smiled sleepily, eyes half closed. He was probably exhausted.

I gathered him against my chest and promptly fell asleep.

29

Apollo

You think you're safe now.

Halsey's words swam in my head.

She was in the window room, and I was in my fishbowl prison. My chest got tight, breaths coming like a panicked rabbit's. This already happened.

I was at home. I'd seen my Mom and Dad. I'd been with Jonah.

As soon as I realized it was a dream, I opened my eyes to my bedroom.

Jonah's arm and leg were thrown over me, caging me in. It was everything I wanted when I was trapped in Caterina's cell. A full stomach, warmth, and perfect sleep with Jonah's hot skin against mine. I'd felt safe—protected—until I'd heard her voice again.

I got out of bed, trying not to wake him. I found my pants and his T-shirt. It made me sad to leave him sleeping, unaware that I'd left. I stood there, unsure of what to do, trying to remember why I had felt the need to get up.

I had no idea what time it was and couldn't tell by the blue darkness of the sky outside. My phone had been dead since . . . well, it must have died sometime while I was locked up. I pulled Jonah's phone out of his pants pocket. 4:45 PM. We'd slept almost seven hours. I was almost certain Mom had come in and seen us tangled up; she was changing her entire parenting tactic, but the fact that she'd let Jonah come up here after how mad the trial had made her meant he was probably excluded from her wrath.

As Jonah and I held each other tighter than the doctor would have advised with my bruised ribs, I understood that thinking he could somehow fix me was childish. I still felt this sense of loss. And it wasn't only because I had a finite amount of time left with my magic.

I was so thirsty. I didn't know if it was the Discernment still, or Caterina drinking from me, or just the waste of it all. I had triggered a chain reaction that had ultimately led to the deaths of Junior, of Gertie, and even of Talbot. Dax, whom Mom made me start having virtual sessions with yesterday, would tell me to step back—don't overanalyze it.

You couldn't possibly be held responsible for any of their decisions. I could just hear the condescending logic in his infuriatingly calm voice.

But, I imagined myself arguing, *if I hadn't been such a fuck-up—*

My brain was caught in this vicious looping cycle Jonah had quieted, for a little bit at least.

I didn't dare leave my room or this in-between space with him. The few times I'd emerged in the past couple of days for something to drink or just to make sure my parents were still there, Dad would be staring at the TV with vacant eyes. Most sapiens who married our kind didn't have to see this much excitement in all of their lives.

"Alright?" he'd ask me, like he was sitting up to keep vigil.

"Yeah," I'd say. That was all we needed.

It was Mom who was still fighting for my life. I was afraid that nothing I could say or do would be the right thing. I didn't want to ruin the miracle of my return. How was I supposed to live up to the same pedestal I held Junior on when he went missing?

I leaned against the window ledge and lit a cigarette. Being in love with my best friend hadn't been a pipe dream after all. Thinking about what Jonah said as he shakily smiled down at me, something rose from the ashes inside of me. This was hope. The real kind. Soft and airy, not sharp. The other bit I'd been feeling had been despair.

Look at that. I'd already learned something from my first therapy session.

Jonah's arm moved over my empty side of the bed. He jerked up, frantically looking around.

"Apollo," he said like a command for me to appear.

"Jonah."

He looked at me, but his face was still etched with fear.

Leaning forward, he pushed his hands through his hair. "Sorry."

After everything he'd gone through, I owed him more than only giving him half of myself. I hated that he was getting this broken . . . aftermath.

I smiled, because it was impossible not to with Jonah, who'd held me all night in my bed, looking at me like I was the sun. "I think I'm flattered actually," I said.

He looked down at the bed.

"Jonah," I said, my voice hard with my fear. "You do remember last night, right?"

His cheeks were as pink as they were last night. "I remember, Apollo. Fuck."

I took a drag, staring back, then a second thought came just as quickly on the tail of the first.

"This is all . . . new for you. I've known how I felt for a while, but you . . . I get it, if . . ." I looked down at my cigarette. "If you're not ready to . . ."

"Not ready to what?" he asked.

I couldn't look at him. I know he noticed me trembling. "To be with me, like this."

"What would you call this?" He spread his arms to the bed, which was a mess, or maybe to himself shirtless in the bed.

I called it my wildest dreams coming true.

"Didn't I seem ready?" His voice dipped lower, which did things to my insides.

"Yeah," I said, swallowing.

From my peripheral, I could see him get up and walk over. He stood in front of me, and I was left staring right at the center of his chest. I was usually self-conscious by my small chest in comparison, the narrowness of my rib cage, but the way he'd looked at me all night, I didn't feel self-conscious at all, even with my scars and bruises.

He kneeled down and took my cigarette to flick it out the window. We both watched it stumble down. He put his hands on my knees, jaw clenching.

"I couldn't think about anything beyond getting you back. It was like, I couldn't wrap my brain around the possibility of living without you," he said, flustered. I always paid attention when Jonah got flustered. It meant that he was talking about something he cared about.

It was like Caterina had somehow pulled out my deepest fantasy and was dangling it before me. I was still in the belly of her lab, dead or dying, living in a vivid dream where my best friend loves me back.

"Is this a little uncanny for me?" Jonah asked. "Yes."

I almost rolled my eyes. There was my proof that it was real. Jonah was the only person who would casually use 'uncanny' in a conversation.

"But only because it's different from everything I've ever experienced. Being with you, like this, is better than . . . everything." He laughed nervously. "Even if I don't exactly know what to do next, I'm in this with you. If I'm not . . . giving you something you need"—we both blushed at that—"I want you to ask me."

"Yes, Jonah. I would never try to make you guess," I said dryly, but I was grinning.

"I'm serious," he said, gently pushing my hand.

Every touch felt like a burst of potential.

"I get it. And that goes the same for me. This is new for me too, remember."

"I don't think I ever really believed that," he said, and we both laughed.

"I'm just saying," I said. "If I'm moving too fast for you, or you're not ready for—"

"Apollo."

I looked at him.

"Can I kiss you again?" he asked.

I waited for the fantasy to dissolve. When it didn't, I leaned in. I kissed him softly, because I was afraid. But he didn't pull away.

He didn't pull away.

"We need to get ready for the funeral, if you're coming with me." I hoped I didn't sound needy. But I couldn't stand the idea of him leaving me alone with my looping thoughts, the memory of the dark.

Jonah nodded. "You okay?"

"Yeah. You're kind of distracting."

He stood up, trying to prove me wrong, but he was smiling. He went over to his pants on the couch and got his phone out. It was strange that he'd been that far from it since he got here. He always had it inches from his hand in case his parents needed anything.

I went to my dresser, trying to find a decent black undershirt. Mom had already put out a black dress shirt and pants. She'd done it without a word yesterday after bringing me soup.

"Mind if I take a shower first?" Jonah asked.

"Go ahead." I turned back to my closet, buttoning the over shirt. The sound of the shower made me stop. I stood there, remembering the static.

My bedroom door opened.

"Jesus!"

"I knocked," said Mom.

"Sorry. I didn't hear you." I tucked my shirt into my pants, then pulled it back out.

"You guys got a lot of rest. You look . . .well."

"I feel better," I said, trying to be casual. Seeing that Jonah hadn't been vaporized after the trial like I'd been imagining certainly helped. Gotta love fever dreams.

She scanned the room, possibly noticing the tidy couch and very untidy bed, and narrowed her eyes. "Do we need to have a talk?"

"What? God, no. He was a perfect gentleman," I said. I was the one that instigated everything, after all.

"Mmhmm." She straightened my collar. "You do look better. Worlds better. Jonah coming with us?"

"Yeah." I wondered if all my secrets were laid bare.

"Be careful with your heart, baby."

Yep, it was all out there.

"I will." I had to believe Jonah was the safest place to keep my heart.

I closed the door behind her.

When he got out of the shower, wet hair slicked back, he was wearing the same pants as yesterday and the long-sleeve shirt he had left over. "Did your mom just lecture you for letting me sleep in your bed?"

"Kind of." I walked over to him. "I told her you were a perfect gentleman, though." I leaned in to kiss his neck. He took a fast breath in through his nose and tightly held me.

"Not a perfect one," he said. Both of our bodies seemed to go hot at the mention of last night.

I laughed against his skin, but he didn't move.

"What's wrong?" I asked.

"Nothing."

"You seem nervous again."

"I'm not nervous," he said indignantly, pulling away. "Just worried about you."

"Well, stop."

"Okay, let me just turn it off."

I opened my mouth, but he held up his hand.

"Okay, I'm done worrying now."

"Smart ass," I said.

He huffed out a distracted laugh and went over to his shoes. I closed my eyes. I couldn't stand the idea that everything had been an illusion.

"Don't do this because you think it's heroic."

He glared at me. "What?"

"Don't pretend you're into this for my sake. To protect me, or . . . save me from myself or whatever."

"Just shut up, Apollo." He sat down on the couch and started putting on his socks. When he finished, he looked up at me. I never wanted to see that look on his face again. "You think I was faking that?" He turned and shoved his feet into his shoes. "That I was lying when I said—" He closed his eyes and took a deep breath. "I know what you went through was awful, but I'm not the same either. You're the only reason I'm able to keep it together right now. Things are going to be hard, but I'm not running. So don't push me away."

"Okay. I'm sorry."

He hugged me tightly, the fingers cupping the back of my neck softer than his words had been.

"You don't have to be sorry. Just don't be a . . ."

"What?" I asked.

"A butthead," he mumbled into my shoulder, but I could hear his smile.

The funeral for Gertie and Junior was held at the records building. Before the entire clan started pouring through the doors, it was obvious the whole place had been transformed. The heat from thousands of candles warmed my face. The flickering candlelight and against the old-style architecture made it feel like some sort of ancient ceremony in a cathedral. It was beautiful and meant more to me than I had a right to claim.

The good thing was that Talbot's funeral would be separate, seeing as how Junior, and Gertie by extension, very probably died because of Talbot. The bad thing was that it felt gratuitous to look at both their pictures up there at once. So I didn't.

When I looked at Jonah, he was already staring at me. He lifted his mouth in that flat, sad way that people sometimes did. And it was suddenly too much.

I focused with a militant-like concentration to hear the words being said about Gertie. Gertie with all her gifts. She came to save me, and this was her payment.

She would probably say something like, 'Don't take it to heart. People make their own decisions.' But that didn't make it any easier to listen to the funny stories Junior's friends and even his mom told. I just kept seeing him saying '*te amo*' before he died, and I couldn't breathe.

Jade found me after the service. She wrapped her arms around my neck and held me for a long time.

"Thank you for trying," she said.

I lost it.

She released me, hand over her mouth and mascara running.

Lupita came over to me to give me his poncho, and I almost laughed because I knew exactly how unattached he'd been to it. But he'd cried into it at a time when he'd felt alone, and that was something I understood.

Before we left, Jonah pulled me against a tree. He put his forehead to mine, arms draped over my shoulders, in view of everyone.

"Are you out to your family?" I asked.

"They already know, Apollo." He laughed like it was a dumb question.

"Hey!" I said, pinching his side. He blocked and stepped back with a grin I wanted to live inside. "I'm trying to be sensitive to your boundaries, man."

He came back and took my face in his hands. He took a breath, looked in my eyes until I was right there with him, and kissed me.

"Thank you," he said.

Our breaths were warm and humid against the cold of the night.

"For what?" I asked, completely stupid from that kiss.

"For considering my boundaries," he said, and that made me laugh.

As he walked away with his family, I heard Maddie tell him, "You shouldn't joke about someone's boundaries," and Jonah's reply, "They're my boundaries! I'll joke about them if I want."

When we got home, Mom asked if I had any requests for dinner.

"Can Dad make his mac and cheese actually?"

"No respect around here," said Mom, throwing her hands up. I think we were all a little shaky from the funeral.

"Get a better specialty than quinoa salad."

She gasped, fists on her hips. I hadn't seen her this relaxed in a long time. I think she was just relieved to see that I was able to joke around. She'd been watching Jonah and me after the funeral but giving us our space.

After dinner, Dad said he'd be in his office reviewing some tracks, but that if I wanted to play, just come in.

"Maybe tomorrow," I said, happy for the offer.

I went into my room and laid back on my bed, on top of all the messed up covers. Covers Jonah and I had shared. I had imagined being with him in so many different ways. But the real Jonah was better than all of the fantasies. I never thought he could look that happy to have me, that easy in his own skin.

I turned on my phone. Tom found it in a Ziploc just outside that window room Caterina had been in, along with my wallet, the necklace I wore with Junior's ring, his wallet, and Lena's belongings, including a photograph of a dark-haired woman. It wasn't mine, and Junior was an Instagram junkie—or, he used to be. He'd probably be surprised physical pictures still existed if someone handed him one.

Would have been surprised, I corrected.

I asked Tom to hold onto the picture for me, since Lena was still recovering at one of the clan's safe houses. I got her information, but I still didn't have the courage to call her. Talking to someone, someone still alive, who had seen the inside of that place, maybe even seen Halsey—I wasn't ready.

When my phone finished booting, about fifteen message notifications went off.

Quinn: *Dad told me what happened. I'm so glad you're okay. You're okay, right?still*

Danny: *Hey man. Why weren't u in school? Quinn said mono. Her and a bunch of other kids who got it were out. Didn't even know that was still a real thing*

Another from Danny: *Wanna hang tonight?*

And one more from him: *Don't get mad, but I think me and Quinn are together now. Kinda hard to tell with her tbh*

I smiled at that.

The next was from Jonah. A response to mine from that night.

Jonah: *Leave, Apollo. Please.*

And the next one, after the trial: *I don't know how you will ever forgive me. But can I please come see you?*

Then Mom's texts from that night. Her first ones telling me to get my ass home.

Then begging me.

Twenty-three missed calls from her.

A voicemail. I cried as I listened to it.

"I'm not mad at you, Apollo. Just please . . . please call me back and let me know you're okay."

I went to the kitchen. She was sitting at the table with her head in her hand, an untouched cup of tea at her elbow.

"Mom?"

She looked up. She was still fighting.

"What's wrong?"

Her soft voice brought me to my knees. I hugged her waist.

"I'm sorry." I cried like I had just fallen off my bike after trying to ride it without training wheels for the first time.

"No, no, no, no." It was an oddly comforting chant as she rubbed my back.

I told her I had found the letter. I don't know why I brought it up. I wanted to give her some kind of explanation for my bad decisions. It felt good. It felt like letting go of something I couldn't hold onto anymore.

"What letter?"

"The one you wrote to Dad apologizing for being pregnant. You didn't want me."

She took my head in her hands, and stared me down with the eyes I stole from her. They were overflowing with tears.

"That is not true. I was scared because of the pressures my parents put on me. It had nothing to do with not wanting you. Your father and I created our life together for you."

I couldn't even absorb that. I didn't know how to take it in and rearrange everything I'd thought.

"Come on, sit down with me." She pulled a chair closer and I pulled myself up into it, embarrassed. I wiped my face with both of my hands. When I finally looked at her, she was watching me.

"When I was your age, I used to gather more than my fill. I knew it would be a problem, even before I could throw. And when I came of age, I took to only letting it out if I felt I deserved it. I used it kind of like a punishment."

Something inside of me clicked in understanding. "Why did you think you needed to punish yourself?"

She smiled. "I really don't know. Maybe because I didn't choose a nice boy your grandparents would have approved of and married a rock star instead."

I laughed. Dad was so not a rock star.

"Maybe because I felt different," she said. "But eventually, I came to accept who I chose, who I am, and what I am. And once you accept that, Apollo, it gets so much easier," she said.

I nodded, looking down at the table. "I'll try."

She got up to pour me a cup of my favorite tea.

Your life supposedly flashes before your eyes before death, but really, in Caterina's lab, I had realized that fighting to live was worth it. Not just because I was a cup that could be filled, but because I breathed, even without magic. I felt and loved even without magic. Without it, I still lived. And that was worth everything. But . . .

"Will it ever be over?" I asked.

Would I ever stop hearing Caterina's voice, feeling her teeth breaking into my neck? It was all healed now, but I could still feel her venom like dry ice under my skin.

"I think you have to be the one to make that decision."

Just like Talbot had decided to side with the *vampiria.*

Just like Gertie had decided to rescue me.

Just like Junior had decided to come after me.

Just like Jonah and I chose each other.

Epilogue

It was a clear day for March but still pretty cold. Craving the sun, we'd met Lena at the park. I stayed on the blanket to catch up on the reading for English while Apollo and Lena's legs swung from the edge of the jungle gym, both their arms threaded through the bars. He was leaning his head against them, turned toward her as she spoke in her reserved way.

Apollo was different since he'd undergone his binding. Everything about him was more purposeful and serious.

He was Apollo to the tenth power, even without his magic.

Being together was even more addictive, because being together reminded us we were still *magikalia.* I didn't regret my choice at all. Every time he smiled at me or let me kiss him helped. But it wasn't easy.

From the moment I got up after the binding ritual, I knew it had worked. There was nothing, but I had tried to throw anyway. It created so much pressure and discomfort, I swore never to even try it again until my sentence was complete.

Maddie said it was called the Leveling Sentence because it was similar to how you measured a cup of flour and you had to shake off the excess. But it wasn't like that at all. It was torture. It was like having a limb you constantly used amputated.

I felt like a bird with its wings clipped. Permanently grounded. Domesticated.

Sapien.

I could see why they considered it an archaic punishment.

When I asked Apollo about not being able to hold his magic in anymore, thinking about what his mom said, he brushed me off.

"It's a good thing I got a head start on my sobriety in captivity." I hated when he blew off what he went through, but maybe he was right in a way. Maybe it hadn't been worse than anything else that could be bad for you. Smoking, eating banana splits every day, pretending to love your girlfriend because that was normal. I was an idiot.

His guilt is another thing we deal with. We've talked about it from every angle, rehashing the things we did wrong. I think he wanted to remember all the ways he messed up, to try to convince me that what I was going through now was his fault. I assured him that even if we'd gone to the adults any sooner, that didn't necessarily mean we wouldn't have ended up in the same exact situation.

He was still recovering. There were days he'd lose himself to what he'd seen there. It tore me up to watch him go through that. All I could do was hold his hand. I wouldn't tell him it was okay, because it wasn't.

We were both broken in a way, I guess. Broken together.

That didn't make me feel any less impotent as I watched him and Lena walk back, laughing, faces flushed from the cold. After he'd returned the picture of her mother to her, they'd become close. Honestly, I was a little jealous, but I think that was mostly because I was afraid Apollo might never see me as an equal. I would never be able to comprehend what he'd gone through as Halsey's prisoner.

Lena hugged us both goodbye. We sat on the blanket after she left. Apollo's eyes turned dusky when they landed on me.

This was why I'd asked for the Levelling Sentence. To be sitting here with him. The dappled shade across his face. The unreachable distance in his eyes that had always been there but stood out a little more now. And now there was the heat of something living alongside it—determination or restraint or both.

He looked like a beautiful, solemn king.

"Do you still think I'm . . . right for you?" I asked.

Everything in him softened like it always did when I got insecure. Sometimes I just wanted to hear him argue. Sometimes I really believed I wasn't good enough for him.

He looked up at the leaves over us. Or maybe he was looking at the sky between them. He looked so much like he did before all this. Capable of anything, ready to spring.

He crawled over me, forcing me to lay back.

"Haven't I already proved there's nothing you can do to get rid of me?"

Touching him now was a whole different thing. Before, I thought it was just the extra breath of life our magic breathed together. It was so much more than that though. It always was.

"I know it's stupid, but I'd do it all over again for you." I rose to kiss him, but he pulled just out of reach.

"The good thing is," he said, his lips and breath soft against my mouth. "I'm not asking you to."

I laughed and forced him to close the space between us.

Acknowledgments

My best friend and partner in writing shennanigans, Lisa, encouraged me to see this magical best-friends-to-lovers idea through to the end. Without our ritual write nights, I would have never finished the novels that came before this one, each of which made finishing The Space Between You and Me possible.

For the spark of an idea that rolled into a full-fledged bonfire, I need to thank Danielle, who asked if I would like to write something for the LGBTQ book box she was putting together. Her enthusiasm and beta read are stones (wood planks?) in the bridge that has brought this novel into your hands.

My little sister Emily has been a fan of my work from the early days of clacking away to my fictionpress stories on ye olde desktop computer. The song she wrote for this novel (!) in an unexpected moment of fangirling makes my heart threaten to tear from my chest and float to space.

As for my light and sound technician behind the scenes, my spouse, Charles, facilitates my writing sessions and encourages me, after work and parenting, to do this crazy thing that I love.

Finally, thank *you,* dear reader. Without you, these are just words on a page, telling a story that lives in my head alone. You breathe life into these words by reading them. And that is the greatest gift an author could ask for.

About the Author

Ashley B. Davis writes about the ordinary and extraordinary. Her work appears in Rainbow Crate's summer anthology, A Queer, Queer Summer, Liquid Imagination, Eunoia Review, Months to Years, The Grey Rooms Podcast, and Trembling with Fear. She manages rental property, consumes way too much coffee, and tames two feral seven-year-olds in Southern California. The Space Between You and Me is her debut.

If you loved this book, please don't forget to leave a review!

For exclusive content and ARC opportunities, subscribe to Ashley's newsletter:
www.ashleybdaviswrites.substack.com
Instagram: ashleybdaviswrites

Resources

If you or someone you know struggles with depression or addiction, please seek help.

Substance Abuse and Mental Health Services Administration (SAMHSA) National Helpline
1 (800) 662- HELP (4357)

National Suicide Prevention Lifeline
Call or text 988

Made in the USA
Las Vegas, NV
07 April 2026

44864054R00152